CW01187245

LUCKY GUY

JOHN O'NEILL

ISBN: 9798872218913

Editor: Kathryn Hall – cjhall.co.uk
Cover art: Joseba Altuna, Selke Designs
Formatting: Elaine Denning – elainedenning.com

Printed in United Kingdom.

CONTENTS

CHAPTER ONE

It was 1988, and close friends, George, Degsy, Stuart and Noah decided to leave school at the age of sixteen. College and university weren't for them; they wanted to start earning, take the first step on the ladder to joining the workforce. Noah tended to take the lead role, he had something about him that made people want to be in his company. He wasn't loud but he stood out, and not just to his friends, either. Most of his teachers liked his determined attitude, the way he got on with the job he was tasked to do. He was a doer, not a talker, a young man with an old man's head on his shoulders.

When their decision had been made to leave, all four boys went to see the careers officer and talked through their options. Most of the jobs on offer for school leavers were typically low paid with a promise of good future earnings if you were lucky enough to land an apprenticeship.

But Noah had since met up with an ex-school friend of his, two years above their year, who'd taken a job at the local coal mine, Clock Face. Simon Campbell told Noah the wages were four-times what they'd get from any of the jobs on offer through the school, and when Noah made the announcement to the others, it was a no-brainer to forget about pursuing apprenticeships and low-paid jobs and apply to the coal mine instead. The fact miners were striking meant the mines needed staff to cover, and so, they submitted applications and within the week, the boys were sat outside the medical room being checked over by the resident doctor, who declared them all fit to work for the mine.

Their first year of employment would be spent working above ground while they got used to working for a living and learnt about how the mine operated, and then they'd be introduced to the actual job of mining. The wages, fortunately for the boys, were still better than if they'd gone for a local job elsewhere, so that first year gave them the opportunity to banish any thoughts of being workshy, giving them a taste of hard work and a realisation that being a grown-up meant grafting through life if they wanted to afford the essentials, not to mention luxuries.

The year flew past, and it was finally time to start work down below. It hadn't been an easy time due to the picket lines and having to get through them each day, not to mention being ostracised and called *Scab* whenever they turned up for work. But they were young and naïve and this was their step into the big wide world. They wouldn't be allowed to work on the coal face, however, as that type of work was carried out only by experienced miners. The boys' tasks mostly consisted of moving coal that had come from the coal face to the surface, and all that heavy manual work meant they were developing into very strong and muscular young men.

One thing they did all agree on was not rushing into marriage. These four friends preferred to enjoy life for a while before getting tied down with family commitments and the expense that came with having kids. Of course, they weren't shy of the opposite sex, and would spend many a night at a house party getting to know the girls better. The fact they were all working and still living at home with their parents, albeit paying rent, meant they could always afford to take a decent stash of booze with them to these parties, and that made them extremely popular!

There was one girl in particular, Carol O'Brien, who had her sights set on Noah. To her, he was perfect marriage material, over six foot tall, well-mannered, and extremely handsome. He was slightly well-spoken, too, and the fact he was earning good money made things even better as far as she was concerned. It wasn't long before she got her way and they became a couple, and soon after they did, things in the bedroom department moved swiftly.

"What about protection?" Noah asked Carol on their first time being intimate together.

"I'm on the pill," she replied, matter-of-factly.

"Already?" Noah asked, a little surprised.

Carol, not wanting him to know she'd been having sex on a regular basis with her boss in the Chinese restaurant where she worked as a waitress, thought quickly. "My mother took me to the doctor's because I was having trouble with my periods," she blurted out in one breath as she registered the shock on Noah's face. "The doctor put me on the pill to regulate them and it worked."

Noah nodded and looked impressed. He was still a virgin and hadn't even begun to think that Carol could be sleeping with other men. Believing her was the only thing he could do, and so he decided there and then to book a cheap hotel room and whisk her away for the night. That first time for him was unforgettable, perhaps not initially because of the passion, but because he only manged to last a few minutes after seeing Carol's naked body and fumbling about to get inside it. Carol wasn't going to let on she wasn't a virgin and so giggled a little when at first things didn't quite go to plan, making it look like she was new to it all, too. She had to be careful not to let him see that she was, actually, very experienced where sex was concerned, fearing it might scare him off if he realised otherwise. But when Noah's first time was over, it didn't take him long to summon up the urge to do it all over again, much to Carol's surprise, and pleasure, of course.

By the time they left the hotel the next morning, tiredness had overwhelmed them both after little sleep and a lot of sex. Carol, however, was more than happy with her enthusiastic boyfriend who was particularly well-endowed and had an excellent physique. She would bring him along slowly and make sure he fell head over heels for her, which was a lot more than her married lover felt, only being interested in using her for his own pleasure. She knew he wasn't interested in her, in what she needed or wanted out of life, and the only thing she benefitted from being with him was an extra two days' wages in her pay packet at the end of the week for giving him what he wanted. It made her no better than a prostitute, but that didn't seem to bother her. She was just glad of the extra money.

Carol and Noah had been a couple for just over three months when he went round to her house one night and she ushered him into the living room. "We need to talk," she said, a nervous look on her face and seeming a bit fidgety.

"What's the matter?" Noah asked, worried she might be dumping him.

They sat down on the sofa and she got straight to the point. "I'm pregnant."

Noah stared at her, his expression a picture of shock. *Shit* was the first thing he thought, then, "I thought you were on the pill?" he said.

"I am," Carol replied, looking down at the floor. "But it's not always guaranteed to work. What are we going to do?"

The silence in the room was deafening. Noah didn't have a clue what to say and just shuffled about on the sofa, averting his eyes around the patterns on the carpet. But Carol wasn't going to sit around in an uncomfortable silence and decided it was time to make her point clear.

"Well, one thing's for sure," she began, "I have no intentions of being an unmarried mother!"

Once more, you could hear a pin drop as Noah became lost in thoughts, realising he'd mightily cocked up along the way, and that his plans to stay single for as long as possible were diminishing before his eyes. It couldn't be happening, he wasn't ready for this kind of commitment, he had too much living to do first, too many places he wanted to go and explore, hell, he even wanted to explore the opposite sex more and have years of experience under his belt before he committed himself to one woman for the rest of his life. And having a child just hadn't been part of his agenda, it was something he wanted in the future, but not right now. Thoughts racing around his head, not realising Carol had played him for a fool, he turned to look at her, unsure whether he could see tears in her eyes or whether she was just as scared as he was.

"Well," she said, breaking the silence, "what are we going to do? I'm not getting rid of it, if that's what you're expecting me to do."

But Noah was a decent young man, he knew he had to do the right thing even if it was going to put an instant stop to all the things he'd got planned, and he took her hand, gently stroking it and trying hard to find the words he needed to say.

"I'd never expect you to get rid of it, Carol," he said. "We'll just have to get married and give the baby a proper home, with a loving mother and father."

Carol threw her arms around him. "You won't regret it," she squealed. "I'll be the best wife to you ever and I'll make you so proud."

The first part of her plan had worked to perfection, and she smiled at the thought of knowing that within the next few months, she would become Mrs Carol Burgess.

"You fucking dildo!" was Degsy's reaction when he heard the news from Noah the following day.

"How far gone is she?" Stuart asked.

"Two months, possibly three," Noah replied.

All three of Noah's friends were thinking the same thing, that they'd only been together just over three months and it was Stuart, the sensible one of the group who said, "What about contraception? Did you not think to use a condom?"

"She told me she was on the pill," Noah replied. "But it doesn't always work, apparently."

All three knew Noah wasn't savvy when it came to girls, none of them were, and they all had the same opinion that he could have been lied to. He wasn't the first and wouldn't be the last, but being married at eighteen with a young family and his future already mapped out was just crazy in their opinion.

It was a few days' later when George was in the kitchen with his sister Debbie and their mum, telling them about Noah's news. Debbie, much to George's surprise, burst out laughing.

"You've got to be joking!" she said between hysterics. "She's been screwing the boss of the Chinese restaurant where I work for as long as I can remember!"

George looked confused. "Yeah, but that might have been before she met Noah," he said innocently.

Debbie sniggered. "Ha, I don't think so. The pair of them go missing every Wednesday afternoon after the lunchtime rush is over. He leaves first followed by her five minutes later."

"Where do they go to?" George asked.

"I'm not sure, but there's a Holiday Inn just up the road and I'll bet you any money it's there, they couldn't go to his place because he has a wife and kids!"

Angie, George's mum, shook her head. "Poor lad," she said. "Sounds to me that if she is pregnant, it's not even Noah's. Listen," she continued, "my friend Sylvia's daughter, Helen, works at that Holiday Inn on the reception, She's there Monday to Friday and I'll ask her if she's seen them going in, she'll know Carol because they were in the same class at school."

And so, that evening, Angie rang Sylvia's house and asked to speak to Helen.

"I need a favour," she said. "You know Mr Chin from the Chinese restaurant on the same road as the Holiday Inn, does he ever come in the hotel with Carol O'Brien?"

"Well," Helen began, "Mr Chin usually comes in first and Carol tends to come in about five minutes later around 2pm. They always have the same room, every Wednesday afternoon." Then she paused. "I'm not really supposed to give out information about people who stay in the hotel, though. You won't tell anyone that I told you, will you?"

Angie assured Helen that her name would never be mentioned and then hung up, passing on the news to

George and telling him he needed to tell Noah as soon as possible.

"Listen mate there's no easy way to tell you this," George began that night when he called round to see Noah. "So, I'll tell you how it is." He paused and composed himself. "You're not the only one who's sleeping with Carol."

Stunned, Noah didn't know what to think and before he could allow any sinister thoughts to enter his head, he asked George, "What makes you say something like that?"

"Mate, I found out from my sister that every Wednesday Carol meets up with her boss from the chip shop where she works, not too far from the Holiday Inn down the road. Debbie told me and my mum, it was as though it was common knowledge."

Noah shook his head, unable to comprehend what his friend was saying.

"It's been going on for a long time, mate."

Looking up at George's face Noah said, "That's where we went the first night we hooked up together."

George couldn't mask his sympathy.

"I know. I'm sorry, and I hope I'm wrong, but there's only one way to find out the truth. We need to be at the Holiday Inn next Wednesday, agreed?"

Noah just nodded.

"We'll catch them out and make sure she knows you're not some easy target."

"What are we going to do?" Noah asked and George told him of the plan he'd concocted, hoping Noah would go along with it.

It was the following Wednesday afternoon when Noah and George were sitting in George's dad's car in the Holiday Inn car park and right on cue, Mr Chin approached the main entrance, followed shortly after by Carol. It was all the proof Noah needed and he and George got out of the car and went inside the hotel.

Helen was sat behind the reception desk, a look of surprise now on her face as they went towards her. "Look, I don't want any trouble, I could lose my job."

"Don't worry," George reassured her, "we're just here to prove a point. There won't be any trouble."

The boys then made their way to the bar and ordered two pints of shandy. They obviously had no idea how long they would be waiting and after two hours and a couple more pints, they went back to speak to Helen.

"We're gonna wait in the car. Can you give us a signal when they're on their way out?"

Helen reluctantly agreed, saying she'd flash the outside lights a few times when they appeared in the reception area.

It was nearly an hour later when the lights on the walls outside the main entrance flashed a few times, and the boys jumped out of the car. At first, Carol and her lover didn't see them as she was too busy giving Mr Chin a kiss and he was too busy patting her backside. Then, just as they were about to leave the car park, Carol turned around in reaction to the voice calling behind her.

"Three hours together in the hotel bedroom, not bad...not bad at all considering his age must be at least sixty plus."

To say Carol was shocked was an understatement as she stared at him. "Noah?" was all she could manage to say.

"Room 117. Say no more," he said, shaking his head, before he turned around and walked back towards the car. Both he and George got in, leaving Carol and Mr Chin standing in the car park, both unable to speak and now neither of them wanting to continue the confrontation.

"Thanks, George," Noah said, as he started the engine and drove onto the main road. "I've just had a lucky escape. Once a cheater always a cheater, definitely not the type to marry."

"Reckon you've been played, mate. I'd say there's a good chance the kid she's carrying isn't yours, that's if she is pregnant."

"Yeah," Noah said, a little crestfallen, though relieved at the same time.

It was eight months later when Carol gave birth to mixed-race baby boy with very clear Chinese roots. Noah had been very lucky; had he married Carol, he would now be in the middle of a drawn out divorce dispute costing time and money.

"Definitely a lucky escape," George said when they found out and were having a drink in the pub. "Imagine if you'd assumed all along it was yours and then found out after you'd married her."

"Lying bitch," was all Noah said.

"Once a cheat, always a cheat. Good luck to them all. I'm sure Mr Chin's gonna need it once his wife discovers he's fathered another kid to a girl young enough to be his daughter."

The boys were all happy again. They were back to being the foursome they'd always enjoyed being, realising they'd become a strong unit that covered each other's backs. As a way of life it came to them naturally and even though it had been a difficult situation for Noah, his friends had helped him through it as a team, making them even closer than they were before. Noah, well aware of how lucky he'd been, made the decision that from now on, whether he had sex with a girl on the pill or not, he would always use a condom!

CHAPTER TWO

The lads had been working at the mine for over two years when tragedy happened. Noah had decided he wanted more than working down the mines, choosing instead to see the world, and so had recently made the decision to see what the army could offer. He took a Friday afternoon off to attend an interview at the local army information centre with a view to joining up, hoping it would give him the opportunity to travel. His intension was to get all the information together before sharing his plans with the others, and possibly find out what they thought about making a change in their future, too.

As was now the Friday routine, the boys arranged to meet for an early couple of pints in the Rose and Crown, their local pub. But half an hour into arriving at their usual time Noah began to wonder where the others were, having still not turned up.

Another half-hour passed before the door opened, and Degsy and Stuart walked inside, making their way to the bar where Noah was standing. Their expressions told Noah something had happened; plus, the fact they were still dressed in their work overalls with dashes of coal and dirt smeared across their faces. Noah also noticed both his friends had been crying as he looked into their bloodshot eyes.

"What's the hell's happened?"

"Pit fall," they replied in unison.

"Where's George?" Noah asked, not sure he wanted to know the answer to that question.

Stuart looked down at the floor. "He's in hospital," he said, quietly. "It doesn't look good. He took a real blast."

"Is he going to make it?"

"The hospital won't give us any information, they're saying it's too soon to tell,"

Degsy replied.

"Was anyone else injured?" Noah asked.

Stuart and Degsy looked at each other, then looked at Noah. Stuart nodded solemnly.

"The three lads working with George were all killed instantly," he said, as total silence now descended between them. The shock that Noah would have been one of the miners killed had he been in work that afternoon was too much to bear and tears glazed his eyes as he looked at his friends standing in front of him, their eyes also filled with tears. Once again, he'd been an extremely lucky young man as he always worked with George, loading the huge containers that took the coal to the surface.

Stuart went on to tell Noah that a further thirteen men were missing, including Simon Campbell, their school friend, and that all were presumed dead. They agreed to meet the next day and go to the mine to see if there was any more information about the missing men, but sadly there was none, and it was becoming more apparent that all those not accounted for had died in the blast.

There was more bad news the following Monday morning when they arrived at the mine, only to be told they had to make their way to St Helens Town Hall as an urgent meeting was to take place at 10am. The outcome of that meeting was that the mine was now closed for at least the foreseeable future and each worker would be paid just one week's wage, which meant having to find alternative employment in the meantime, or, if they could afford to, wait until the mine reopened and they were reinstated.

Each of the lads had some savings, but they all knew it would take at least three months, so they tried to get employment in other local mines. Unfortunately, as they feared would be the case, there was now a surplus of experienced miners looking for work due to Clock Face Mine being closed. Over a pint after the meeting, the boys needed to work out what to do next, all feeling very despondent after things had been going so well for them.

"What do you think about joining the army?" Noah asked, pulling out the brochures and information leaflets he'd collected from the recruitment office. After going through all the pros and cons, it was agreed that they had nothing to lose and so they decided to go for it.

But first, they needed to check up on George. Their visit to see him in hospital made it clear he wasn't in any fit state to join the army with them, even though he was out of intensive care. His injuries were too severe and there was a possibility he might never walk again.

Six weeks later, Noah, Degsy and Stuart were staying in barracks at Aldershot Army Training Camp. The shock of the blast at the coal mine was still a talking point and had been a devastating blow for the mining community. Families had been bereaved and some miners still hadn't been found beneath the rubble, but the boys had to get on with their lives and couldn't keep dwelling on what had happened.

Their sorrow lay with George, who was still in hospital and had been diagnosed with permanent paralysis from the waist down. He would never be able to join the others in the army now and would be dependent on a wheelchair for the rest of his life. Noah couldn't help but feel guilty every time he visited his friend, knowing that if he hadn't taken that Friday afternoon off, he would be where George was now, or even worse, he could have been dead.

It was a few weeks after the boys attended their passing-out parade, proud parents and families watching on, when they got their first posting. It was in Cyprus, and even though a bittersweet time for them all having been lucky to be army recruits now, and not affected physically by the tragedy at Clock Face, they enjoyed the leaving party, and managed to have a great time with their friends and families.

Their parents' pride shone through as they recalled tales of themselves being in the army during the second world war and the hardship they went through to protect their country.

"It won't be a bed of roses," Noah's older brother Bram, told him. "My mate was based in Cyprus, and it's always been trouble with the fanatical archbishop organising terrorist action against the British army."

But none of the boys believed they'd come across much conflict while they were there, even though they now felt a bit flat about the prospect, after hoping to be living it up. As far as they were concerned, the British had won the war and Cyprus was only a small island, so there should be no problem.

However, they realised Bram's army friend had been correct when, after being on the island for almost a month, the troubles began to increase daily. It had been fifteen years since the conflict began between the Turks and Cypriots, but for the last few years things had calmed down somewhat.

Most of the operations the boys' battalion carried out were setting up roadblocks and doing 'stop and search' and it was at one of these stop and search roadblocks that a mass killing took place. Twelve soldiers were killed in an explosion, the details sketchy, however, as there were no survivors, and anyone who did survive the blast had been shot in order to leave no witnesses.

The investigating officers were confused. They'd expected to find that a car bomb had caused an explosion of this size, but no evidence was found. When the same thing happened a week later, again with no survivors, there was panic amongst the ranks as nobody knew how the killings were being carried out. The powers-that-be then decided to increase the numbers of soldiers on each petrol.

Noah, Degsy and Stuart were now panicking at the thought of having to dodge bullets, and what made things worse was that they'd been split up and had to man separate roadblocks. Those odds meant that now, at least one of them could be the next target. Things had escalated along with the protection required, and now, before setting up any roadblocks, soldiers had to do a full sweep and search of the area to check for explosives.

It had been a week and there had not been any more explosions. The roadblock Noah manned had been busy all morning before coming to a lull, and the soldiers were instructed to scan the surrounding hills for any movement. Unfortunately, nobody took any notice of the woman walking towards the roadblock pushing a pram with what they presumed was a baby inside.

A shot rang out, causing everyone to dive for cover, and as the soldiers turned to see where it had come from, they were surprised to see the woman who'd been pushing the pram lying dead on the floor. Standing close to her body was their sergeant major, holding a smoking gun that had just been fired. The soldiers began to make their way towards the woman's body, until the sergeant began shouting his orders.

"Stay where you are. Keep your eyes on the road. The next vehicles could be accomplices to finish off the job if this bomb had gone off!"

The soldiers peered into the pram and realised the woman had been hiding a significant number of explosives. There would have been no survivors should she have detonated what was in that pram and everyone stood back, their own thoughts racing at the realisation that they'd just escaped death. The bomb disposal squad arrived on the scene shortly after the sergeant had put out a call on his radio, and they were just about to cut the cable that led from the bomb to the detonator held in the dead woman's hand, when the sergeant stopped them.

"I want you to do a controlled explosion," he said, before turning and pointing in the direction of a hill.

"I'm going to move my troopers up there so we're at a distance when it goes off."

It was a few minutes later when the sergeant and his men took cover and were told to expect a follow-up by the enemy who would kill off any survivors. Sure enough, a short time after the bomb was detonated, a car pulled up and five men jumped out holding machine guns and looking for anyone who had not been killed. In a matter of seconds, all five gunmen were lying dead on the floor having been shot multiple times by several British soldiers, including Noah.

It was the first time he'd shot a man and it had no effect on him. In his mind, if it hadn't been for his sharp-eyed sergeant noticing the detonation wire hanging from the pram, it almost certainly would have been him and his colleagues lying dead on the floor. Once again, Noah was a lucky guy, as, for the second time in his short life, he had cheated death.

There was back patting all round when his group returned to the barracks, Degsy and Stuart having heard about another bomb attack and feeling a huge sense of relief on seeing their friend again.

The British army now had enough evidence to know how the Cypriots had been getting close to the roadblocks: suicide bombers. It was a new threat, but from now on they would be more aware.

Later that day, Noah sat in the canteen with Degsy and Stuart, all three of them starting to have second thoughts about their decision to join the army. They all knew they would almost certainly see more killing during their tour of duty and all they could do was keep their fingers crossed it would never be them.

In the six months that the lads were based in Cyprus, they had changed from carefree young men without a care in the world, into hardnose soldiers. Relief, however, was the emotion they all felt when they were informed they would be going home for Christmas and the regiment they'd replaced would be returning to the base in Cyprus. The conflict was bound to get a lot worse before it got better, but they wouldn't be returning for a while and they looked forward to spending some time with their families instead.

Back in Liverpool, relieved parents, wives and girlfriends welcomed the soldiers home, greeting them with open arms as they arrived once more on British soil. Noah's parents flung their arms around their son, tears flowing after they'd witnessed the atrocities on the television and followed the constant stream of bad news about dozens of soldiers being killed by the terrorists.

Noah's mother Hellen, a non-practising Catholic, and his father, Abraham, a non-practising Jew, had married after a whirlwind romance, They'd been lucky enough to get a three-bedroom house on the outskirts of Liverpool not far from the Ford factory where Abraham worked as an engineer, and apart from Bram, their first born, and of course Noah, they also had twin daughters, Violet and Lisa, who were still at high school.

Hellen prayed Noah wouldn't go back to the army after Christmas and hoped he'd follow in Bram's footsteps and go into accountancy. Bram had done well for himself, starting out as an accountant and now running his own business.

Christmas and New Year went by too quickly and the celebrations were over too quickly, and it was time for the lads to report back for duty. Reluctant to let him go, Hellen held on to her son for a long time, wondering if she'd ever see him again, but she knew he had to go. They weren't going to Cyprus, however, and were instead posted to Belize in South America, then known as British Honduras.

No explanations were given as to why a change in their posting and all the sergeant was prepared to tell them was that it was classified, not to ask any questions, and it was only to be revealed on a 'need-to-know' basis. Instructions would be given once they arrived at their base in Belize. And although they had experienced the heat of Cyprus, nothing could have prepared them for the humidity of the jungle in South America.

They were given two weeks to adjust to the conditions before being told what their duties would be and the reason they were there. Split into groups of ten, their job was to go out into the jungle and locate the numerous cocaine farms currently in operation, and when they discovered them, it was to be their job to destroy them. None of the soldiers really knew anything about cocaine and at first, they found the idea exciting, but it was hard work. From the outset they were given just enough supplies to last two weeks; one week out and one week back, which sounded all good on paper but in reality was a lot harder.

On their first trip into the jungle, they found no active camps, the only ones having already been burnt out. They'd run out of supplies two days before making it back to camp, but what the patrol didn't know was that they were supposed to have had a local guide with them, leading the way. The sergeant who sent them out was a Mancunian and had a dislike of those from Liverpool. His intention to send out his scouse troopers backfired on him, however, when they wearily walked back to base, albeit alive and well. Their journey through the dense jungle could have had tragic circumstances, which was why a guide should have accompanied them.

Hungry and tired, the soldiers were desperate for some food, to take a shower and then go to bed. The last thing they needed was Sergeant Chambers ordering them to give in their location sheets indicating which areas they had covered. His voice rising and his temper beginning to show, he demanded they be handed in immediately, but unbeknownst to him, Captain Harris, Chambers' superior, had heard the commotion and approached Noah.

"Where's your guide?" he asked.

He could tell by the look on the soldiers' faces they didn't have a clue what he was talking about, and the captain then turned to the sergeant.

"Sergeant Chambers," he bellowed, "did you send this rookie group of soldiers out into the jungle without a guide?"

Chambers had been caught banged to rights, and he knew it.

The captain then turned back to the soldiers.

"You men get something to eat and take your rest. I will see you all first thing in the morning for a debriefing."

"Yes, sir," came the replies in unison from each soldier, now desperate to make their way to the canteen for their first hot meal in two weeks.

After ten days of carrying out local duties, they were ready to go back out on tour again, only this time they had maps that showed where the streams ran and any imminent dangers they may face. They also had an experienced guide who knew his way around the jungle. He led them on a six-hour hike, using pathways that were well-used, and they advanced more in six hours than they had done in two days on their previous mission.

Noah's fellow troopers were pleasantly surprised when they came across a clearing that had obviously been used as a camp, alongside of which was a running stream with fresh water. The guide told them this would be a base from where they would go out on patrol, a six-hour duration ending back at the camp to eat and sleep. The guide then made his way into the undergrowth, returning ten minutes later to a sea of puzzled faces as the soldiers wondered what he was up to. He was carrying two large holdalls each containing ten hammocks. He then made his way around the trees where hooks had been fitted from his previous times spent at the camp, and hung them in place.

The guide also had a map, which had been marked out in grid sections. This was to let headquarters know the location of any cocaine farms they had destroyed, even though, after searching for three days, they hadn't found any. It was on the return to camp on the third day that they got a smell of smoke coming out of a dense area to the left of the trail. It was late and getting dark and they marked the area with a circle of twigs with a view to returning and exploring at another time.

Back at camp they spread out the maps and were able to work out where the smoke had more than likely come from, and then, with the expert help of their guide, they found their first farm. It wasn't like anything they had expected.

There was no factory like they assumed there would be and instead could only see bamboo-type shelters where the coca plants were turned into pure cocaine. What the soldiers didn't realise as they made their way towards the farm was that coca plants were growing wild. It was an impossible challenge as everywhere you looked, another coca plant was growing.

Expecting resistance, the soldiers had guns at the ready not knowing what to expect and were shocked when they finally came across a group of scruffy and unkempt people, mostly men, who looked a sorry bunch and put up no resistance whatsoever. They just packed up and left after speaking to the guide.

Not knowing what to do next it was the guide who took charge, instructing the men to grab all supplies of food and other items they would use back at base. The camp was well-stocked with different ingredients and tinned soups, rice and potatoes. It was something the soldiers found fascinating, knowing these people had been living here for probably months on end, harvesting the purest cocaine that would amount to millions of pounds, whilst they lived in quite filthy conditions, albeit with enough food to last them a lot longer than they would be staying.

The next thing they did was count how many kilos of cocaine were stored on the farm, which turned out to be in excess of one hundred kilos. Because they knew very little about cocaine, they had no idea what it was worth.

After photographing the product, they then set about destroying it and were just about to burn down the sleeping area when their guide stopped them, pointing to the dozen or more hammocks hanging between the trees, all covered by netting to keep out the bugs, and in his broken English he indicated the soldiers should stay here for the time being. That afternoon, they had a hot meal for the first time since leaving their barracks, curtesy of the guide who used the confiscated supplies to their fullest.

The next day they radioed back to base, informing them of what they'd found, and within an hour, the noise of a plane could be heard flying above, confirming the information by the smoke coming out of the jungle.

They spent the next three days in the camp before making the two-day journey back to base, but before they left, they buried all the tinned goods. When they came this way again, they would then have extra supplies, including a good amount of food, which gave the platoon more incentive to find the cocaine farms.

They had been back at base for a few hours when the group were called into the canteen where they saw a display of all the photographs they had taken at the cocaine farm. It was confirmed this was the largest farm that had been destroyed to date. The captain was a lot happier, as he'd been under pressure from his seniors who had been telling him that their US counterparts had been destroying farms at the rate of two a month, and questions were being asked about the British capability. But a haul of this size would help put that to bed.

The platoon was given their next set of areas to be investigated and were disappointed that it was in a totally different direction to where they'd hidden the tinned rations. When given the area they were to patrol they had hoped it might have been towards the areas where the US troops had been finding farms to destroy, as they'd been so successful in finding so many.

After two days in the jungle, trudging through dense bracken and avoiding the dangerous and venomous creatures that were a constant threat, a strange thing happened to them and although they didn't know at the time, it would change their futures in a way they would never have thought possible.

Brown sugar how you taste so good. Brown sugar just like a young girl should.

A song was being played from a speaker not far from where they stood and they froze, fearing they could have wandered into enemy territory. It could be anything in this incredibly thick jungle, and on their guard, weapons raised, they slowly advanced towards where the music was coming from. But as they got closer and the music got louder, the other thing they noticed was the smell of cooking; a strong smell of meat and vegetables, not something they experienced often in these parts. Then, more music rang out.

This could be the last, this could be the last time, maybe the last time, I don't know.

Mick Jagger was roaring out the words and the soldiers begin to wonder whether it was some sort of joke. But once they got close enough to the camp, they could see soldiers in what appeared to be American combats scattered around a makeshift camp and sitting upon benches, drinking what looked like beer. But the biggest shock they had was the sight of all the women, very scantily clad and seeming to wait on the men.

Not knowing what to think, most of the British soldiers wanted to make their way into the camp, but Noah stopped them.

"They might be working for the Columbian cartel," he whispered. "We might be their enemy or the target."

Everybody stopped in their tracks and continued to watch what seemed like a party taking place just a few yards away. After a few minutes, more women came out of a hut holding plates of food and handing them to the soldiers who began eating hungrily. It was at that moment one of the men stood up and looked towards the British troopers on the other side of the trees. He smiled and waved his arm about, beckoning them to come forward before picking up a handheld speaker and shouting, "Hey, you Brits, come on in, dinner is being served!"

Somewhat apprehensive, but knowing they'd been spotted anyway, the soldiers began to make their way through the trees where the US troops waved and encouraged them to sit down.

And that decision to join those US soldiers would lead them on the path to a way of life they could only have dreamed of, not just here in the jungle, but one which would follow them all the way back to the UK.

Noah couldn't believe this was happening as he, like some of his fellow soldiers, lay on his stomach, completely naked, being given his first massage. Noah's masseuse was a stunning Brazilian teenager, one of twenty young women who'd been sent to the soldiers by the cartel bosses to keep them happy and cater for their every whim, and that included sex.

"Enjoy yourselves, guys," Sergeant Harper told them. "The girls are there for your benefit, so take advantage!"

At first the soldiers were a bit hesitant to take advantage but not being with a woman for such a long period of time, it didn't take long for their resistance to break down, especially when all the girls showed no signs of shyness when they bathed in the local stream totally naked as if they didn't have a care in the world. It became almost impossible to resist their advances, which, of course, they didn't.

Sergeant Samuel Harper from the US army went on to explain he and his men had been the ones to burn the cocaine farms to the ground, living on minimal supplies as they trudged through rough terrain. He also told them it had been a pointless task due to the fact there were so many in South America, that they hadn't even scratched the surface. Noah and Degsy agreed and so just went with the flow, making their way to the American camp and spending their days being spoilt and pampered.

To make the powers-that-be think they were doing their job, the local natives would go deep into the jungle, make a clearing, and start a fire, and the soldiers would then radio their superiors and give them the location on the grid of the latest so-called, burnt-out farm. It worked like a charm and they were getting praised by the higher-ranking officers at headquarters!

CHAPTER THREE

It was two months later when the group were told they were due some leave and were given a choice of where to spend their two weeks off: Brazil or Mexico. It was Samuel Harper who helped them make up their minds by suggesting a fortnight in Rio, asking them to drop off a parcel in the city centre.

"You can keep the money you get for this," Harper said. "Just make sure it gets to the address on the front." And so, Noah, Degsy and Stuart, along with another soldier from their group called Archie, got their backpacks ready and made their way to the airport.

The parcel, labelled and neatly wrapped in brown paper, contained a kilo of the purest cocaine and because they were soldiers, they were fast tracked through customs and chauffeur-driven to a rather swish hotel, organised by Sergeant Harper. He had pre-paid for everything, or the cartel had.

A couple of hours later, after showers and a drink at the hotel bar, the four of them set off from their hotel and walked through the streets of Rio, looking for the address on the parcel. None of them knew what kind of money would be passed over, but if it was a few hundred dollars each, they'd be more than happy. As they reached the address, the first thing they noticed was how upmarket the building was, with a sign fixed above the door advertising a beauty parlour and hairdressers. Degsy knocked on the door and the lads stood back, not knowing what to expect, and within a few seconds, a young woman appeared and invited them in.

"How can I help?" she said, looking them all up and down with an expression that made them wonder if they'd been sent here for something other than just dropping off a parcel.

Noah held the parcel out, showing her the label. "We've brought this for Shelley. Is she here?"

The lady nodded. "Follow me," she said, leading them through a door at the back of the room and along a dimly lit corridor.

When she got to another door at the end, she knocked gently and a voice called out, "Come in."

She opened the door and stood aside, making enough room for the lads to walk through. They entered a large room that had a huge desk over the far side and a bar to their left. Leather sofas were positioned in the middle of the room and a giant oak coffee table in between them. But what their eyes were immediately aware of was a good-looking brunette woman sitting behind the desk in an executive leather chair, and she stood up when the door was closed and walked towards them.

"Alright, lads, how's it going?" she said, in a strong Liverpudlian accent.

The four lads smiled, surprised to hear what sounded like a friendly voice amidst this rather dark and somewhat seedy-looking building.

"You're a scouser," Noah said. "What are you doing here in Rio?"

"Married to the owner," Shelley replied, taking the parcel from his hands and putting it on the desk. Then she took out a bundle of dollars from her desk draw and started to count it in front of them. Dollar notes were being placed on the desk in four bundles and she continued to pile them up, the lads looking on in complete amazement. They had never seen such a huge amount of money in their lives.

She then picked up the money and handed a bundle to each of them in turn.

"There you go, boys," she said. "Enjoy!"

They took the cash from her and stared at it. "How much?" Stuart asked.

"You've got five grand each," Shelley said. "Make sure you put it in the hotel safe. There are a lot of thieves about in this city and foreigners round here stand out."

Putting the money in their pockets, each of them couldn't help but grin as Shelley went back to the other side of the desk, made herself comfortable in the chair, and put the parcel in the top drawer. "Off you go, then," she said, unable to hide her own grin as it became obvious to her that the lads were new to all this.

They left the office and were escorted by the lady who'd let them in, back to the door where she offered a smile before ushering them through.

"Is there a decent place to have a pint around here?" Noah asked her as they stood on the pavement.

"Juan's Bar, just down that way," she answered in broken English. "Expensive, but you can afford it." And then she closed the door and put the bolts back in place while the four lads set off with a spring in their step.

What they didn't know, however, was that Sergeant Samuel Harper was heavily involved with a Columbian drug's cartel, that were making plans to flood Europe with pure cocaine and heroin. He'd built up a working relationship with Shelley who had become the main distributor in Rio, and she and Harper had high hopes that they could get the lads involved in getting a supply chain back into the UK. Liverpool was the perfect location with it having a major dock, as well as being central in the U K.

They found Juan's Bar and had a few drinks, shocked at how much they were, but it was a pleasant place to spend a few hours and they were well looked after by a very appealing waitress who made a point of showing off her cleavage every time she bent down to place their drinks on the table. They were lapping it up and when she arrived with a tray filled with tapas dishes, they were even more pleased.

When they got back to the hotel, there was a message waiting for them behind reception. It was from Shelley, requesting they join her that evening for dinner.

Seven o'clock prompt, they were sitting at a table in Marco's restaurant, a plush glass-fronted building with modern interior décor and a grand piano being played in the far corner. Six places had been set and they assumed Shelley's husband would be joining them. But they were shocked when she walked towards them ten minutes later followed by Sergeant Harper.

Although the exchanges were friendly, it was plain to see they had an agenda, and so Noah asked straight out, "So, what's all this about? It's obvious you two have a plan, so why don't you just get to the point and let us in on it?"

Harper looked at Shelley, impressed by Noah's forthright questioning, and Shelley looked from each lad in turn.

"Now you have an idea what kind of money can be earned from dealing in cocaine, it won't be long before all of Europe is swamped in it. There's a lot of money to be made here. Would you be interested in getting involved?" Harper asked.

There was silence for a few moments before Noah once again spoke up.

"What would we have to do and what would the risks be?"

"There won't be any risks if you're organised and do it the way we tell you to do it," Shelley replied.

"And what way would that be?" Noah asked.

Harper shuffled in his seat and rested his elbows on the table. "Before we go any further," he began, "is it something you would be interested in?"

Noah looked to his three companions for guidance, and each one gave him the nod. "We are interested," he said. "What would be required from us?"

"As we have said," Shelley replied, "the cocaine market is growing in Europe, and we have a window of opportunity to build up a substantial reserve of the product ready and in place for when a bigger demand comes." She hesitated, then added, "And it will come."

Noah nodded. "How would it work and what would you want us to do?" he asked again, a little impatient that his questions hadn't yet been answered.

"So," Shelley started, "first, you'll need to get a group of soldiers around you that you can trust and would be interested in making money. It would be an advantage if you could recruit someone from a high rank, like a sergeant or an officer." She stopped and looked at them all again, as they continued to stare at her with intent. "There are five thousand soldiers based in Belize. Every month, five hundred go home and five hundred new soldiers arrive. We are prepared to give every returning soldier one thousand pounds each time they take two kilos of product back to the UK."

That amount of money got everyone's attention. Considering their current annual salary was around ten thousand pounds, it seemed like a very tempting offer indeed.

This would be like getting several weeks' worth of tax-free wages in one fell swoop! Nobody had a clue about the epidemic that was planned, not just for the UK but the whole of Europe.

The cartel wasn't worried about making money now, but once they had their supply lines set up in England, they had other means of getting the product into the country, and hoping to set up a base in the UK first could mean it would become their gateway to Europe.

On their return to the army base, the boys had a lot to think about. They still had no real idea of the journey they were about to embark on. Noah, however, was more aware than the others about what they were getting themselves into. He knew the rewards would be high, and his thoughts drifted to trying to decide which of the officers he would approach to bring on board. Most weren't the type you could ask, being married to the army, but there *was* one: Sergeant Adrian Chambers.

Chambers was pissed off as he'd just returned from a two-week stint in the jungle having failed to find a single farm to destroy. He couldn't understand how a group of soldiers whom he had no time for could manage to destroy not one but sometimes two cocaine farms every time they went on patrol. Upon returning to base, Noah decided there was no time like the present and went to see Chambers in his office.

"When are you due to go out on patrol again?" Noah asked.

"Why?" Chambers answered.

"I've got a proposal to put to you. I think it's something you'll be interested in."

Chambers looked Noah up and down, an expression of annoyance covering his features as he wondered how this young soldier had the cheek to speak so openly. "Like what?" he asked.

"I'll show you rather than tell you," Noah replied. "Can you come with us on our next tour?"

Curiosity getting the better of him, Chambers nodded slowly, his eyebrows knitted together. "Yes," he said, "but it'd better be worth my while."

Noah saluted and turned towards the door. "It will be," he said, before adding, "sir." Then he walked out and went back to join his comrades.

Not one to miss out on an opportunity, especially if it meant making money, Chambers couldn't concentrate for the rest of the day, knowing that these four likely lads from Liverpool were obviously onto something and needed him to help them do whatever it was they'd signed up for. It was four days later when he was sitting at a table eating freshly cooked chicken and drinking an ice-cold beer after a short tour through the jungle with the four scouse soldiers, that he couldn't believe his good fortune.

He was even more impressed when they introduced him to Sergeant Samuel Harper, and he then realised they were dealing with a professional organisation.

The operation was set up. Cocaine was supplied to the UK free of charge for the first six months while the cartel organised permanent bases and agreed terms with their counterparts in Liverpool.

Over the next six months, a regular routine was built up where twenty kilos a month arrived in the UK, all financed by the Columbians, who had also, by now, opened bases throughout Europe. It was at this time the lads' tour of duty in Belize was coming to an end.

A good working relationship had been built between Noah and Sergeant Chambers, and he was satisfied that between Chambers and Shelley they would have a steady supply of the cocaine. The money the cartel was paying out was, of course, pocket money to their business, but to Noah and Chambers, it was a small fortune.

When Noah met up with Shelley in a restaurant on his two-day leave, he asked her what the expected turnover would be in the next twelve months. To say he was shocked would be putting it mildly as she told him they would be dealing in tens of millions of British pounds. Shelley noticed Noah looking apprehensive at these huge amounts and the last thing she wanted was for him to cock all this up by being naïve.

"Everything's going smoothly," she said. "There's no need to look so worried, this is very normal."

"Millions?" was all Noah could think of to say.

"Yes, millions. Have you any idea what coke is worth?" she said, smiling as she hoped her words were reassuring him. "These cartels are dealing in high-end drugs and these amounts of money are part of it." He nodded and she added, "I'll be in Liverpool when you return to the UK, I'm needed to make sure things are in place just the way we want them to be. I had to arrange things for when the cartel break into the States so if we do it the way we did it there, you'll have no problems with the law."

It was clear to Noah now that they were onto something big, but he also knew it would come with risks. He'd seen the news reports from the US that cocaine was now flooding every part of the country and it wouldn't be long before the government acted.

"So," he said, "what action do I take to keep ahead of the game?"

They were words Shelley was happy to hear, as she realised he wasn't just seeing pound signs but was looking at the pitfalls so he could avoid them.

"First thing," she said, "is to never become a user. That's a big mistake that many dealers make. You don't mix with users at all, if possible. And whatever you do, whoever you meet, don't go splashing the cash. Set up a cover business. Don't invest it in flash cars and expensive homes. But don't keep any cash on the premises or let anybody hold on to it on your behalf. Okay?" Noah nodded and Shelley was satisfied he was listening to her every word.

"Once established," she continued, "I'll show you how to set up as many layers and dealers between you and your suppliers as you can. But disassociate yourself from the drug scene as much as possible." She took a sip of her drink before adding, "I will be putting a structure in place that works, but you will have to make sure your three colleagues follow suit. Money corrupts, it gives people delusions of grandeur, but it also makes a lot of people jealous, and jealousy makes people do silly things like informing the police on dealers. So, low profile right across the board as much as possible. Got that?"

The risks were high, and Noah was very much aware, but he was also aware of the high financial rewards that were going to come his way. He'd made a lot of money on the drug runs he'd done over the past six months, but he realised that was nothing compared to what he was on the brink of now. Shelley impressed him. She knew so much about the trade, she was clever, too. She had an air about her which showed she pulled no punches or took any shit from people.

"How long have you been involved with the drug trade?" he asked.

Shelley gave it some thought before giving her answer. One of the rules was not to give away too much information about yourself and as a stickler for rules, she wondered just how much she could reveal.

"Six years, give or take," she replied.

Noah was surprised, assuming she was much younger than she appeared to be. "You look no older than twenty-one, twenty-two at most. So, how old are you?"

Shelley smiled cutely and put her head to one side. "It's rude to ask a lady her age."

Noah tried another question. "What part of Liverpool are you from?"

But again, Shelley wasn't prepared to give him the answer he really wanted.

"The suburbs," she said, looking away from him and hoping her vagueness would discourage him from asking anything else of a personal nature.

"Anyway," she said, "when are you due back home?"

"February third," Noah answered. "I'll be discharged out of the army by March. Our time in the army will be over then."

She took a small notepad out of her handbag and fumbled around for a pen, then wrote a phone number down, ripped the piece of paper from the notepad, and handed it to Noah. "Here," she said. "This is my number in Liverpool. Call me the week you get discharged and make sure you ring at exactly at 12pm. I'll be in Liverpool and will arrange a meeting to get the ball rolling."

Noah looked at the paper. "This is a Liverpool city centre number," he said. "Is it an office?"

Shelley put a finger to her lips, nodded, then put the notepad and pen back in her bag. "Yes, it is. It's my contact in the Colombian embassy. Don't look so worried," she said, as she noticed Noah's expression suddenly turn to one of concern.

"He's on board with it all. Just say you want to arrange a meeting with Shelley. Say nothing else, just that, then hang up."

Noah swallowed and put the piece of paper in his pocket before Shelley continued.

"Then, you need to call back the next day at exactly the same time and you will be given a time and a place to meet."

The fact that the cartel had a member of the Colombian embassy on board impressed Noah. To him, it showed how big their plans for the UK and Europe really were.

When he caught up with Degsy and Stuart later that day, he filled them in on every detail about his meeting with Shelley, telling them about the rules they would all have to follow, how the operation was huge and even though the risks involved were dangerous, if everything went to plan, as it should, those risks would be minimal. He also asked about Archie, as he wasn't sure he trusted him. After their first drop off, that time in Rio when they met Shelley, it hadn't gone unnoticed that Archie seemed a little too excited about spending huge amounts of money and the fact one of the rules was not to go splashing the cash and drawing attention to themselves, it was a worry. None of them knew much about him and they all decided it was better if they met up with him soon and got to know him a bit better.

They went to find Archie after supper, slouched in a hammock, holding his tin cup filled with water. After going through the rules, updating him on what was going on and what would be required, Noah decided to ask the question he'd been wanting to ask for some time.

"Anyone of you been in trouble with the police?" he asked. He knew Degsy and Stuart hadn't, but he didn't want to aim the question at just Archie for fear of causing offence.

"No," Degsy said, and Stuart shook his head and said the same.

"How about you, Archie?" Noah asked, looking at him.

"No, never," Archie replied. "Good as gold, I am."

That was just what Noah and the others wanted to hear. Noah went on to tell them the set of rules they would have to keep to so as not to attract the attention of the police or anyone that might get jealous of their newfound wealth and grass them up.

"Why us?" Degsy asked. "With that kind of money on offer they could recruit just about anybody!"

CHAPTER FOUR

Noah

Back in Liverpool, George was getting used to life in a wheelchair. Even though he'd rather have been working for a living, he was grateful for the compensation he'd received from the coal mine as he was able to buy himself a smart bungalow in a nice area. He and Noah had been writing to each other since Noah joined the army, and knowing George wasn't shy to a good financial deal, he thought it might interest his friend to include him in their new business opportunity. George was very interested. Making money was what he needed to do.

He'd spent most of the compensation on having the bungalow adapted, door frames widened and the garden levelled out to accommodate the wheelchair, and now it was time to start finding another way to access an income. Noah's proposal had come just at the right time.

Noah sent George two hundred pounds which enabled him to have a phone line installed, as Noah knew he would have to get in contact directly once he had everything in place. It was also an advantage to have George's sister Debbie on board, as she was able to drive him to the south of England each month once they had the operation working. He was instructed to pick up twenty kilos of cocaine from ten soldiers who had just returned from Belize and they were to meet in a local pub in Brize Norton.

Noah told Shelley that he had everything in place to start what he needed now that the cash was available to pay the soldiers when they brought the cocaine into the country. And Shelley made sure the money was put into George's account to pay the soldiers and a good payment for him for his involvement, too.

Debbie didn't know what the packages contained and didn't want to ask, even though she had an idea, but each month after they'd made the journey, somebody transferred a thousand pounds into George's bank account and all Debbie asked for was to be reimbursed for the petrol.

It was helping George out quite nicely and he was once more content whenever his bank statements came through the letter box. The cocaine was stored in his garage and locked away and none of his neighbours were any the wiser.

By now the boys were aware of the way cocaine was swamping America and had started to creep into Europe via Holland and Spain. They also knew the goods that were stacked in George's garage were strong drugs as one day, just before the team were getting ready to go back to the UK, Noah phoned George's bungalow and could immediately tell by the tone in his voice there was something wrong.

"What the fuck is in the stuff in the garage?"

"Why?" Noah asked.

"Rats got in there and have been eating into one of the packages. They went crazy, running all over the place."

"You're keeping it in the fucking garage? For fuck's sake, George, anybody could spot it and report it to the police."

"Don't worry, Debbie moved it into the bedroom when it went dark."

"Thank god for small mercies," Noah said with a sigh.

It was February, and the boys had been home for a week when Noah made the call to the number Shelley had given him back in the fancy restaurant in Belize. It was obvious as he spoke to the receptionist that she'd been expecting his call and he promptly hung up after requesting a meeting with Shelley. The next day, as instructed, he did the same thing and was told by the lady on the other end of the phone to meet Shelley the following day at the Adelphi Hotel. "Be in the bar 12pm prompt," she added.

The next day, Noah showered and chose one of his best suits, taking a little time over deciding which tie to wear with it. A quick shave and a splash of Brut finished off his transformation and he went downstairs to the kitchen where Hellen, his mother, was standing by the sink.

"Got a job interview?" she asked, thinking how dapper her youngest son looked.

He nodded and grabbed his car keys. "Yep, a security company," he said, hoping she wouldn't ask any more questions because he hated having to lie to his mother. He gave her a peck on the cheek and left the house.

"Good luck!" she shouted after him as he closed the front door.

In his heart, he knew this could lead onto something big, and especially after he'd seen George's bungalow and the setup he had there. That double size bedroom was ideal, and he was more than grateful to Debbie also, for helping the way she was. Poor George couldn't drive; he'd never had the chance to even learn. She was a godsend in more ways than one.

He'd seen the boxes, each filled with ten kilos of cocaine, stacked up in the bedroom, and had been extremely impressed at how Debbie had managed on her own, most likely with George's supervision. He might have been wheelchair-bound, but he was still sharp and sometimes a bit bossy. Noah, of course, knew the true value of the cocaine, but chose not to tell George just yet. Per kilo, it was worth twenty-five thousand pounds, but that price would rocket once it started hitting the market. There were currently a hundred and fifty kilos in that double bedroom, and George had no idea he had product worth well over three and half million pounds inside his property.

Noah felt a bit over dressed when he met up with Shelley in the bar at the Adelphi. She was wearing jeans along with a casual denim top and she smiled at him as he approached, looking him up and down and raising her eyebrows.

"You look like a car salesman," she said, then added, "a good looking one at that."

"Thanks," Noah said, sarcastically. "Thought I'd dress up for the occasion. This is a nice joint, not like some of the shitholes we used to frequent in South America."

"I've ordered afternoon tea for two," Shelley said with a smirk as he sat down on the stool next to her.

"Nice," Noah said, wishing she'd ordered him a pint. He then took his wallet out of his jacket pocket and put it on the table.

"What did I say about flashing the cash?" she said, noticing his wallet looked like it was bulging with notes. Then she smiled. "Put it away. These are on me."

The meeting went well, and Shelley's afternoon tea turned out to be a few pints for him after all, and a gin and tonic for her. She told him that she'd got an opening in Jersey, a gang that wanted twenty kilos of product, worth half a million pounds. They were one of the major dealers in Europe and had associates in place in all the major capitals.

"I've got five families in place to carry ten kilos each to the island in a hire car. They'll get a free holiday in return and plenty spending money, so they're happy to do it."

"So how does that work, then?" Noah asked.

Shelley looked at him as though he was a school kid who'd just starting learning a new subject.

"Well," she began, "they'll arrive at their hotel, someone will meet them in reception after they've checked in and give them a set of keys to another hire car the same make and model as their original hire car. It'll even have the same number plates. Then, before the car gets returned to the hire company the following week, a member of staff exchanges the spare wheel and replaces it. The removed wheel will then be given to George, who will take it to you. The happy holiday makers aren't told anything about the operation or the spare tyre that's been replaced with a hundred thousand used pound notes inside. I must make sure it all runs smoothly, as you know." She took a sip of her gin and tonic then added, "Anyway, I heard your big brother is an accountant, is that right?"

Noah nodded. "Yeah, and a good one, too. He's honest as the day's long, though. Why are you asking?"

"Might he want to join us, come on board and work for us?"

"I'm not sure," Noah said, taking a gulp of his pint and wiping his mouth with the back of his hand. "He doesn't know about the drugs operation. I've never told any of my family. My mother thinks I'm having an interview at a security company right now!"

Shelley laughed. "You do look like you're dressed up for an interview, I have to say. Not like you're meeting me for a few drinks in a casual setting."

Noah looked down at his recently pressed trousers. "I'll tell her I didn't get the job," he said, replacing the now-empty glass on the bar and signalling the barman to get another round.

"Well, anyway, have a chat with your brother and see what his reaction is. You never know, he might be up for it. I can't imagine being an accountant is much fun!"

"He's done well for himself, thank you very much," Noah said, taking the fresh pint of beer from the barman. "He always worked hard at school. I couldn't wait to leave!"

When all the money from the Jersey operation was back in Liverpool via the hire car, Noah had a get together with his crew, which now included George along with the four lads that had been in the army. He gave each of them a folder that contained twenty thousand pounds, and also gave them a stern warning not to go flashing the cash around but to open as many bank accounts from different addresses as was possible. They were also to recruit a family member to each bank every Friday to deposit a thousand pounds in cash, as this was the first of their monthly pay days. And it would start to get even bigger as the months went on.

"The biggest problem we can create is to let people see all these bank notes. One thing you need to think about doing is investing in property abroad, Spain or Portugal are the best places, as they accept used notes. Some places call it black money. You need to make sure you keep your heads down, stay on the ball, and be clever. We don't want any fuckups."

He then glanced at each of the lads, resting his eyes on Archie, who looked a bit eager to get spending.

"You got that, everyone?" he asked, and they all nodded. "Archie, are you on board?"

Archie nodded too, quite enthusiastically, and Noah realised he'd have to keep a close eye on him.

That night, Noah decided to tell his brother what was happening in his life, cautious as he had a feeling it might not go down too well. Bram, who was knowledgeable and had dealt with dodgy businesses before, pulled his face.

"I don't know, Noah, this is big business and I know for a fact American drug dealers are the number one target for government agencies. These people do nothing but bring misery to people's lives. They're not good people to get involved with."

"I was hoping for some advice," Noah said. "The amount of money we're talking about is huge to say the least. We're talking millions."

He hoped that might tempt Bram, but when he didn't say anything, Noah continued.

"A friend of mine told me the easy part is getting the cash, but the hardest part is cleaning it up and hiding it. She told me the downfall so far in the States is that too many dealers flash the cash so much they stand out like sore thumbs, attracting the wrong type of attention."

"Who is this friend?" Bram asked. "Can you trust her?"

"Her name's Shelley, she's very well connected. She has a degree in business studies, and she's my one and only contact to do business with. And yeah, I do trust her."

"How old is she?"

"Early thirties, or thereabouts. When I first met her, I thought she was in her twenties but as I got to meet with her on a regular basis, I realised she was older after she told me a few things about herself. She's a very well-educated lady, too. Speaks three different languages."

"Three? That's impressive," Bram said. "What are they?"

"Spanish, Portuguese, and English."

"And where's she from?"

"Liverpool."

"What part?"

"Jesus, Bram, quit with the twenty questions, will you," Noah said, feeling a little irritated now. "Anyway, I don't know which part she's from, she won't say. She doesn't have to give out all her personal details to me, it's not how these people work. The less we know about each other, the less the risks are."

Bram went quiet. He wasn't sure he wanted to get involved, even though he knew the rewards would be high. But he also knew the jail sentence that followed would be high too, if or when they were caught.

Something he was aware of, however, was that without his help, he was quite sure Noah and the others would end up serving a very long time inside and that was something Bram wasn't going to allow to happen to his younger brother. If he was to get on board with this, he'd need to lay down a few ground rules and make sure Noah understood it would be for his own good. Apart from which, their parents didn't deserve to be visiting their youngest son in jail, not now and not in the future.

"Right," Bram said, sighing heavily and reaching for the glass of whisky in front of him. He took a large swig then carried on. "Come to my office at two o'clock on Monday and make sure you come on your own. Don't let anybody else know about me getting involved, especially this Shelley woman. Okay?"

Noah nodded. His brother was serious and now expressing the business side of his personality, something he'd never seen before. Then both men finished their drinks and Bram poured another glass for each of them.

The following Monday afternoon, Noah found himself sitting in Bram's office reading a list of conditions that he'd been presented with, drafted up in secret by Bram himself.

1. *Nobody, absolutely nobody is to know that I am involved with your dealings in any way whatsoever.*
2. *After a period of two years when you have accumulated enough clean money, you will cut all ties with everybody connected to the business you are in at present.*
3. *Any systems that I set up for you are not to be shared with any of your associates. None whatsoever.*
4. *You will move out of our parents' house and relocate to a moderate apartment in the city centre.*
5. *All records of dealings will be kept away from George's bungalow and kept in a secret location only known by you.*
6. *You will arrange to have monthly meetings to discuss the business. These meetings will be held in different locations; no location being used twice in a six-month period and the address will only be given on the day of the meeting, to be arranged by you.*

Noah read the conditions to himself then put the sheet of paper back on the desk and sat back in the chair, looking up at his brother.

"That all seems fair," he said, realising this was the first step to getting Bram involved.

"I would suggest you get your Liverpool associates to recruit a right-hand man, an intern who does the same. The chain of command needs to be moved as far away from the top as possible and it should be made clear to that person the name of his boss should never ever be disclosed to anyone. The same conditions should be passed on down the line. This is for your benefit, Noah, so you need to be sure they understand.

"All these conditions need to be carried out, they're all high importance. You need to build as many barriers as possible with no paper trail that could lead to you. Anonymity is everything and this is something you need to drive home to your colleagues, too."

Noah nodded and they shook hands over the desk.

"Right then," Bram said. "Fancy a pint?" They both stood up and walked towards the door, and Bram patted his brother on the back. "It's important you don't get caught, mate," he said, as he opened the office door and beckoned Noah through first.

CHAPTER FIVE

Shelley

Shelley Helm was born in Liverpool, the youngest one of eight children. Her upbringing was a happy one and she was loved unconditionally and spoilt rotten. Her dad, Richard, was of German descent, whose family name was shortened when his parents had decided to move to Liverpool. The name Von Helm would not have gone down well with the locals after the first world war.

Shelley decided she wasn't going to follow in her parents' footsteps like most families did in those days. She didn't want to marry young and have a big family, she wanted a career, one where she could travel and see the world, meet interesting people and climb the ladder in her chosen occupation. It had been an old-fashioned geography teacher who had first got her interested in travelling, once a merchant seaman who had spent years exploring the world. He had advised his class that they would be better off learning Spanish as a second language, as French wouldn't help as much due to so many parts of the world being able to speak Spanish.

Shelley made her decision from his advice and went on to study Spanish language and business studies in college, then got a place at Liverpool University where she took a degree in international business studies. She had a good grasp on Spanish, enough to hold a conversation, and eventually changed her language studies to Portuguese after having a holiday in the Algarve. It was a move that would prove to be a good one later in her life.

She had a good social life with many friends, most who were like her and aiming for a successful business career once they'd left university. They all knew it could be a gamble for a woman in those days to get that lucky break and land the job of their dreams, but they had drive and ambition and were all prepared to go the extra mile if it was needed. One of Shelley's closest friends was Rita, who she'd gone through college with and into university, and they both left education with firsts in their chosen subjects. They were inseparable and even bought a flat together.

Rita started work for a company called Avison and Lowness, based in the city centre. Wages were low in those days for interns, but it was a good start and would give her the experience of being in a busy workplace. Life at university had been easy compared to the tasks she was given on a daily basis and even though she would have appreciated a better salary considering the amount of work she'd put into her degree, she was grateful for the opportunity of building a career. Shelley, on the other hand, landed a job with a well-paid salary in a larger firm and that meant with their joint income they could easily afford the flat. Another plus was that both companies were based in a part of the city only minutes away from one another, so they could take the twenty minutes' walk to and from work together.

Shelley enjoyed her job. She got on well with her colleagues and was keen to do a good job of whatever was needed of her. Most of them, except her boss, Lenny, were married, so she didn't have a great deal in common with them, but nonetheless, it was a good place to work. Her main job was to make sure freight ships had a full cargo on their return to base and she would spend most of her day creating forecasts and liaising with freight companies to make sure the vessels were ready to sail. It was an interesting job to have, one which required her to use her degree to its full potential and one which she did extremely well. But after six months of working there, she was asked to replace one of the women in the office who was leaving to have a baby.

This meant being trained up in a completely different department, one which, fortunately for Shelley, was just as interesting. She was now in charge of ensuring containers reached the port efficiently and were checked in through customs without needing to queue. Each contained perishable goods, such as fruit from Italy and Spain, and flowers from Holland. Shelley was now responsible for each container being checked at the point of unloading by customs where they would fix a government seal on the container doors. It was a highly responsible job because if these containers didn't get through quickly, the goods inside were in danger of being ruined, which in turn would cost the company a huge amount of money, not to mention embarrassment to the supplier.

One morning, Lenny approached her with a look of panic in his eyes, placing a business card in front of her on the desk.

"Call this number later today," he said. "The man that answers is called Pepe. Tell him we have been raided. Then hide this card somewhere, but not in your purse."

Just as he finished talking, the office doors burst open and a large contingent of police officers flooded in, instructing everyone to stay at their desks and not to touch their computers.

The sergeant in charge then approached Lenny, pulled his hands behind his back, and roughly handcuffed him. The next thing the office heard was Lenny being read his rights and arrested for the import of cannabis.

The other police officers then approached each member of staff and began leading them downstairs to the awaiting police vans, where they were taken to the local police station. None of them seemed to know what was happening, all in complete shock when they arrived and were checked in by the desk sergeant.

They'd been in the police station less than an hour when a rather overbearing female solicitor turned up demanding to see her client, Leonard Homes. Angela Rylan was a hardnosed criminal lawyer who was well known for representing high profile criminals. It didn't take long for the police to realise that most of the employees were innocent. It was obvious after brief interviews took place and no explanations were offered, due to the fact no one knew what the hell was going on, that they dealt in high sea import and exports and mostly had nothing to do with the fast imported perishables. To think some dodgy dealings had been taking place under their noses while they worked innocently at their desks, was something none of them could comprehend.

When everyone turned up for work the next morning, the talk was inevitably about Lenny, and they learnt that Elaine, his wife and an employee of the company, was helping the police with their enquiries. It was later that afternoon, just after 2pm, when Elaine turned up at the office, her attitude nonchalant as if nothing had happened.

"I'd like to see you all in the conference room in half an hour," she announced.

Gossip started again amongst the colleagues, and they began to wonder if the company would close, but what Elaine had to tell them surprised them even more.

"As you know, Lenny has been arrested for smuggling cannabis into Liverpool. He did it as a favour for a friend of his, stupidly perhaps, but has now been caught. The operation was a large scale one and has earned him a lot of money, hence why he can pay you all so well."

Everyone looked at the floor when she said that, knowing they were all earning a good wage and knowing how big Lenny and Elaine's house was; a huge mansion set back from a leafy suburb street with electronic gates and a Bentley in the driveway.

"There will obviously be some changes made around here in the coming weeks and I would appreciate your cooperation in helping me turn this company around so we can continue providing the excellent service we do. Some of you will be taking on extra responsibilities and some of you will carry on doing the job you already do. But I'll be requesting a meeting with you individually to go through what will be required." She looked around the room at the sea of faces, realising the responsibility she now had. "Can I rely on you to stay discreet about this, not to answer any questions from the press?"

Everyone nodded.

"And if you receive a phone call from a reporter," she added, "either transfer it to me or hang up. We don't want this company to fail just because Lenny is unable to run it." Then she smiled and said, "Thank you, that'll be all."

Everyone stood up and went back to their desks, hushed tones emitting as a few wandered towards the coffee machine and others sat down and continued their tasks. Shelley wasn't sure what to expect, but she knew her skills could help Elaine and she decided she would accept whatever task her new boss had in line for her to do.

It was the next morning when Elaine called Shelley into her office, the one that used to be Lenny's. Seeing Elaine sat in his executive leather chair, Shelley went in and closed the door, then made herself comfortable in the chair opposite.

"Shelley, thanks for coming to see me," Elaine began. "This has been such a shock for all of us and we now need to keep things running as smoothly as possible. That's why I need you to take charge of the new position of importing soft perishable goods. I know it's something you've been doing, but we weren't sure if it would continue. However, we have orders to fill and I'd like you to get on and run it to your efficient standard."

"Of course, Elaine," Shelley said, nodding. "I'd be happy to keep this position running smoothly. Does this mean you're promoting me?"

Elaine smiled, knowing where this line of questioning was heading.

"If you like, you can consider it a promotion. I'll make sure you receive a pay increase as from your next pay packet."

"Thanks, I appreciate that. Anything to help the company." And with that, Shelley stood up and left the office, heading back to her desk and taking a slight detour to the coffee machine on her way.

Things in the office soon settled down and it seemed like everything had gone back to as near to normal as possible under the circumstances. Lenny never did get back as he received a ten-year jail sentence for the illegal importation and distribution of a Class A drug. Elaine was lucky. She had known about the operation, but Lenny denied that she knew, managing to convince the jury he had kept his drug dealing from his wife in case he was unfortunate enough to get caught. He had a business to keep afloat, after all, and as Elaine knew the business inside-out, it made sense that she would continue running it, with the help of their loyal and somewhat naïve employees, of course.

Over the next twelve months following Lenny's arrest, Elaine had built up a good working relationship with Shelley. She was impressed with her work and the fact she could speak Spanish and Portuguese, knowing it would be helpful in her next business venture, which was scheduled to take place in New York, along similar lines as the setup she had in the UK. So, when she offered Shelley the opportunity to go with her to the States, she jumped at the chance.

Elaine, however, hadn't been totally honest. She'd managed to gain Shelley's trust and admiration and had often relied on her to be next-in-line if she ever needed to leave the company, either in a hurry or to attend a meeting elsewhere. Shelley was confident she could take over at any time and was grateful for this further opportunity to climb the ladder.

She'd become very career orientated, which was something else Elaine liked about her. It meant that this next phase of the business would be something she was sure Shelley would pull off to perfection. In a nutshell, Elaine had been given the opportunity to get in on the next big change that was about to take the world by storm: Cocaine. She already had contacts in the States and had been liaising with several cartel members in order to set up new businesses and therefore increase their turnover.

Something Elaine didn't realise at first, though, was that Shelley was no fool. Her salary was now twice as much as it was when she first joined the company just eighteen months ago, and she'd since moved out of the flat she lived in with Rita, buying her out and leaving all the furniture, and purchased a very nice dockside apartment instead that she could now easily afford. She and Elaine spent many lunch hours eating in fancy restaurants and she'd been to Elaine's house several times for dinner, seeing how her boss lived in luxurious surroundings, being chauffeur-driven to work each morning in her own Bentley.

Shelley wanted to get involved in whatever Elaine was doing, even though she was quite sure it was probably a lot worse than what Lenny had done by importing cannabis for a so-called friend.

Elaine felt she could trust Shelley and she knew she'd need right hand man, so she decided after her first meeting with a cartel member in New York to hire an Italian named Franco. Elaine took Shelley to New York with the intention of getting her on board and when she asked after the meeting with the cartel if she was happy to join them, Shelley nodded and offered a smile. "Yeah, count me in," she said.

The meeting had gone well, and the head of the cartel was impressed with both Elaine and Shelley, quite sure a mutual trust would soon be reached along with a good business rapport and an efficient service, and so Shelley's new life into the murky world of drug dealing began and over the next five years, she built up an impressive profile and large list of contacts, enjoyed living a life of luxury, and was wined and dined by some very influential drug lords.

Her fortune was increasing by the day and her interest in property meant she was able to build up a decent portfolio. She was always one step ahead, learning from the mistakes she saw others make, especially Lenny's where he got caught for being a little too complacent. But by the time she turned thirty, she felt it was time to go it alone, perhaps look for that husband she'd told everyone she had. This was brought forward faster than she expected when Elaine told her Lenny was due out of prison and she was pulling out to live in the apartment she had bought in Portugal. She told Shelley she had the best part of two million spread around several bank accounts all over Europe, and the main reason she was getting out was because a contact she had in the police force had told her that she was being investigated for importing Class A drugs. She had no intention of going down the route Lenny took. He'd been warned and didn't take action to avoid being arrested. But before she pulled out, she introduced Shelley to other members of the cartel she had never met before.

Shelley was now making plans for her own safety and to keep ahead of the police. She'd left the employment of Elaine's company and decided to take Franco's advice and move her operation out of England. The two had formed a good working relationship and trusted one another completely. It was Franco who advised her to relocate to the States and cut all ties with the UK as there would be a good chance the police would have her name in the frame, as they almost certainly knew she was an associate of Lenny and Elaine's.

The supply of cocaine that they had been bringing into the country was a trickle. Franco told Shelley that the American connection to the cartel was setting up a brand new way of bringing in the supply at ten times the rate they had been importing currently and she it would be better that she relocated to somewhere like Rio de Janeiro. He went on to tell her that he owned the perfect place and it would be perfect to run the business from for a year or more, and that by the time she was settled in, the new drugs operation should be set up.

And now she was meeting with Noah to explain how they were going to distribute the cocaine and that they had everything set to go. Shelley had just sat down by the bar at the Adelphi when the barman took her order.

"Gin and tonic, please," she said with an air of confidence. She was giving out the image of a hugely successful businesswoman now and was having another meeting with one of her new recruits, Noah Burgess.

"You look like a car salesman," she said, trying not to laugh as her approached her.

Noah sat down, and she went on to tell him about the apartments she leased, all located in the city, each block holding around twenty dwellings. She rented them out to various couples and some families. The buildings would be constantly busy with people coming and going, so using a few empty apartments to hide the product wouldn't attract any unwanted attention.

"How many married couples with kids do you and your friends know?" Shelley asked.

The question confused Noah and he gave it some thought before answering. "Why?"

"We have our first drop off lined up," Shelley said, taking a sip of her drink and reaching for some peanuts in a dish on the bar. "We have a new buyer lined up for twenty kilos at thirty thousand a kilo."

"Why the married couples?" Noah asked, still a bit puzzled.

"I need five families in place to carry two kilos each to Jersey in a hire cars. They'll get a free holiday in return and plenty spending money, so they'll be happy to do it."

"So, how does that work, then?" Noah asked.

Shelley couldn't help thinking he was quite naïve, and smiled, wondering if the suit was for her benefit. "Well," she began, "they'll arrive at their hotel, someone will meet them in reception after they've checked in and give them a set of keys to another hire car the same make and model as their original hire car. It'll even have the same number plates. Then, before the car gets returned to the hire company the following week, a member of staff exchanges the spare wheel and replaces it. The removed wheel will then be given to George, who will take it to you. The happy holiday makers aren't told anything about the operation or the spare tyre that's been replaced with a hundred thousand used pound notes inside. I must make sure it all runs smoothly, as you know."

"I take it the product would be hidden in the hire cars?" Noah said.

"Yes, the spare tyre holds at least six kilos of coke."

"What are the risks? What would happen if they got caught?"

"Nothing," Shelley said, with a confident shrug. "If they get caught, they will be squeaky clean and innocent, they'll have nothing in their luggage to suggest they knew they were carrying drugs. The smuggling will be attached to the car hire company and more than likely pinned on one of their employees."

Noah gave it a bit of thought then asked, "Will we be paid in the same way?"

"Yes, but with a few exceptions, but that's on a need-to-know basis. Half will be brought back in the spare tyre and the rest delivered using other methods, and as this will be the first time this has been done, using your people it should be risk free."

Shelley was assessing Noah's expression, needing to work out what effect all this was having on him. It was going to be the first of many big cash deals in the future and this deal alone would bring in the best part of six hundred thousand pounds, less expenses, of course. The boys should clear at least five hundred and fifty thousand pounds between them.

This would make or break the team depending on how they handled such a huge amount of cash, and Shelley needed to make sure handling that amount of money wasn't going to go straight to the boys' heads. So far they had done well with the cash they had received.

"The first transaction using the stock you have will be yours and the cash you receive will be yours, and after that, the cartel get their cut," Shelley reassured him, seeing Noah's puzzled look etched on his handsome face and thinking she needed to soften him up a bit.

"Shall we sit at a table?" she asked not waiting for answer, and stood up from the bar stool, making her way towards a table in the corner. He couldn't take his eyes off her as she walked elegantly in front of him, her pert backside and long, slim legs looking very tempting in the tightly fitted skirt she wore.

Shelley had already made her mind up that she was going to seduce Noah. She'd already done her homework on him and discovered he was still single. He ticked all her boxes and was the kind of man she liked, tall and good-looking, and a considerable amount of years younger than a lot of men she had dated. She normally dated men that were a lot older. She'd made her mind up at an early age that she never wanted children and as far as men were concerned the size of his wallet was more important than his looks. She'd met a few that fitted the bill but hadn't fancied settling down on a permanent basis.

She'd booked a room for the night, and it was now time to get to work as they sat at a table and ordered an expensive bottle of wine. The waiter nodded and went rushing off to fetch it, and within a few minutes they were sipping one of the more exclusive bottles of Sauvignon Blanc the bar at the Adelphi had to offer.

It was good, and it wasn't long before they ordered another. A few people were milling around but Shelley and Noah could have had the whole hotel to themselves for all they cared. They were enjoying each other's company and talking about family and business and how life was so much different when they'd met in Rio some years ago.

At 11.30pm, Shelley told Noah about the room she'd booked, an executive penthouse suite, and offered him the chance to see it before he went home. The look in her eyes told him she was offering more than just a tour of one of the Adelphi's high-end suites, and once again he followed her as she led him to the lifts and towards her luxury accommodation. He wasn't disappointed as his eyes scanned the sumptuous surroundings with a stunning view of Liverpool city centre from the floor-to-ceiling window, and when she approached him and put her hand on his, he knew he wouldn't be going home that night.

The next morning, as Noah was leaving the hotel, he couldn't believe what had transpired the night before. It was something else. Shelley had shown him just how experienced she was in the bedroom as they made love many times throughout the night. At one o'clock, they had phoned down to reception for another bottle of wine to be delivered, and had lay in bed, the wine in an ice bucket at the side of Noah, drinking it in their luxury four-poster bed. It was a lifestyle Noah could get used to and one he felt he deserved. As for being with Shelley, he wanted her, and they agreed to meet up in Jersey in a few weeks' time after the first shipment had taken place involving his people.

While still in Liverpool, Shelley met up with her old friend Rita, who was now a well-established solicitor in the city. Having heard that Rita worked for Angela Rylan, the lawyer who'd represented Lenny after his arrest, she thought it would be a good idea to catch up and see if there was a way she could hire her to do a little underhand work with the purchase of a few properties she had in mind. One of those properties was Shelley's mother's house, a council house that her mother had been renting for over twenty years now and one she had the right to buy at a reduced rate.

"I want to buy it for cash," she told Rita. "I don't want to attract any attention and I want the deeds and all the papers drawn up as quickly as possible and put in my mother's name."

"I can help you," Rita said, much to Shelley's relief. "You might know my boss, Angela Rylan?"

"Yes, she did a lot of work for my boss Elaine Pursell, when her husband Lenny got sent to prison. I know Angela. She's a good lawyer, though she couldn't get him off," Shelley said.

"Larry was caught red-handed, he thought he was above the law," Rita pointed out. "Anyway, if you want this done on the quiet, Angela is the right person. Lenny managed to keep a stash of cash and started buying houses and Angela has a way of filtering cash through client accounts before completing the sale. I'm sure she'll do the same for you, at a cost, of course."

"I want the house to be put in my parents' name for three years. After then, I want the deeds to be changed over to the Liverpool letting agency. Mum and Dad will still live there rent free, for the rest of their lives."

"Have you discussed it with them? Is it something they want?"

"Not having to pay rent again at their age alone is a no brainer."

What Shelley didn't tell Rita was that if this scheme worked, she had several other houses in her mother's street that could take advantage of the right to buy and make money as well as live rent free. After all, if they didn't take advantage of what was on offer, the property would eventually go back to the council.

Shelley had become at top player in the cartel organisation. She and Franco were in a league of their own. They both knew once all the supply routes into Europe had been consolidated, the number of imports that would come in would go through the roof as everybody in Europe were watching Amsterdam and Spain. None of the authorities were expecting Jersey to be the main supplier to the whole of Europe.

But Shelley was no fool. She was investing in property mostly in the UK and she had a solid list of people who were in a position to get the council homes they had lived in for most of their lives but would never afford to buy due to being too old to take out a mortgage. So the opportunity to live rent free for the rest of their lives was obviously going to be appealing as it meant their pension would go a lot further when they retired.

CHAPTER SIX

A second meeting was arranged between the boys at the Hilton Hotel in the Liverpool city centre where Noah passed all the information on about the first deliveries to be made to Jersey.

"We can expect a decent pay-day," he said, "but we need five families to recruit and as I mentioned, they'll each get an all-inclusive holiday and a grand in cash a week before they go."

"I wouldn't mind a free holiday," George said. "Count me as one of the families."

The boys looked at him as though he'd just grown two heads.

"You're not married or is there something you're not telling us?" Noah asked.

"Our Debbie's a single mother with two kids and could do with a break. She's got a full clean driving licence, so if I go with her, we'll look like your average family."

He smiled and looked at the others' faces, but Noah wasn't too happy, he didn't want any of the lads getting involved in that way. But he knew Debbie, and he also knew George was right; she did need a holiday and so did the kids. Debbie had done her fair share of storing the product and meeting the soldiers coming home from Belize.

"Okay," he said, "but it will be a one-off for you and Debbie. We need to be as far away as possible from the supply chain, is that understood?"

George nodded. "Yeah, I know, don't worry, we won't ruin anything."

They all knew what Noah was saying made sense. Archie, though, was not happy when Noah proposed they just take ten thousand pounds each when the first cash came in.

"Only ten grand? Why?" he asked.

"Look, each of us," Noah began to explain, "will need to come up with a way of cleaning up money without attracting attention." He then passed a sheet of paper to each of them across the table. "Have a look at what I've drafted up; these are your targets and suggestions on ways to recycle the cash. We can't go splashing it around, you all know that. It'll only cause waves and have people asking awkward questions that we don't need."

Archie shook his head. "How much will be coming my way, apart from the ten grand?"

"I don't know that yet," Noah said, still not sure if he could trust Archie.

The problem with him was he wanted to enjoy what money was coming his way, live his life to the full and splash it on luxuries he wouldn't otherwise have had. He had his own ideas about this operation, apart from which, he wasn't happy that it was only Noah who dealt with Shelley and Franco. He didn't like being kept in the dark and only told what was happening at these meetings. Archie didn't trust anyone, it wasn't in his nature to, and he was wary that Noah could be keeping a considerable amount of cash for himself, taking the lion's share. It was the way his mind worked; he wasn't a team player and always put himself first.

Bram was taken aback by the amount of money his younger brother was expecting on his first three months from the outlets in Jersey. Noah had asked his advice on how to clean up his cash and make it legit, and not wanting to put a damper on Noah's enthusiasm, Bram told him he could possibly have a solution to a part of his problem. Ever since the conversation they'd had, when Noah signed his brother's list of conditions, Bram had lined up one or two companies where the owners could be persuaded to sell up, as they were getting on in years and looking at retirement.

One such place was an engineering company called Kirby Engineering, a medium size firm that made bearings for the car manufacturers in the local area. The owner, Thomas Hobart, had run the relatively profitable business for just under forty years. Bram had been doing his accounts for the past ten years and they had a close working relationship with him. Thomas was a family man and devoted to his wife, who he'd told Bram had recently been diagnosed with a lung disease, which was another reason he thought Thomas would probably be a good prospect to approach with a view to selling his company. What Bram didn't know was that was just a front. Thomas Hobart had been offered a huge amount of Spanish grants to relocate his entire engineering business to Spain to an area of high unemployment, enabling him to get top European grants.

His tale to Bram was that the doctors had recommended it would help his wife's health if she spent the winter months abroad, and Spain had been mentioned once or twice. Thomas was able to afford a place there, but only if he sold their current house in the UK or his business, and the downside on selling the business would mean a huge tax bill on the profit from the sale. To Bram, this was a perfect opportunity to buy a well-established company with a good trading reputation and an above-board business reputation. Bram had connections in Spain's banking industry and connections who would take cash.

The following day, Bram put his proposal forward to Thomas, asking if they might want to think about their idea of moving abroad.

"We'd love to," Thomas said, "but right now, we're not sure how we can. We need to finance a move like that and it's a case of selling the house over here or a quick sale of the business."

This was music to Bram's ears. This business ticked every box he needed to bury the money his brother would need to have as a front and this would be perfect. A deal had been put together in principle and he called his brother.

"I might just have the solution for you," he said, then went on to explain his plan to buy the business so Thomas and his wife could move to Spain and keep their house in the UK to use during the summer. It was the best of both worlds as far as Thomas was concerned. An agreement was reached during their meeting and the outlined paperwork signed, and they shook hands on the deal that two hundred thousand pounds would be drip-fed into Thomas's account in the bank of Sole in Spain over the next six weeks.

Bram also agreed to Hobart's request to keep Thomas's daughter Gabriel on board, as the general manager of the company. Gabriel, a divorced mother of two, ran the factory to perfection having a good knowledge of the engineering business. She'd been trained by her dad over the years, and it was ideal to have her there, keeping everything ticking over. It also suited Noah's plans, as his business acumen was limited and his knowledge of engineering even less. But Noah decided to keep his new business to himself, not wanting to tell any of the lads what he was doing with his cash, particularly Archie, who might slip up in the pub one night and reveal more than he should. He didn't want anyone to know he'd bought a factory outright and Bram agreed, insisting he kept tight lipped and didn't even tell Shelley.

Shelley and Noah were in Jersey two days before the first delivery was to be made. Shelley told Noah that she would be meeting a French contact in a local pub, and she wanted to meet him alone.

"I want you to sit in the pub, far enough away that he won't suspect you're with me, and then I want you to discreetly follow us when we leave the pub to see if we're being followed. This is the first time I've had contact with this French connection, and I need to be sure I can trust him."

"You can count on me, Shelley," Noah said, before taking her back to the room and showing her just how much she could count on him.

He was quite enjoying the thought of him and Shelley becoming an item and was starting to get rather smitten with her. She was sexy and adventurous and had just the right personality that he admired in a woman. She looked good on his arm, and he was proud to walk through the hotel with her, as he had been at the Adelphi back in Liverpool.

This could be the start of something special, he kept thinking to himself, and when he got her back to the hotel room, he made love to her that day more passionately than he had the first time. He held her in his arms, kissing her and staring into her eyes, knowing they could be good together as a proper couple one day. But what he didn't understand was that the tear in her eye was one of sadness; her time with him was just a stop gap, something she didn't want on a permanent basis.

For Shelley it was just sex. She liked the feeling of being wanted and she knew Noah was perhaps getting a bit too close. But she wasn't going to rock the boat. She enjoyed their intimacy and liked the thought of having a younger man in her bed. Not only did it make her feel good about herself physically, but it made her feel powerful knowing that he wasn't as experienced as she was and still relied heavily on her for the industry they had embarked on.

It was Friday morning when the first family arrived at their hotel. They were greeted by the French contact and handed over the keys to their hire car. Then they checked in and took their luggage to the room. The Frenchman then took the car to a designated garage where an identical hire car was waiting, with the same the number plates, and then it left the garage and drove a few miles up the road to a local hotel where he was joined by what would appear to be his wife and two daughters, before they were to catch the afternoon ferry to France in the car that been carrying the cocaine.

This would be repeated twice in the next two days. The route to supplying the product into Europe was now established from an area that nobody expected. Rather than thinking that was the end of the deal it was not, and they were given another thousand pounds for their trouble.

Each were happy to do it all again and were under strict instructions not to tell anyone about the operation they were now involved in. They knew better than that. They also knew the price they'd pay if they broke their agreement.

Two weeks later, the boys were having their monthly meeting and when Noah gave each of them a folder containing ten grand in cash, in used notes, all five were happier than they'd been for a long time,. He also gave each of them a key to two safety deposit boxes located in train stations in and around Merseyside. He went on to explain that one key was to a safety deposit box where the money for the goods would be left, and the other was a key for a second deposit box which contained two kilos of cocaine ready for collection. No person-to-person contacts, no face-to-face recognition; a dead end trail set up thanks to Shelley.

"Remember what I told you: don't flash the cash. This isn't a game and I don't want any of you fucking it up for us all. Got that?" They each nodded, and once again Noah looked at Archie for his reaction. "Got that, everyone?" he asked, staring straight at Archie. Again, they all nodded, including Archie, and Noah felt satisfied they all had taken everything on board.

In no time at all a routine had been set up consisting of minimal contact with their dealers, who themselves had dealers that distributed the cocaine all over Merseyside. Within six months, each of the boys had over a dozen safety deposit boxes each scattered throughout the county to avoid using the same box more than once every three months.

CHAPTER SEVEN

Noah was happy. The business transactions were complete and everything had gone through, which now made him the proud owner of Kirby Engineering.

From day one, Gabriel was on a charm offensive making sure Noah knew she was a main part of the company, and not only that, but she liked the look of him as well. Thomas, her dad, had already told her Noah was single and a good future prospect, so it was only a matter of time before she set her sights on him. It didn't go unnoticed by most of the office workers that she had started dressing up more than usual, wearing business suits and low-cut blouses, parading around in heels when she usually wore dowdy flats. She openly flirted with him, and she was quite good at it, too.

Someone else who was happy was Bram. The business's accounts were plain to see that Noah was sitting on a lucrative deal and would be earning a top salary. Just one new customer, the Nissan motor company, would determine Noah's wealth would be made legit and could be used to finance future investments legally.

Shelley had begun her operation in Europe, including Spain and Holland. All the players were in place to flood the whole of Europe, just like they did in the States, which was now being swamped and was out of control with huge amounts of money being made.

Noah, however, was a bit disappointed she hadn't been in contact with him for the best part of a month, and especially after the time they'd shared together in hotels, sharing meals and drinks before retiring to their room where they'd make love into the early hours and then start again when they woke up in the morning.

He was confused. Was this the way they did things in this industry?

Shelley was doing extremely well with her right to buy from the council and in a short space of time, she had a lot of new enquiries her mother's neighbours in the same street. Her money was being well-invested and she was constantly thinking that if things continued going this well, she could get out of this business within the next year or so and move on to much more lucrative business deals. She wasn't greedy, she had enough money to last a lifetime, but one of the main reasons she kept coming back to Liverpool was to see her parents.

She knew the lifestyle she was leading could only last so long, even her lawyer, Angela Rylan, had told her that, saying she'd be bringing the current arrangement to an end by the end of the year as it would be too risky putting cash through client accounts for too long.

The boys' next meeting was held in the bar at the Atlantic Tower Hotel in Liverpool, where each of them was given the opportunity to discuss their own business ventures. They'd all taken care to adhere to Noah's advice about not splashing their cash around and buying into firms without bringing attention to themselves. Their plans had been to install at least two layers of people between themselves and the dealers and distributors. They seemed excited, happy to talk about what they were doing, how they were spending their cash, and how well they'd managed to get everything up and running efficiently and smoothly.

Stuart had invested in a local building company and now had a well-paid position as a director. He was in the process of buying his first house and rather than just buy it outright, he'd done the sensible thing and taken out a mortgage to make everything look above board and normal.

Degsy had bought out a taxi company and renamed it Red Lion Taxis. He hired drivers and bought a fleet of used low-mileage cars that were reliable and well-serviced, and then gave one to each of his employees. They would have to refuel the cars themselves out of their salaries but would keep any tips and get a weekly wage, keeping the accounts straight and allowing each driver to use the car as their own, even when they weren't working.

Archie couldn't wait to tell the lads where he was investing. "In sunbed tanning shops," he said with a huge grin. "All over Merseyside. I've bought a few rundown shops and fitted them out with top of the range tanning beds, along with the very best fixtures and fittings. You'll have to try them, they're the bee's knees!"

Funnily enough, the lads had noticed that Archie looked tanned and wondered if he'd been away for a few weeks on holiday.

"The way it works is, I've got a manager in each shop, running the day to day stuff, they bank money every Friday even if the shop hasn't made much." He sat back in his chair, a smug look on his face as though to say his idea was by far the best.

George hadn't been as active as the rest of the boys, mainly because of his disability. He had, however, bought another detached bungalow for him and his sister to live in, fully adapted for his wheelchair and with a lot more land around it than his previous one.

"I'll be spending some time in a clinic in Germany that specialise in spinal injuries," he said. "I'm starting to get a bit of feeling in my legs so I've decided to get it looked at and see if there's anything they can do."

"That's brilliant news, mate," Noah said, and the others smiled, genuinely pleased for their friend.

"Who knows," he added, "I might be running marathons this time next year!"

That made them all laugh and Stuart, who was sitting next to George, patted him on the back.

"Good on you, George. We're all behind you."

"So, what's your story?" Archie asked, looking at Noah.

"Ball bearings," Noah replied, smiling at the confused look on everyone's faces. "I bought a major share in Kirby Engineering based on the outskirts of Liverpool. They're the biggest manufacturer of ball bearings in Europe and I am now on the board of directors." This was, of course, his cover story as he had no intention of giving any true information to anyone letting them know he actually owned the company.

It was agreed that there was no need to meet again for six weeks as everything was working as planned, and they would only meet if there was some sort of emergency. Noah was happy; he knew he was lucky having Shelley and Bram around him. They'd given him good sound advice, and he in turn had passed his good luck on to his comrades, who seemed to be taking full advantage.

Noah had started putting more time in at his factory and was spending a lot of time with Gabriel getting things up to pace.

"So," Gabriel asked him one morning in the office, "how did somebody as young as you be in a position to buy my dad's business?"

Noah had expected this question and he already had an answer. "Part inheritance and part investment," he told her, then asked, "So, what's your story, then? Your dad told me you're divorced."

For a moment, he thought he'd overstepped the line when he noticed the embarrassed look on Gabriel's face.

"I am sorry, that's personal," she answered, and then she smiled at him, realising she'd embarrassed him. "It's a long story," she continued. "Same old story, married young, and as in many marriages everything is perfect for the first couple of years, that's until the kids come along and your love has to be spread around." She sighed, then added, "In my case, a boy and a girl."

"I thought that would bring you closer as a family unit?" Noah enquired.

Gabriel was looking out of the office window, deep in thought.

"You would have thought so, but my husband had other ideas."

"I'm all ears if you want someone to talk to," Noah said, wondering if she had any friends and was perhaps struggling.

"It started with little things at first. He wanted me to be a stay-at-home mum and that suited me at the time. It was something I wanted but it didn't take long for him to find fault in everything I did. He didn't like the food I prepared, his shirts weren't ironed properly, it just went from bad to worse really, anything he could find fault with."

"You don't seem the type to take that sort of shit," Noah voiced.

Gabriel turned to him and smiled. "Giving birth to two children takes a lot out of you, not only financially, but emotionally, too. That's when a woman is at her lowest, her weakest."

She looked embarrassed again and after a quiet moment, Noah asked, "What about your parents? Could they not get involved?"

"Mum wasn't in the best of health and in any case, I was too embarrassed to let anyone know, and he took full advantage of that. It was then when the violence started," she said, a sad tone in her voice now.

"He hit you?"

"Well, it started with pulling and pushing me about, pulling my hair."

Gabriel's voice faded as if remembering the horrors her ex-husband had put through. Turning to Noah and giving him a tearful smile, she asked, "So, what about you? No Mrs Burgess?" Then she realised she was prying. "I am sorry, I didn't mean to pry into your private life."

"No problem," Noah said kindly. "I've lived a boring life, really. I left school at fifteen, started working down the coal mines where I spent a year above ground then a couple of years below, then I joined the army and spent three years abroad. I haven't had time to have a serious relationship."

Noah was wondering if Gabriel had a boyfriend in tow, assuming a good-looking woman like her would have no problem finding a new man to spend her life with. Finding a man for Gabriel was never a problem; finding one she wanted to be with, however, was.

"I'm sure it'll happen," she said, fluttering her eyelashes at him, and Noah stood up.

"Shall I get us a coffee?" he asked. "I'm dying for one."

She nodded and smiled. "Sounds like a great idea. White, no sugar, thanks. I've got some chocolate biscuits in my drawer, too."

A woman after my own heart, Noah thought.

The next meeting with the boys had been arranged, this time at the Holiday Inn in the city centre, where Noah had pints lined up for everyone and a few plates of crisps and nuts. They were all in high spirits, ready to talk about their businesses and how well things had been for the last three months, that was until Noah had a phone call. It was Shelley, and she wasn't happy. He finished the call and went back to the lads, raising his arm to attract their attention and hush them as they talked excitedly. They all knew immediately something was wrong by the look on his face.

"That was Shelley," he said. "We have a problem."

There were a few moments silence as the boys put their drinks on the table, and then Noah continued. "One of the courier families never brought back the hire car. It's gone missing."

The boys all looked puzzled as this news sunk in, and it was Archie who was first to speak. They all knew that the returning car from Jersey would be carrying a large amount of cash.

"What's the name of the courier?" he asked.

"Dave Granger," Noah replied.

The name meant nothing to four of the five lads, but it did to one, and all eyes turned to Archie. In a very quiet voice, he said, "He's my brother-in-law."

Again, silence descended. Noah was furious. One of the conditions that was agreed on by all of them was that if family were ever used, it would be once and once only, to prevent such a thing like this happening.

"How much?" Stuart asked.

"Five hundred thousand," Noah replied. "The problem we have is part of that money was meant to be a payment for the cartel."

The consequences of a non-payment were evident. At a push they would have to dig into their own cash, which they had plenty of, but it wasn't what they needed.

"Get on the phone to your sister and find out what's happening," Noah instructed Archie, who then left the room in a hurry and went to use the payphone in reception.

"What happens now?" asked Degsy.

"Not too sure," Noah said. "I'll know more when I catch up with Shelley on Saturday."

"Can't we just make up the payment out of our own assets?" George asked.

"The deal we have is the cartel get paid by associates of Shelley's. We are kept completely out of the loop."

At that moment, Archie re-entered the room and the look on his face said it all.

"She's not answering her phone," he said, a panicked expression clouding his features.

"This isn't looking good," Noah said, voicing what everybody was thinking.

What nobody in the room knew, and what Shelley had kept from Noah, was all the hire cars had tracker devices fitted in case something like this happened. The hire cars were also followed from the moment they landed back in the UK until they reached their destination.

The minder following the families had done this run over twenty times and knew he had a problem when Dave's hire car took a totally different direction that was the normal route. He called his contact informing him they could have a problem and was told to follow at a distance, using the tracker.

After travelling for about an hour, the hire car pulled into the car park of a country pub alongside a large saloon car. By this time, the minder had been told to recover the goods at any cost. He also pulled into the car park and parked up to see what was happening. He knew there could still be an innocent reason for the diversion, but that thought was soon put to bed when the two occupants, a man and a woman, got out of the car and started to transfer their suitcases into the waiting saloon before the male then removed the spare tyre. Just as he was about to put the tyre in the boot of the saloon car, the minder pulled up next to him and jumped out holding a handgun and pointed it at Dave.

"Give," the man said. "Or die. Your choice."

Dave handed over the tyre containing the cash, and he just stood there, relieved that he hadn't been shot. Shelley had been informed the money had been recovered, but she decided not to pass the information on to Noah. She wanted him and the boys to sweat a bit, make them realise how serious these operations were and that anybody messing with the cartel would be playing with fire. In other words, they wouldn't get to see another day. She had toyed with the idea of just keeping the money and make the boys pay it back out of their own stash but had second thoughts, as part of this money was the cartel's payment, and the minder was one of theirs, so the money was to be paid to the cartel through the usual channels.

The lads met again the following Friday in the Big House pub in Lime Street, and Archie was the last to arrive, sauntering in and approaching their table, shaking his head and looking thoroughly pissed off.

"That bastard Dave told our Maureen that this trip had been cancelled and she believed him. But the prick took his new girlfriend in her place. I'll kill him!"

"Calm down, Archie," Noah said, trying to defuse what was already a dire situation becoming even worse. "You might not have to. He must be an idiot thinking he could get away with it. The cartel is worldwide, there'll be nowhere for him or his fancy piece to hide, and believe me, it won't be a slap on the wrist he'll receive if they find him."

"I am sorry," was all Archie said.

Nobody else said anything. They all knew he had broken the rules by using the same family member on more than one occasion, with a direct paper trail back to them if anything went wrong.

"What about the payment to the cartel?" Stuart asked.

"Won't know until I meet Shelley tomorrow, that's if she has the answers," Noah replied. "We might not have to dig deep from our reserves to make up the loss." He took a long swig of his pint then said, "We need to use new families to do the next drop off in Jersey. Everyone agreed?"

"Yeah, agreed," Stuart said, and the rest nodded and muttered their responses.

"That's if we get away with this fuck-up," Noah said, giving them all food for thought.

"What's likely to be the amount we'll owe to the cartel?"

"Only Shelley will know the answer to that question. It's something we've never discussed. All I know is that the balance after the cartel take their cut is fifty thousand per trip, so I would imagine it would be double that amount."

CHAPTER EIGHT

Shelley had booked a luxury suite at the Hilton Hotel in the city centre for a couple of nights and arranged to meet Noah at 3pm, telling him to make his way to room 714 and give three quiet knocks on the door. He almost skipped through the main entrance, past the concierge, and straight to the lift where he pushed the button to take him to what he hoped was going to be an afternoon and pleasurable evening of mind-blowing sex! Much to his disappointment, Shelley answered the door wearing a business suit, her hair immaculately styled and looking like her only intention was to discuss their business arrangement.

"Come in," she said, moving aside for him to enter. "Can I get you a drink?"

"Er, yeah, sure," Noah said, wondering when the lecture might begin.

Shelley went to the drinks cabinet and poured him a large measure of whisky from a decanter. Passing it to him, she beckoned with a nod for him to sit down on one of the sofas that looked out over the iconic Liverpool city centre buildings. Still not sure what to expect, Noah gingerly sat down and took a sip of the drink, awkwardly crossing then uncrossing his legs and throwing his arm across the back of the sofa as though trying to act nonchalant.

She glared at him and sat down herself, before moving a few strands of hair behind her ear.

"You owe me, big time," she said, as she watched Noah's expression change from confusion to embarrassment. "The cartel has been paid. You're in the clear."

She didn't tell him how she'd retrieved the money; she didn't feel that was something he needed to know. The relief on his face was plain to see. She could have made him grovel a bit, of course, Noah knew how ruthless the cartel was, and she could easily have put the fear of God in him with talk about killings and revenge and torture, but she wanted to move on from this unfortunate incident, not wishing to dwell on it when much more important things needed discussing. The cocaine industry had now spread throughout Europe and was big business and even though Noah and his team had been a part of the operation for a couple of years now, he still felt out of his depth from time to time, especially when mistakes such as the one Shelley just rectified were made and he knew his life could be on the line. Perhaps it was time he moved on too, get out while things were good between them. He'd made a fortune in assets and had enough cash stashed away to keep him comfortable for many years.

"So," he asked, "what happened to Dave Granger?"

Shelley sighed and took a sip of the red wine she'd poured just before Noah arrived.

"He wasn't killed," she said. "It would have drawn too much attention. Let's just say, he was lucky."

She looked at Noah, noticing the relieved expression, deciding that toying with him perhaps wasn't working anymore. It was time to get on with business.

"Look, things are growing at a rapid rate. The operation in Belize is coming to an end and you're lucky. A new potential import base has been identified but before we go any further, I need full commitment from you and your team that you will not make any mistakes like the one you just made."

This didn't bode well with Noah. Instead, it made him realise walking away from this was going to be far from easy and probably not even an option. He and the lads had been exemplary in their actions, one or two mistakes made through teething problems, as Degsy said one day, but they'd worked hard and made their money and Shelley's words weren't making Noah feel confident about his future.

"I want your team here tomorrow at twelve," Shelley instructed. "We need to go over the new arrangements of what's going to happen in the future."

"New arrangements?" Noah asked.

"This is an ongoing operation, Noah, things change all the time. You're working for some very dangerous people now, people you don't want to be messing with."

Noah gulped down his whisky. "Yeah, I know that, just thought I'd ask what you had in mind."

"We can discuss it all tomorrow when everyone's here," Shelley said, standing up and reaching for the decanter to fill Noah's glass up. "Are you driving back?"

He shook his head. "I can get a cab if you're planning on filling my glass up again."

"I've booked a table at Shanghai Palace for five. In the meantime, make yourself comfortable while I go and shower."

Noah sat in the luxurious suite, whisky in his hand, wondering how on earth he'd allowed Shelley to take control of him the way she did. He fancied her like no other and admired the way she asserted herself, and to think he was the one escorting her to one of Liverpool's fanciest restaurants excited him. He knew heads would turn, like they always did when she walked in anywhere, and it was his head that turned when she came back into the room wearing a satin green dress, hugging every curve of her body and her hair flowing in cute curls against her shoulders.

"Wow!" he said, unable to help himself, and she smiled at him then reached for her bag.

"You like?" Shelley asked, doing a twirl.

"Er, yeah, you look incredible," he said.

"Thanks. It's new, cost a fortune, but I knew it'd look good on me the moment I saw it.

"You could wear a sack and look good," Noah said, and Shelley smiled again and shook her head at his cheesy line.

"Come on, Casanova, let's get to the restaurant, I'm starving."

Noah was so engrossed in Shelley, walking behind her and watching the satin material shimmer gracefully over her stunning figure, that he didn't notice the four people sitting at a table they had to pass, all sets of eyes apart from one, staring at the beautiful woman in a green dress.

Gabriel stared in amazement at Noah, wondering who the woman he was with could be. She was having a meal with her brother, his wife, and a male friend of theirs to make up a foursome.

"That's my boss," she said to the others, and they looked at her.

"Which one?" her brother asked.

"Noah Burgess. Obviously with his girlfriend, the one in the green dress."

Gabriel's brother looked at his friend across the table as though to say, *lucky bastard.*

It was obvious to Gabriel now why Noah didn't seem interested in her in the way she would have liked. She wasn't even in the same league as this woman, and her thoughts wandered to how easy it must be for Noah to mix with women like this one.

He was sophisticated and wealthy, and a nice person with it, but perhaps he was popular with the ladies, too, and this was just one of many he enjoyed wining and dining in high-end restaurants like this one, places where Gabriel wouldn't normally choose to come. It was obvious to her brother that she liked Noah, she never stopped talking about him half the time!

But even though they'd worked together for almost two years now, seeing him here tonight with a woman who looked like a Hollywood actress attending the Oscars, she realised she didn't really know him at all, and that intrigued her more than ever. Getting to know the real Noah Burgess was now her mission, and as she watched them both take their seats at a table at the other side of the restaurant, being fussed over by two waiters, one who was holding a silver ice bucket containing a bottle of champagne, she picked up her glass of white wine and turned her attention back to the three people she was sat at her own table with.

The following day was Sunday, and Noah found himself luxuriating in the shower in Shelley's hotel suite. He felt as if he'd spent the night with two different people: Shelley the astute businesswoman who took no shit, and Shelley the wild sex machine who left him feeling like he'd been eaten alive and spat out for breakfast. She was sensational in the bedroom, well, the whole apartment in fact, as they'd only managed to close the door after returning from the restaurant the previous night before she threw her bag on the sofa and began tearing his shirt from his back. Noah didn't complain, of course. He'd hoped he'd be invited back to her room and wouldn't be expected to call a cab to take him home.

"You can't go home," she'd told him when the waiter hurried off to get their bill. "I have plans for you tonight."

With an excited grin and a large swig of his champagne, the last of a second bottle, he felt an instant stirring in his trousers and silently urged the waiter to hurry up. Shelley paid the bill with her credit card then they stood up and made their way to the main doors, where a maître-d stood, wishing them a good evening. The five-minute journey back to the hotel gave Noah a taste of what was to come as Shelley continuously rubbed her hand against him, making him strain even more as the erection grew.

Once back at the hotel, the concierge called the lift and they rushed inside, where Noah pulled Shelley towards him and nuzzled her neck whilst pressing himself against her. They started off in the lounge, clothes discarded on the floor, before Noah sat on the sofa, naked, and pulled Shelley down to sit astride him.

"I want you all night," she whispered into his ear. "You still owe me."

That was fine by Noah, he was more than happy to owe her for the rest of his life if this was how she expected to be repaid! They soon moved into the bedroom, where he pushed her onto the bed and lifted her legs, diving in between them and causing her to moan with ecstasy as he guided his tongue all around her sensitive areas. When he lifted his head, his chin glistening and his eyes glazed, he looked at her lying there, naked and aroused and full of lust. He had it bad. He wanted to be inside her right that very moment and so lifted himself from the floor and entered her, watching her breasts move up and down as he pounded into her with everything he had.

Sweat poured off him and he needed to explode, then she put her arms around his neck and pulled him towards her, kissing him passionately on his lips and exploring his mouth with her tongue. And then it happened, he could contain himself no longer as he finally released himself inside her, closing his eyes and groaning at the eventual climax he'd built up to.

"Fuck!" he exclaimed, as he rolled off her and lay against the mattress, trying to maintain his breathing to a normal rhythm as she turned over and faced him. Shelley sat up slightly, resting her elbow against the bed and leaning her chin on her palm.

"That's just for starters," she said. "I don't forgive easily, and you still owe me."

He turned to look at her and kissed her softly. "I need another drink," he said, before throwing his legs off the side of the bed and standing up on the expensive carpet. "Want one?"

Shelley nodded. "Bring that bottle of champagne in and hurry up!"

Suffice to say, Noah didn't get much sleep that night but his ability to satisfy Shelley made up for the trouble his team had caused. And once out of the shower the following morning, he rang George using the phone in the room.

"Gather everyone together and be at the Hilton by 4pm," he said. "Room 714. Knock three times so I know it's you."

"What's going down," George asked.

"Shelley wants to move forward, got stuff to discuss. Don't be late cause she's still a bit pissed with us," he added, assuming that didn't include him anymore.

Sure enough, at 4pm on the dot, Noah answered the door to suite 714 after hearing three knocks against the heavy-duty wood. George in his wheelchair, together with Degsy, Stuart and Archie were ushered inside like they were spies and Noah told them all to sit down before asking if they wanted a drink. They all opted for a beer and as neither Shelley nor Noah had touched the several bottles of beer chilling in the fridge, there was plenty to go around.

Shelley loved being in control. She now had five pairs of eyes watching her every move as she entered the room, looking business-like and assertive dressed in another expensively tailored suit. The men took swigs of their beer and waited for her to begin.

"As you know, we've had a good run with the supply of the product from Belize, but that will come to an end within the next six months. The British base located there is closing the UK operation and so the UK dealers are pulling out altogether."

The men looked around at each other, wondering if this meant the end of their journey with the cartel and their career in cocaine. It wouldn't have been an issue for any of them as they were all in a better place in their lives than they could have ever expected to be in. Millions in the bank, with business projects on the go, each now enjoying the high-life and not having to scrimp and save like they did when they were in the army. Then Shelley stood up and put her glass of wine on the coffee table.

"Gentlemen," she began, "the organisation I represent are very happy with the way you've all conducted yourselves in the last two years. You took on board all the advice given and have been rewarded well." She gave them each a few moments to digest that, nodding their heads with appreciation at her praise. "There was, of course, the one mistake last week that could have been detrimental to you and the way you carry on in this business. Noah may have told you it's been sorted, which you should all be grateful for because believe me, your error of judgement could have cost you a lot in more ways than one."

Another pause as each of them were now beginning to realise this perhaps wasn't going to be all about praising their achievements so far.

"Did you not think my organisation would take precautions to protect our interests?" she asked, looking at each of them in turn and resting her eyes on Noah, but it was Archie who spoke up.

"So, what happened to the cash my shithead of a brother-in-law stole?"

"You can rest assured," she said, "the income you would have earned from the last Jersey operation has been used to pay off your debts. All four hundred grand of it. Your brother-in-law, Archie, got off light, he was lucky. This time. It's not good to attract attention to the organisation and if they were to carry out what they really wanted, it would have no doubt led to all sorts of difficulties and bad publicity, bringing attention to the way we do business." Pouring herself another glass of wine, she carried on.

"As you might be aware, the cartel is now well-established in the UK as well as all of Europe, and we now have numerous ways of importing the product. I suppose you all know the government have ordered the army based in Belize to return home, so, as I said, our supply from there will come to an end in six months." This had been something they'd heard on the grapevine through various contacts still involved with the military, though now that Shelley was reiterating it, they realised it wasn't just a rumour.

"Each of you now have individual bank accounts in the Cayman Islands and as you know, each account has up to two million dollars in credit. You now have some big decisions to make about your future in so far as you can pull out now or continue in the business. It's your choice and I'm going to give you some time to talk it through. But whatever decision you make, you will either be all in or all out."

Shelley sat down again and crossed her legs, letting her announcement sink in as each of the team shrugged and wondered what the best thing would be for them to do.

"Any more beer?" Degsy asked, tipping the rest of his bottle down his throat.

"Help yourself," Shelley said, and he got up and walked to the fridge, taking out five more bottles and handing them out.

"How will it work from now on?" Archie asked, popping the top of his bottle with the bottle opener Noah passed to him.

"We have advanced plans in place," Shelley replied. "But until I know your decision, those details won't be divulged. It wouldn't be professional of me to do that."

"If you have plans in place," Noah asked, "why do you need us? Surely you've got other supply routes into the UK, so why use us?"

Shelley put her glass down and glared at Noah. "You lot have impressed. You've kept completely under the radar and every one of you has invested wisely. Even when Degsy and Stuart got married you didn't go daft. You each had a big wedding but never went over the top, and that's what worried me. I needed to know you would do as I instructed right at the beginning, as in not flashing the cash and drawing attention to your new-found wealth."

"We've been living in a goldfish bowl the last two years," Stuart said. "Obviously we haven't been living a private life and your lot have been watching every move we've made."

"That's true," Shelley confirmed. "But it's only to be expected. The cartel won't have anyone working in their organisation that they don't trust, and you have all proved to be reliable and trustworthy, which cannot be said for everybody who came on board. So, I'll leave you gentlemen for a while so you can discuss your next move. I'll go to the hotel bar and have a drink and I'll be back in half an hour. When I return, I expect you to have made a solid decision so we can start moving this forward." And with that, she stood up again and left the room, leaving the five men swigging their beer, deep in thought.

"We've done well out of them so far," Archie said, breaking the silence. "I think we should carry on, see what Shelley has in store for us next."

Noah shook his head. "We're in a safe place now," he pointed out. "We're all very rich and can walk away from this with enough money to keep us going for the rest of our lives. We have good businesses, we've no need to continue. Let's remember we got away with probably being killed, thanks to your idiot of a brother-in-law," he said, looking at Archie. "I think we should call it quits."

Assuming everyone would agree, he offered a slight grin and took a swig of his beer. But nobody spoke for a few moments until Stuart finally said, "Let's take a vote."

Noah looked around at them all as each one nodded, and Archie grabbed the notebook that sat on the table in front them and ripped a sheet out, tearing it into five pieces.

"Write 'in' or 'out' then put your papers into that bowl over there," he said, pointing to a glass bowl sat on the bar. "It needs to be unanimous. As Noah's our leader, he has the final say if it's equal, so Noah, you will vote last and keep hold of your vote till we've seen the others. We need to stay together now."

"Pen?" Degsy said.

"Got a pen, Noah?" Archie asked, and Noah went to the writing desk in the opposite corner of the room and picked up the pencil that rested on top of it.

"Here," he said, handing it to Archie. "Pass it round, that's the only one."

"Turn your backs when each of us writes our vote," Archie said, as he started to write on his piece of paper before folding it up small and placing it in the bowl. Then he passed the pencil to Stuart who did the same, followed by Degsy, George, and finally Noah, who kept his vote securely in his hand.

"Right, that's all of us," Archie said, walking over to the bowl. "Shall I do the honours?"

They each nodded and watched Archie empty the four bits of paper into his hand then bring them back to the coffee table which the others were sat around. He started to open the folded papers in turn. Two said 'Yes', and two said 'No'. They all looked at Noah and he handed Archie his vote.

But before he got the chance to open it up, the door opened and in walked Shelley.

"Time's up," she said, making her way back to her armchair where she sat down and looked at each man in front of her, including Archie, who was still standing up in front of Noah.

"So, what's it to be?" she asked. "Are you in or are you out?"

The room went silent for a few moments before Noah snatched the piece of paper from Archie's hand and screwed it up, then put it in his trouser pocket.

"We're in," he said.

Shelley smiled, impressed at their decision. "Good. In that case, gentlemen, I can tell you that in two months' time, we will be taking ownership of a timber yard in Widnes. The yard has a licence to import hardwood timber from South America and that will be the next way we are going to import the product."

The cartel already had a timber yard located in Bristol that imported hardwood tree trunks, one of which had a six-inch hole drilled out of the middle from one end, leaving enough space to put one hundred kilos of cocaine before being sealed closed. Liverpool had the advantage of being more central to supply Scotland and the Northeast, as well as the Midlands, which were all becoming fast growing markets, though Shelley decided to keep that information from them for the time being.

"We'll meet again here next Wednesday," she told the group, adding, "I have a new contact I want to introduce you to." Then she turned to Noah. "I'm going for a shower; you're taking me for a Chinese tonight so make sure you're back here by eight o'clock."

CHAPTER NINE

Over the next few days, Noah stayed at the Hilton with Shelley, living it up in her suite, having expensive meals in upmarket restaurants, and getting through enough champagne in the hotel bar to sink the Titanic. They'd also visited the new hub in Widnes, the timber yard which would be used to operate their cocaine shipments. When Wednesday came round, he was ready to greet the others and let Shelley once more do the talking. When they arrived, she was in the bedroom, and Noah told everyone to take a seat while he passed them a beer each.

"Are you giving her one?"Archie asked, his usual lack of decorum making everyone snigger.

But before Noah could answer, a voice from behind him said, "Of course, he is! It's something I look forward to when I'm in Liverpool. I'm a girl with needs and your friend here is making sure I have those needs satisfied, aren't you, Noah?"

All five men had the decency to blush, much to Shelley's amusement. Shelley, as usual, was dressed to kill and more than happy with the way the boys were looking at her, five sets of eyes undressing her as she reached the wine bottle and poured herself a glass.

"So, down to business," she continued, making everyone snigger again. "This will be one of the last meetings I'll be having with you as I'm relocating to New York. My services are now required there. I have a replacement called Franco, who's been working in Liverpool for the past two years. He has good working knowledge of the business and will oversee the supplies coming into the timber yard in Widnes."

She let that sink in, giving them a few moments to gather their thoughts, not to mention allowing Noah the chance to compose himself. It hadn't been a pleasant announcement that she'd made a few nights previously after one of their mammoth sessions of sex, and she'd started to understand that her part-time lover could want something more than just sex in a posh hotel room every now and then. Chances were that he would meet somebody and that would be it.

"The Widnes factory is one of biggest importers of hardwood timber in the UK. One of the trees they stock will be hollowed out and one hundred kilos of cocaine will be placed inside it. This will happen once a month and will be taken off the premises within twenty-four hours and delivered to the five safe locations you now have. From there, your couriers will meet out-of-town couriers and pass on the product. No money will exchange hands on the day, and the payment will be made separately at another time.

"The only exception to this will be the Campbell brothers from Glasgow. They must pay cash when they get delivery of the product. They normally collect two kilos, which is worth one hundred and twenty thousand pounds. This money will then be yours to use as working capital to pay your couriers and connections. Is all that understood?"

They all nodded, making Shelley happy that this operation was on and with their help, the money would carry on rolling in.

"One question," Stuart asked. "Who are the Campbell brothers and why them?"

"Not very nice people," Shelley answered. "Dodgy as fuck and a couple of scallies you need to keep a close eye on. That's why they pay upfront. If it wasn't for the fact they're the biggest dealers in Scotland they would be out." She then waved her hands in the air and added, "Right, gentlemen, I'll leave you in the capable hands of Noah as I need to finish packing. Help yourself to another beer."

"I think we'll leave you to it, Shelley," Noah said. "Who fancies a pint in the bar?"

The others nodded and all stood up, placing their now-empty beer bottles on the table and making their way to the door.

"Safe travels," Degsy said as Noah opened the door, and Shelley turned around and smiled before disappearing into the bedroom.

It was busy in the bar, but they managed to find a table and sat down just as a waiter hustled around them and took their drinks' orders.

"You're one lucky bastard," Archie said to Noah. "How long have you been hooked up with Shelley?"

Noah smiled smugly. "Over a year or so, something like that."

"No wonder you know everything before we do. If you two have been shagging for a year, that explains a few things. So, how long will she be in New York?"

Noah shrugged. "Don't know. She only told me the other night and didn't want to discuss it, so I didn't ask any questions."

"Reckon you'll miss her, mate," George said as the waiter returned with their tray of shots and beers.

"Yeah, reckon I will," Noah replied, taking a shot and knocking it back, with the others doing the same. "Anyway, until the new timber yard is up and running properly, I say we meet here once a fortnight to keep us all updated with progress and what's going on with businesses and stuff, agreed?"

They all raised their glasses and nodded and George shouted over to the waiter to bring them all another round of shots.

It had been just under two weeks since Noah had been to the factory. Gabriel was starting to think he must have been travelling abroad as she hadn't heard from him at all.

He hadn't even rung the office to check everything was okay, but that must have meant he trusted her to keep things running smoothly, so it wasn't something she was too worried about. However, she missed him. She missed him being in the building and she missed their coffee breaks together in his office, sharing chocolate biscuits and putting the world to rights.

She liked it better when he was around. It hadn't gone unnoticed by other colleagues that she had a soft spot for him and not one that could have just been mistaken for admiration as her boss. Noah had allowed her to do so much more in the company since he'd bought her dad out, and it was becoming clear to her that it had been the best thing all round when he moved to Spain.

In Noah's absence, Gabriel and the factory foreman Brian, had been working closely together, working out what advantages there could be by extending the factory. Brian had mentioned it before Noah had done his disappearing act, pointing out it could mean increasing turnover by at least twenty-five per cent. It was just another reason why

Gabriel couldn't wait for Noah to return, so she could give him the good news about what she and Brian had calculated, knowing Noah would most likely give the go-ahead to start work.

Unable to hide her delight when he finally did arrive back at the factory, Gabriel drew up in the car park and noticed his car, a smile from ear-to-ear and a spring in her step as she walked briskly through reception and made her way to the offices. There he was, sitting at his desk, a pile of paperwork in front of him.

"I thought you'd been kidnapped by aliens!" she retorted, walking into his office and sitting down in the chair opposite him. She noticed plans were amongst the paperwork, the proposals she and Brian had requested be drawn up along with costings and preparation to get the ball rolling.

He looked good. She clocked the smart suit and expertly knotted tie, along with the smile he gave her when she sat down. Her first thought was how much of a shame it was to think he was way out of her league; knocking about with women like the one she'd seen him with recently meant, to her, they would only ever be work colleagues and possibly just friends.

"Coffee?" he said, and she couldn't help but detect a tone of annoyance in his voice, which made her wonder if he hadn't appreciated her comment about his long absence.

"I'll get them," she said, and jumped up out of her chair, hurrying to the newly installed percolator, filling two mugs. "So," she said as she placed the coffees on the desk and resumed her seat. "Have you had a nice holiday?"

"I haven't been on holiday," he said. "I had a business colleague over from New York." *So that's who she was,* Gabriel thought. "She kept me busy with work as she's moving on, doing something different when she gets back to the States. We had a lot to catch up on before she left."

"She's a looker," Gabriel said, and watched a confused look come across Noah's face. She knew she had put her foot in it again. "I was in the restaurant when you came in with her," she added, praying she'd got out of another awkward exchange.

"The restaurant?"

"Yeah, The Grand. I was there with my brother and his wife and a friend of theirs."

"You should have said hello," Noah said, much to her surprise.

"I thought you were, you know, together, on a date perhaps. I didn't like interrupting."

"Oh well, I would have introduced you," Noah said, secretly grateful that Gabriel hadn't said hello but just trying to sound polite. "It was my friend Shelley. She's gone back to New York now. I doubt I'll see her for a while. And no, it wasn't a date." *Just a mere business arrangement,* Noah thought. *Perhaps unconventional, but pleasurable at the same time.*

Gabriel decided it was time to change the subject. Talking about Shelley, whoever she was, made her feel even more out of Noah's league when she thought about that satin green dress and those killer heels, not to mention every man's eyes on her as she paraded through the restaurant like she was on the red carpet.

"I see that you were looking over the figures Brian's estimated for the extension. It'll create a massive increase in turnover besides other advantages," she said.

"Such as?" Noah asked.

"Well, we have a limited storage space for stock but if it was increased it would mean more efficient deliveries."

Noah nodded and shuffled a few papers before taking a swig of his coffee. "I have a friend who has a building company. I'll be meeting him on Wednesday to get an estimate on what the cost to extend the factory will be and we can start the ball rolling. Let Brian know and we can all go in my car."

"You want me there, too?" Gabriel asked, surprised but feeling quite excited at the prospect of spending time outside the office with her boss.

"Sure. You and Brian have done a great job here. I've looked through all the proposals and the architect's drawings and I can see you've done some costings."

"Right, well, I'll go and tell him now," she said, springing up from her chair and reaching for the mug of coffee that was still steaming. Before she left the office, she turned around to look at him. "Anyway, it's good to have you back," she added, and with that, she went back to her own office and left Noah with a smile on his face, intrigued as to whether she meant that as him being her boss, or if she was trying to tell him she'd missed him being around for other reasons.

It had been a couple of months now since Shelley had gone back to the States and the first shipment had gone through the timber yard and been dispatched. Everything had gone smoothly, no hiccups this time, and the team of five men organised their regular meeting to catch up with progress at the Hilton Hotel, one of their favourite venues, mainly because they were treated like royalty because of all the money they spent there. It had been a relief that even the Glasgow connection had gone without a hitch, and the Campbell brothers had paid in cash without an argument.

The meeting started with the waiter scurrying around the table, passing out pints of beer to six thirsty men, which included their new contact Franco, Shelley's replacement.

He'd settled in well with the team and his efficiency and determination matched Shelley's without a doubt.

Then Noah started the meeting by asking, "So, anything important to tell us?"

George spoke first. "Yeah, me," he said.

Everyone looked at him taking a gulp of his pint whilst sitting in his wheelchair.

"Go on…" Noah said.

"I'm getting married!"

They were all taken aback. It was news they didn't expect to hear from George, not now at any rate.

"Mate, that's fucking amazing news," Noah said, getting up to shake his hand, and the others followed.

George had been seeing a girl called Wendy for a while, but he'd never let on that it was serious. He'd always wanted the others to believe it was just a casual sort of relationship, knowing it would probably be impossible for him to father a child and it would therefore fizzle out before long. But it seemed things had changed in their romance as George went on to explain.

"Well, you all know I went to the clinic in Switzerland to see if they could do anything with my paralysis?" Everyone nodded. "The downside was they can't sort my legs out. I'll never be able to walk again."

"Aw, mate, sorry to hear that," Stuart said.

"But," George continued, "they did give me some news that I wasn't expecting."

"What?" everyone shouted in unison, causing a few heads in the bar to turn in their direction.

George smiled and took another swig of his beer, making them wait as long as possible before he announced his news.

"The specialist told me it wasn't impossible for me to become a dad and I could very easily get feeling back down there..." he said, nodding his head towards his crotch area.

"Anyway, when we got back to the hotel, I ordered a bottle of champers and got in the mood, like, if you know what I mean." He winked and the others starting grinning, eager to hear the next bit. "I got a stiffy, for the first fucking time since it happened. Wendy reckons it must have been the excitement about what the specialist had told me, but she was lying on the bed at the time, stocking and suspenders and looking amazing, and maybe it was psychological, who knows, but I managed to get it up. We had the night of our lives!"

"Jesus, George, I'm thrilled for you," Noah said as the other raised their glasses.

"There'll be no stopping the pair of you now," Archie said, laughing.

"Does Wendy know what she's in for?" Stuart said. "I mean, you always were a randy bastard!"

"Just don't overdo it," Degsy said, rolling his eyes, knowing how good this news would be for his friend.

"Well, that's the thing," George said. "Wendy's pregnant!"

"Fucking hell!" was the exclamation from four mouths all at once.

"Congratulations, mate." Noah turned to attract the waiter's attention, signalling to him for another round of drinks. "So, is she gonna move in with you?"

"Well, that's my other bit of news," George began, now beaming with excitement. "We've decided to get married before the baby comes!"

Four sets of eyebrows were raised and a few heads were shaken as they took in George's amazing announcement. The others couldn't have been happier for him. What he went through after his accident in the mine had been life-changing and he spent many months in a state of depression, wondering if his life would be worth carrying on. Helped mainly by Noah to keep going and never give up hope, he'd picked himself up and done just that, and it was now Noah who once again left his seat and gave George a hug.

"When?" Noah asked as he pulled away and sat down again.

"Three weeks' time," George replied, another shock for everyone to absorb. "I know it's not much time to prepare, but Wendy's already showing and she doesn't want to waddle down the aisle. It'll be a small registry office do, just family and close friends."

"By close friends, you mean us?" Stuart said, chuckling.

George nodded. "I wouldn't get married without you lot there."

"To George and Wendy," Degsy said, raising his pint glass, waiting for the others to join in.

"And the little one," Noah added, before they sat back in their chairs and digested George's plans for a new life.

It was the next day at work when Noah asked Gabriel to pop into his office. "And bring us a couple of coffees," he added.

"Everything okay?" she asked.

"Yeah, I just wanted to ask you something, but I won't be offended if you say no."

Intrigued, Gabriel plonked the mugs on the desk and sat down. "Fire away."

"One of my best mates is getting married in three weeks and I wondered if you fancied accompanying me to the wedding?"

Gabriel had not expected that! Noah had being lying awake most of last night wondering whether to ask her. He was quite sure she didn't have a boyfriend, or at least there was no one serious in her life, as she'd never mentioned anyone. And the other thing was that all the others would be turning up with wives or girlfriends and he didn't relish the thought of looking like a 'billy-no-mates'.

After the shock had worn off, Gabriel smiled and nodded. "I would love to!"

"There's just one thing," Noah said. "My mates don't know about my involvement in this business as the owner, so it won't be a topic of conversation. You're just my friend if they ask, and if they want to know what you do for living, just say you work with me."

A bit confused, Gabriel couldn't understand why Noah wouldn't want his friends to know how successful he was, but she was happy to go along with anything if it meant going on a night out with him. She'd need a new dress, of course, and heels to go with it, possibly a new bag, too. And she'd need to make a hairdresser's appointment.

If that wasn't exciting enough for her, Noah decided to throw all caution to the wind and ask her something else.

"How are you for babysitters?"

"Oh, I can sort someone out, no problem," she said.

"Well, I was asking for this Saturday as well. It's my brother's birthday and he's having a bit of a bash at Alma de Cuba. I was wondering if you'd like to join us?"

Noah mistook Gabriel's shocked expression, thinking he might have overstepped the line as her boss. "Look, it's fine. If you're busy, I understand."

"No, no, I would love to go with you! It's just I was…well, I wasn't expecting that," she said, much to his relief.

Noah had only ever seen Gabriel dressed in office clothes, so when he turned up at her house the following Saturday to pick her up for their 'date', he was completely gobsmacked at her appearance when she walked into the lounge to greet him. Her aunty was babysitting and had led Noah inside, telling him to wait as Gabriel was putting the finishing touches to her makeup, rolling her eyes as she said it. Noah was somewhat surprised as even though he always thought she looked good at the office, he couldn't imagine her being the kind of woman who went to too much trouble with her makeup. But she looked incredible in an off-the-shoulder black cocktail dress, showing off her slim figure to perfection.

When they reached the restaurant Noah introduced her to Bram and his wife Lydia, and it was a surprise to discover that this was Noah's brother. She'd met Bram only once, at the meeting where he'd negotiated the deal for her father to sell the factory to Noah, but the fact they were brothers had never been mentioned. There was a family resemblance, though. And Gabriel soon settled into the conversation with Lydia, who she found great to chat to.

The evening went well and when Noah drove Gabriel home just after eleven, he pulled up outside her house and turned the engine off.

"Do you want to come in for a coffee?" she asked. "My aunty will want to go home and get to bed so she won't bother us."

Noah thought for a few moments, contemplating whether it might seem a bad idea for him to be going inside this late. It had been a very enjoyable night and he was looking forward to taking her to George's wedding in a couple of weeks. But coffee at 11pm after a perfect night out could also lead to coffee at 8am after a night between the sheets, and Noah wasn't sure it was what he wanted, or indeed needed right now. Especially when they worked so closely together every day.

"I don't mind if you want to get home," she added, a little embarrassed that he seemed to be hesitating on giving her an answer. But then he shook his head, took the key out of the ignition, and unbuckled his seatbelt.

"I'd love a coffee," he said, and opened the car door, rushing round to the passenger side to open that one, too. Gabriel was delighted and couldn't get up the drive quick enough!

As she predicted, her aunty was more than ready to get home and didn't even give them chance to get in the lounge before she was putting her coat on and reaching for her handbag.

Even though it was just a coffee that night, and an hour sat on the sofa discussing work, to Gabriel it was so much more. She began to realise that Noah wasn't out of her league at all but was a genuinely nice man who was most likely just very popular with the ladies. And when he announced he should leave at just gone midnight, she walked him to the front door and leant towards him, planting a shy kiss on his cheek.

"Thank you for a lovely evening," she said. "I've really enjoyed myself."

Noah looked into her eyes before averting his gaze to her lips, and before she knew what was happening, he pressed his lips against hers and kissed her passionately. She responded, wanting it to last forever, but eventually he pulled away and smiled down at her.

"I've enjoyed tonight, too. I'd like to take you out again soon if that's okay, other than George's wedding?"

Gabriel nodded and he kissed her again, this time a brush against her cheek before he opened the front door and walked through it towards his car.

One week before the wedding, the Campbell brothers arrived in Liverpool from Glasgow to pick up their cocaine in exchange for one hundred and twenty thousand pounds in cash. As was the norm, they paid with Scottish notes, then they left for their journey back to Scotland. A few days later Stuart pulled Noah to one side.

"Have you spent any of the Scottish money we got from the Campbell brothers?"

"No, why?" Noah asked.

"I've had my building contractors going crazy with me. Nearly all the Scottish money we have are forged notes. The fucking city's flooded with them."

"Do the lads know?"

"All but George," Stuart confirmed.

"He hasn't paid for the wedding in forged notes, has he?" Noah asked.

"I don't know. I know he was talking to Degsy about the costs the other day, I'll ask him." Stuart phoned Degsy and asked the question casually, before returning to give Noah the news.

"No. They had to pay everything in advance when they first booked is as it was too near the date."

"Have you been in contact with the Campbells?" Noah asked.

"Yes, I called Jimmy Campbell, but he didn't give a shit. He told me it wasn't his problem."

Noah shrugged. "Well, no more supplies for them, in that case."

"I told them that, but it appears they have another source."

"Who?" Degsy asked.

"I'm not sure, but I reckon Franco might know. I'll contact him first thing."

"Do that. In fact, meet me at my place and we can put him on loudspeaker."

Franco didn't know off the top of his head who the other contact was, but he told them to leave it with him for an hour and he'd do some digging. Sure enough, within sixty minutes, he rang Noah's house phone.

"Do you know a man from Manchester who goes by the name of Adrian Chambers?" he asked.

"Yes," Noah said. "He was the sergeant who kept the supply coming from Belize. Why?"

"It looks as if he's the new supplier. Seems like some of our customers might be using him."

"Bastard," Stuart said. "What are we goanna do?"

"I'll sort the Campbell brothers out first," Franco said. "Then I'll move on to the Manchester problem. No one walks over our patch," he added, before hanging up and leaving Noah and Stuart staring at each other with concern etched on their faces.

Noah and the others had already planned to meet up at the Adelphi that Friday, as it would be George's last night of freedom, according to Archie, and so they booked a couple of two-bedroom suites on the top floor and met up at 4pm in George's room. The beers were flowing, as was the champagne, and five suits hung up in the walk-in wardrobe, along with five navy-blue ties and five pairs of black patent-leather shoes. George was excited about marrying Wendy, it was the beginning of his new life, a life he never thought he'd have, and so his friends were determined to give him a good stag night, even though he'd asked them specifically not to hire strippers or dancing girls, and he didn't want to be pushed around pubs and clubs in Liverpool, instead insisting they stay in the suite and had a huge feast brought up to them.

As the best man, Noah finally relented and agreed to go along with most of George's wishes, arranging for a meal to be delivered at 8pm and a stripper at ten.

But the previous day he'd heard the news within the drugs cartel that two men from Glasgow had been gunned down in a disused multi-storey car park as though it was an execution-style killing. Both were known to the police as John and Jimmy Campbell, and it was reported that the killings were quite obviously gang related. To add to this, a news report was broadcast on Thursday night that the body of Sergeant Adrian Chambers had been found dumped on wasteland on the outskirts of Manchester. This wasn't what Noah wanted to hear.

"I don't like this," he said, when the others arrived at the hotel and sat down at their usual table. "We didn't go into this for execution killings, or any killings for that matter."

Stuart and Degsy agreed with him.

"Look," Stuart began, "we've all got, what, well in excess of two million in our offshore accounts, plus our independent business dealings. We're rich, we don't need to be involved with this game anymore. It seems to be getting too dangerous."

But it seemed George and Archie didn't agree.

"Why stop now?" Archie said." Everything's going well, it'd be daft to walk away at this stage."

"Well, I for one..." Noah said, looking at Stuart and Degsy in turn, who both nodded, "...don't want to be in this business within the next six months. First chance I get, I'll be pulling out."

Unbeknownst to George and Archie, Stuart had started developing a new housing project consisting of twelve four-bedroom detached houses, which was of interest to Noah as he was considering buying one himself. Angela Rylan had been filtering cash into his client account over a long period of time now and had come to an agreement with him to charge twenty per cent for her involvement, which suited both parties.

"Let's keep things as they are for now," Noah said, not wanting to be at loggerheads with his mates, especially tonight when it should be all about George.

He decided not to mention his plans with the others about buying Stuart's biggest plot and having the house built to his own specifications, adding a couple of extensions which he would use to keep laundered cash. He also had plans to ask Gabriel to move in with him at some point, and all this talk of killings and guns and pissed off cartel bosses wouldn't have boded well if she were to move in, especially with her two young kids.

The food arrived on time at eight o'clock and the men tucked in, now quite loud and drunk after getting through three bottles of champagne, several shots, and a couple of crates of beer. But the night was young and when another knock on the door came at 10pm, Noah jumped up to answer it to a slim, long-legged blonde, wearing a navy-blue mac fastened up to the neck, and a pair of stilettos. He ushered her inside and when the others looked around to see who their visitor was, Stuart, who'd been in on Noah's secret, pressed play on the sound system and the girl slowly began to unbutton her mac, revealing a black Basque, stockings and suspenders. George's face was a picture.

"Fucking hell, Noah, what did I say?" he said, but the smile on his face told Noah there was no need to be worried. He'd done the right thing, because George lapped up the attention the stripper gave him, especially when she sat on his knee and started kissing his neck, before she pulled his face down towards her cleavage and rubbed her breasts against him. It was the wrong place and the wrong time, but George's erection appeared once again and he could only blush with embarrassment as he realised it was protruding through his jeans.

"Someone's excited," the blonde said, touching the bulge in his pants, and the others fell about on the sofas, laughing until they cried. It was a good night all round.

The wedding went without a hitch the next day, as George and Wendy made their vows in front of their guests, Wendy looking beautiful in a beige dress, just about showing her bump. It was agreed the stripper would be the lads' little secret, as George preferred his new wife not to know he'd managed a hard on for another woman only the night before their nuptials!

But apart from Wendy stealing the day, it was also Gabriel who turned heads when she walked in on Noah's arm, looking every bit as glamorous as the bride. Noah introduced her to everyone as his 'girlfriend' and the only time he left her side was to make his best man's speech. They were quite the couple, and he was more than proud to have her there with him.

"You kept her a secret," Archie said. "Between her and Shelley you have been a busy man, you lucky bastard!"

What he didn't know, of course, was that she worked for Noah, but Stuart did. He'd been to the factory to work out the cost of extending it and had met Gabriel on a few occasions. And quite frankly, he wasn't a bit surprised that they were together.

CHAPTER TEN

Bram rang Noah the following Monday morning and asked him to visit his office as he had a friend who had a business proposition to put to him. It was an old university associate who'd gone on to become a successful property developer and had over stretched himself financially. He'd already invested one and a half million pounds into the project and his bank had refused to extend his credit as he'd reached his limit. The project was going to grind to a stop if the builder didn't have a cash injection. The development of forty, two-bedroom luxury apartments in the upmarket area of Southport was a winner.

It turned out to be a worthwhile deal and Noah was impressed with his brother's initiative, agreeing to go with it and make his investment, getting ten apartments in return that he would rent out. The builder needed five hundred thousand pounds. Things were put in motion and Bram showed Noah the paperwork with the new company name, *Liverpool Letting Agency Ltd* scrawled in a fancy font across the top.

"It'll be long term," he told Noah.

"This is brilliant," Noah said. "Let's get it finalised. I'm assuming he'll accept cash?"

Bram nodded and passed a pen to Noah so he could start signing documents. "Yes," he said.

"Great, but there's one thing I want to change," Noah said, while looking through the terms and conditions. "I want somebody to come on board with me. A manager, someone to get the rent in and manage the tenants, maintenance, that kind of thing."

"So, do you have somebody in mind for the job?"

"Yes, but it won't just be a job, as such. The person I have in mind, if she's agreeable, will be a fifty per cent shareholder, drawing down a good salary as well as making the company into a long term successful profit-making business."

"Who?" Bram asked, thinking it was this Shelley woman or maybe Gabriel from his office.

But he was taken aback when Noah said, "Lydia."

"Lydia? Why?"

"Well, I'm useless at this sort of thing and now your kids are both at school it'll give her something to do. She'll be perfect. It's something she's done before, and it'll give her a good salary, extra funds for your family pot, so to speak. And who knows what the apartments will be worth in say twenty years' time when it's time to retire?"

Bram gave it some thought. He couldn't deny it was a good idea and would definitely help increase their pensions. The company would be set up legitimately and there wouldn't be any cause for concern from the taxman. He nodded and leant back in his chair.

"I think it's a good idea. But we need to run it past Lydia first. I'm not having her entering something she's not sure of."

"Of course. It won't be a difficult job for her. And we'll always be on hand if she needs us."

Lydia didn't have to think twice when Bram mentioned it to her that night over dinner. It was a no brainer as far as she was concerned. Earning a good salary and only needing to work two days a week was a dream job and so Bram got the ball rolling the next day and had Angela Rylan draw up a new contract. He was grateful to Noah; this meant some decent money coming their way, and it was arranged that Lydia would share Noah's office at the factory to run the new business.

"Have you given any thought about pulling out of the drugs business?" Bram asked Noah when Angela and Lydia had left the meeting room after signing the paperwork.

"We discussed it," Noah said. "Even had a vote on it, but it was a three to two in favour of staying in."

"You need to be careful," Bram warned. "This letting agency is a legit company now, and if the authorities start sticking their noses into your other business arrangements, it could mean we'd be in a right mess."

"It won't happen," Noah reassured him. "I've got it all in hand. We've been doing this a few years now and we're not novices, you just think about the money Lydia will be raking in from these apartments and stop worrying about me."

Bram, however, would always worry about his younger brother and his shady business dealings, even though he himself was up to his neck in it now and would probably be classed as an accessory if the shit hit the fan. He wanted to make sure Noah knew exactly what he was involved with. The conditions he'd set at the beginning of their dealings together had been long since forgotten!

Noah patted Bram on the back. "Come on, I'll buy us all lunch at the Adelphi. The ladies are waiting for us in reception."

And with that, they left Bram's office and went to join Angela and Lydia, who were more than happy to be taken out for lunch.

Noah's intention to ask Gabriel and her two children to move in with him was foremost in his mind, and now that the house he'd signed for on Stuart's development was well underway, he thought it was time he broached the subject. He and Gabriel had been together for just over six months and even though they'd talked about how nice it would be if they ever lived together one day, it hadn't really been a discussion between them.

Noah had everything in life, he was in position that most men would die for, but in his late twenties, there was one thing missing, something that money couldn't buy, and that was his own child. Being a father was something he was ready for. He adored Gabriel's children and treated them like they were his own when they were all together, but he wanted to hold his own son or daughter, and knew it wasn't something Gabriel would entertain unless they were married.

Gabriel wasn't only his girlfriend, though, she was his business manager, too, and she did an amazing job keeping the company running efficiently. She ran it herself and only involved Noah in any decision making if it was something he needed to be involved with financially. Her only bugbear was that she'd never be the true owner of the company, or at least partner, not unless she married him. She was smitten with him, felt good when they were together, had no qualms about him spending time with her and her kids as if they were a proper family. But she didn't love him the way she loved her first husband, the father of her two children.

Everyone had, of course, assumed she'd go on to own the company one day once her father retired, but that changed when he went ahead and made the decision to move to Spain, selling the company to Noah and only keeping his house in Merseyside for Gabriel. That was the story they told everybody, but it was nowhere near the truth.

One weekend, when Gabriel was staying at Noah's, he finally made his mind up to propose to her. They'd shared a special evening once again, having dinner in a fancy restaurant while her aunty babysat and then left as soon as they arrived back, and he did his usual going inside for a 'coffee', which resulted in him staying over and them making love all through the night.

This was it, time to get on with it and make his dream come true. She was still young enough to bear another child, but he wasn't oblivious to the fact her biological clock was ticking, apart from the fact she might not have wanted to have another baby.

Her birthday was approaching, and it would be the perfect time to ask her. He had no reason to doubt that she might turn him down.

Everything was falling into place when Gabriel told him, "Mum and Dad are missing the kids," as they lay together in bed, her head resting on his chest. "They're looking forward to seeing them again and want me to take them to Spain for a couple of weeks."

The invitation didn't seem to extend to Noah, and he said, "Oh? When are you going?"

"I've decided to spend my birthday with them."

This wasn't what he wanted to hear, having made the decision to ask her to marry him on her birthday. Now he didn't know whether to ask her before she went or wait until she came back.

"Is that okay?" she said, noticing that he'd gone quiet.

"Yeah, of course. You must do what you feel is best. I guess I was looking forward to us spending your birthday together. I had something planned."

Gabriel sat up. "Really? What?" she said, a smile now plastered on her face.

"A weekend in a nice hotel. If your aunty can't have the kids for a couple of nights then we can find somewhere to take them, too."

"That's a lovely idea," Gabriel said with a sigh before lying back down.

"But I really should see Mum and Dad. I miss them too, you know."

Noah kissed the top of her head. "Yeah, I know you do. We can go away when you come back. That way you can have two birthdays!"

"I like that idea," she said, snuggling back into him and closing her eyes.

Noah went to Stuart's development site the following day to see how his new house was progressing, impressed at how far on they were. Even the false wall that he'd requested had been erected off the utility room, a manoeuvre that would be operated by an unusual-looking switch on the wall. It was all very state-of-the-art.

"Don't worry," Stuart said while Noah examined the high-tech switch. "The builder signed a non-disclosure agreement, so if there's any comeback, he knows he'll be out on his arse and find it impossible to get work in the building trade again."

After his visit, he went to have Sunday lunch with Bram and Lydia and their kids, which as usual was deliciously cooked and complimented with a very nice bottle of Merlot.

"I've got something to tell you," he said when their meals were finished and they'd moved into the lounge.

"Go on…" Bram said.

"I'm going to ask Gabriel to marry me." He looked at them both and smiled, expecting them to smile back and offer him their congratulations. But their expressions told him they weren't too happy at this news.

"Isn't it a bit soon?" Lydia asked.

"Not at all. We've been seeing each other a while now."

"And what about the kids? She's got baggage there, Noah. Is that something you want to take on?"

"I adore the kids, they're great fun. We all get on well."

But Bram and Lydia continued to appear unimpressed.

"Don't you think it's a good idea?" he asked, feeling a little impatient now with their reactions. "She's a sharp, intelligent woman, good-looking, and we get along so well, we have the same values in life, too. I know she's got baggage with the kids, but maybe one day we'll have one of our own to add to the family."

"Look, Noah," Lydia began, "Gabriel's upbringing was different to yours. You've come from a working-class family who had to work hard to make a living."

"And what's that got to do with anything?" Noah asked, perplexed at Lydia's outspokenness.

"Well, she's mixed in high profile business circles, and to be honest, I've always wondered if it's why she's taken to you because you own the company."

"What do you mean, Lydia? Can't you be happy for me?"

"We are happy for you," she said. "But..."

"But what?"

"Have you already asked her?"

"No, I intend popping the question on her birthday in two weeks."

Lydia didn't want to burst Noah's bubble, but she'd never felt comfortable in Gabriel's company and was struggling to say this to him. She had seen how Gabriel had become smitten with Noah, and she'd also seen how quickly she seemed to have fallen for him after knowing about his wealth. But Lydia couldn't help wondering that if Noah hadn't come into money, if he hadn't bought her father out of the business and was now sitting on a fortune, would Gabriel have still wanted a relationship with him? In other words, was Gabriel with Noah for his money? It was all too convenient for her liking, and Bram agreed.

His and Lydia's marriage had been based on pure love and trust right from the start, and Lydia's intuition was telling her that Gabriel wasn't in love with Noah but was giving out the impression to everybody that she was. But was she just interested in the money, and possibly the business?

It wasn't something Noah wanted to discuss in front of Bram and Lydia, but he'd also made up his mind that once he and Gabriel were married, he would pull out of the drugs operation and start living his life on the straight and narrow. He shrugged as he sat in the armchair facing his brother and sister-in-law.

"I feel it's the right thing to do," he said. "I have feelings for her and I want to be with her. I hope one day you'll understand."

"We do understand you want to be happy, mate," Bram said. "Just think it through a bit more. That's all."

Noah left soon after, wondering what the hell that had been about. He'd been excited about telling them, looking forward to their happy smiles and reactions and perhaps bringing out the champagne. But now he felt deflated, unsure as to why his family weren't too keen on him marrying the woman he really wanted to be with. His intention to leave the drugs trade had been an easy one to make. He wanted out anyway, but Gabriel knew nothing about this other side of him and he wanted to keep it that way. What Noah didn't know, however, was that Gabriel had a dark secret of her own, which was the real reason she was going to Spain. She had something important to sort out before moving on with her life.

CHAPTER ELEVEN

Sat at home on his own the night Gabriel flew out to visit her parents on the Costa Blanca, Noah couldn't stand it any longer and made the decision to go in the travel agents the following day and buy a return plane ticket so he could surprise her on her birthday. It was a week away and while in the shop, he booked himself a room in a hotel in Benidorm. He had Gabriel's parents' address and knew their villa was about a twenty-minute walk away from his chosen hotel, so with the arrangement made, he let Brenda, his secretary at the factory know he'd be away for a week as from Friday. Brenda was known as the office gossip and it would have been a bad idea to tell her about his plans to turn up at the villa on Gabriel's birthday with an engagement ring, so he told her he was going to Scotland on business.

He was excited and rang George to tell him, who at least sounded pleased for his friend, unlike Bram and Lydia. And so, that Friday morning, he set off for the airport and eventually boarded his plane that would touch down in sunny Spain in the next three hours or less. The ring was safely stored in his suitcase, nestled in a little navy-blue box, and he couldn't have been happier as he sat on that plane being served whisky and dry by the friendly stewardess.

It was just over an hour's journey from Alicante Airport to his hotel in Benidorm, and he tipped the Spanish taxi driver handsomely with ten thousand pesetas, which worked out at around fifty-five British pounds. The driver got out of the car and shook his hand, bowing and thanking him profusely, before getting back in the driver's seat and speeding off in case Noah hadn't realised the amount he'd handed over had been so generous! Noah checked into the hotel and went to his room, a plush suite overlooking the pool area, and even though it was only February and still chilly, people were sat around the outdoor bar drinking beers. That was going to be his first stop, he decided, as soon as he'd unpacked his holdall.

That night, he ate a selection of tapas in the hotel restaurant, washed down with a few more beers, and then left the hotel to have a wander around the town, checking out a few bars with the intention of finding a nice restaurant to take Gabriel and her family to for her birthday, quite sure they'd also be celebrating their news about getting married.

The bars were quiet. It was out of season and some of them weren't even open. But the ones that were offered cheap beer and a nice atmosphere and he managed to find a couple of nice-looking restaurants that he would mention to Gabriel's parents to make sure they were suitable. *Brown sugar, just like a young girl should…* was ringing out from a bar across the street from where he sat, bringing back memories of his time in the jungle. A large neon sign above the door read 'Union Jack Bar'. He finished his beer then got up and made his way over, opening the door wide for a young couple who were coming out, obviously drunk as the girl fell about on her high heels and giggled as she landed in her boyfriend's arms.

He ordered a beer at the bar and sat down on one of the stools, tapping his foot to the music, which was being played by a tribute band. Again, it was only half-full and there were plenty of empty tables, and Noah ordered another beer as the band continued with their Rolling Stones songs.

After finishing the second beer, he decided to move on and stood up from the stool. He threw a tip on the bar for the waiter, nodded, and made his way to the door. Once again, he opened it and stood back, allowing a couple to enter. The dark-haired man who walked in first acknowledged him with a nod and *gracias*. Then a woman walked in behind him, lifted her head, and Noah nearly fell over in shock.

"Noah!" It was Gabriel. "What are you doing here?"

The man she was with stopped in his tracks and looked at Noah. "Who is he?" he asked in broken English.

Noah looked him up and down then turned to Gabriel, who was now as shocked as he was. "I was about to ask the same thing," Noah answered.

The man put his arm around Gabriel and guided her away slightly, offering Noah a stern look. "She is my wife. I am her husband!"

Gabriel closed her eyes for a moment before she opened them and looked at the man with her. "This is Noah. He's my boss."

The man grabbed hold of Gabriel's hand and began to pull her away from the door before turning around to look at Noah and saying, "Not for long."

Noah left the bar in a daze. What the fuck had just happened? He couldn't even get his bearings and apart from the urgent need to have a strong drink, he paced quickly back to the hotel needing desperately to be alone and allow what he'd just seen sink in. Gabriel was still married, that much was obvious. But something he couldn't understand was the way she was dressed, in a very short skirt and a skimpy blouse, high heeled boots and caked in makeup. She looked like a prostitute and Noah began to wonder if he even knew her at all.

He got back to the hotel and went straight to bar where he ordered a straight, double Jack Daniels, which he poured down his throat in one gulp, beckoning to the bar tender to pour him another. It was 1am when he went to his room, hardly able to stand up.

"You want me to escort you to your room?" the barman said after he'd left a large tip on the bar before leaving.

Noah turned around and shook his head. "I'm fine," he said, and staggered towards the lift.

The next morning, after a restless night's sleep and a full English breakfast to help him cure his raging hangover, he got a taxi to the airport, went straight to the ticket sales office, and bought a plane ticket to Liverpool Airport. He was still in shock, not only at seeing Gabriel with her husband but at seeing how she looked. He'd never seen her dressed like that before and it upset him to think she had another side to her he had no idea about.

When he arrived back in Liverpool, he rang Bram and asked if he'd pick him up from the airport, and half an hour later, he was sat in the back of Bram's car with Bram driving and Lydia sat in the passenger seat.

"Fucking bitch," he mumbled. "I can't believe I didn't know I was being played. The bitch was still married to a Spanish twat, not divorced like she told me. What is it with me and women?"

"I had an inkling something wasn't right," Lydia said. "But love's blind. Bram and I knew you wouldn't have listened to us."

"Hindsight's a wonderful thing, isn't it," he said, staring out of the window at the passing fields as they sped along the motorway.

"What do you mean?" Lydia asked.

"Well, in hindsight, if you had warned me about your suspicions, I might have acted on them. Now I just feel like a fucking idiot."

"It isn't your fault, mate," Bram said. "You were taken in and at least you've found out before you popped the question."

"Yeah, you're right. I wonder what she'd have said if I turned up at her parents' villa and popped the question there!"

"So, they never got divorced, then?" Bram asked.

"I assume not. But she told me she'd mentioned us to her parents and now I doubt that's even true."

"You've had a lucky escape, Noah," Lydia said. "You can stay with us tonight if you like. I'll make your favourite, chicken curry, and we can have a few drinks, too."

Noah appreciated that offer and decided to accept. He didn't want to be on his own tonight, stewing in what Gabriel had done to him. But those words *not for long* wouldn't leave his head as he kept going over it, wondering what Gabriel's husband had meant.

The following day, Noah met up with Stuart and Degsy for an afternoon session in the pub and told them what had happened.

"I thought she was okay," Stuart said. "Nice girl, to be honest. Just shows you don't know anyone properly, not really."

"I certainly didn't know her, did I," Noah agreed. "She's had me good and proper."

"You'll bounce back, mate," Degsy said. "You've got a way with the ladies. It won't be long till you're back in the saddle!"

But Noah wasn't in the mood to laugh and just gulped his pint down instead, leaving the other two to shrug and change the subject.

Monday morning came round and Noah went to the factory early, deciding to ring the bank as soon as they opened to arrange to have Gabriel's name taken off the business account. He was in his office when Brenda walked in and he knew immediately from her expression that she'd heard about what had happened on Friday night, most likely from Gabriel.

"You're back early," she said, placing a mug of coffee on the desk for him.

"We have a meeting with the company accountant this afternoon," he said, "and I want you to take notes." Brenda nodded and scurried out of his office and back to her own.

Because the offices were glass partitioned, it was like working in a goldfish bowl where everyone could be seen, and it was obvious to Noah when he watched Brenda go back to her desk and pick up her phone that she was calling Gabriel. He'd trusted Brenda too and was annoyed to think she was liaising with Gabriel, updating her on events after Gabriel had obviously rung her and told her about bumping into Noah when she was with her husband.

When Brian, the chief engineer, walked into his office, Noah felt as though everyone knew, that people were laughing at him, as he noticed Brian's expression looking like one of sympathy.

"Are you okay?" Brian asked, "you don't seem yourself. I thought you were away for a week?"

"I was. But plans change. It's been a shit weekend and the accountants are in today doing an audit. I assume Gabriel must have forgotten after arranging a fortnight's holiday in Spain." He studied Brian's face again, wondering if his first instinct was right about him also knowing what had happened, but if he did know, Noah couldn't tell.

But then Brian said, "We need to talk in private, it's important. Let's go to the canteen."

Noah stood up and followed Brian in silence. They got two cups of tea and sat down. Brian had a very serious expression on his face now, and Noah began to worry he could have been right all along and everybody knew Gabriel was still married.

"This is one of the hardest things I have ever done," Brian said. "But you've been more than fair with not just me but all your employees since you took over eighteen months ago."

"What is it?" Noah asked, thinking Brian was about to reveal that he'd known from the start that Gabriel had never got divorced. But what he told him instead, shook him to the core.

"When Thomas Hobart sold the factory, he told everybody, including your contacts, that it was because his wife was in ill health and had been advised to move to a warmer climate." Noah nodded and Brian continued. "That was a load of rubbish. Thomas Hobart was offered a huge grant by the Spanish government to relocate to Spain and set up a replica company in a brand new factory twice the size of this place. It would treble production for a lot less than what we charge."

Noah sat there in silence, not knowing what to think or say. This was the last thing on his mind. Brian took a drink of his tea. "We got told by Thomas that if he didn't take up this offer, his competition would and it would be only a matter of time before we went bust, which, if what he was saying was true, would happen. But when I went out to the site in November to have a look at the new factory, Gabriel's husband was interviewing local labour at much less rates of pay than what we offer."

"Husband? So she is still married," Noah said, hoping for more clarification that the dark-haired man he'd seen her with a few nights ago was in fact her husband.

"Yes, her husband, Alfonso, was in jail for dealing drugs. And he got out two months ago."

This sent a shiver up Noah's spine. "How long was he in for?"

"Sent down for six years, got out in just three," Brian confirmed. "They were never divorced, he was released in September and as was part of the plan, he moved in with her parents and Gabriel was joining them when production in the new factory started, and the last of the start-up European grants had been paid some five million British pounds."

Noah's head was in a spin. This was turning out to be one big set up as he began to realise that Gabriel had stayed with the old factory to make sure they never got any idea what was going on in Spain.

"I presume they've asked you to join them?" Noah asked.

"Yes," he answered. "Once things are set up, they intend to provide free accommodation for me and any of the other fitters that move over there."

"Have you asked anyone?"

"No, what's the point? I was waiting to see if it happened. You never know, it could all have been pie in the sky bullshit."

"Who else have they got on board?"

Brian went quiet. Noah understood he didn't want to say which of his colleagues were involved, but Noah already knew one of them. "Brenda," he said, matter-of-factly.

Brian nodded. This was a game changer. Brenda, it turned out, was a main player, the one who maintained the contacts with the company's biggest customers, the biggest one being Vauxhall Motors. When Brian relayed this information, Noah was really pissed off. This was now an all-out war.

For the first time in a long time Noah had fire in his belly. He had not been so motivated in years and though he didn't want to get the lads involved, he did have a contact who could be the ideal one to help him: Franco.

"So, what are your plans now?" Noah asked.

"If you want me to stay, I would like to remain here," Brian replied, an awkward curl of his lips hoping Noah would agree.

He did, and Noah held out his hand to shake on it. But what to do about Brenda was on both their minds. She was a key worker in the factory, and they had no idea how much damage she could do if she was playing for the other side.

Bram had arrived and been told Noah and Brian had gone to the canteen, so he made his way there and ordered three more teas. He couldn't believe what Noah told him, as Brian sat at the opposite side of the table, nodding and confirming it was true.

To Bram, this was the worst-case scenario, knowing that Thomas Hobart had sucked him in as well as Noah. After all, Bram was supposed to be the cleverer of the two brothers, he was the qualified accountant with the brains and the business know-how, while Noah had always been known as the brawler. Furious, not only with Hobart but with himself for being taken for a complete fool, he banged the table with his fist.

"We need a plan," he said, and Noah and Brian nodded.

That Friday, Gabriel and Alfonso were with her mum and dad at the villa. Thomas, having only done dealings with Bram and not having met Noah, told his daughter she needed to return to Liverpool and find out what Noah's plans were now things had gone pear shaped.

"Who is he, anyway?" Thomas asked.

"I told you; he was part of the ex-army lads and came into some money, that's when Bram got involved and you sold the business to him."

"I know all that," Thomas replied, raising his voice in annoyance.

"But we need to know what he plans to do now he knows Alfonso is still your husband. He could be unpredictable."

"I've done my part of the deal, Dad," Gabriel said. "I kept the business running to perfection and have kept you updated with everything going on financially. We should have done more homework on him. He's quite a secretive person. Keeps himself to himself. He's well-connected and not in a nice way."

"Well, whoever he is and whatever he's planning to do next, you need to get on a flight as soon as possible and get back in that factory," Thomas said, much to Alfonso's annoyance. "You're running the place after all, and you need to keep doing that for the time being."

Noah arranged to meet up with Franco, not too sure whether he could help him with the situation he found himself in, but knowing he more than likely had contacts that could. At first, Franco wasn't too responsive when he found out what this meeting was about, but when Noah told him the amount of money that was on the table and the country it was in, he changed his mind and told Noah to leave it with him, saying he'd get the ball rolling as he had a lot of contacts in Spain.

After the meeting, Noah felt as if he had the power behind him, power he'd never felt before, not even when the Glasgow problem was taken care of. Franco was quite obviously a hard-hitting criminal, and a violent one at that, and even though it had never been Noah's style to settle something with Franco's methods, he felt it was necessary now and intended doing it without mercy. He was hurt deeply for being taken as a soft touch again by a woman he trusted.

Back in the factory, things were still running smoothly, despite the absence of Gabriel, who had only been gone two weeks. However, her temporary replacement, Sandy, had taken to her role quickly and, supported by Lydia, who was now getting more involved as an overseer making sure the basics were being taken care of, they swiftly built up a good working relationship, something Brenda wasn't too happy about. Without Gabriel there, she'd wrongly thought the place would fold, but realised that was now far from the truth. She found it hard to tell Gabriel that she wasn't missed much at all and worried that all the top customers of hers might think twice about joining a new company away from the UK and possibly lose a top reliable supplier.

At the first opportunity, she cornered Brain and told him of her concerns that pulling out of the company might not be such a good idea. Brain didn't tell her that he'd already told Noah what was going to happen in Spain and that he'd been set up. He just told her he was having second thoughts himself and that as Noah had deep pockets and would not take things laying down, they finally agreed to keep one another up to date on everything that was happening.

CHAPTER TWELVE

In Spain, things were going to plan for the Hobart family. The factory had been completed and was ready for the machinery to be installed so they could start producing bearings and other parts needed in the production of cars and other machinery. It had been a month since Gabriel had been caught out. She'd managed to avoid going back to Liverpool, even though her father was adamant she returned, but she still had to collect all her furniture and belongings from her Liverpool home, plus she felt she owed Noah an apology and perhaps an explanation about her husband and why she'd called him her ex.

And so, one Friday afternoon, she booked herself a plane ticket for the following day to return to Liverpool and sort things out. It wasn't easy saying goodbye to Alfonso, who was angry that she was going back, knowing she'd be in the company of Noah again. He hadn't liked the way Noah had looked at her as if she was *his* woman, or the way she had seemed upset when she had been confronted by her new boss. He knew straight away in his heart that she'd slept with him but let it lie as he was on to a good thing working with her and her family. To make him feel better she only packed a small suitcase to let him know she wouldn't be staying in Liverpool long, but when he dropped her off at the airport, he turned his head when she went to give him a farewell kiss.

"For fuck's sake," she moaned. "I must go back, you know that. Give me a break, will you!"

"And what if he wants to be with you?" Alfonso said, sulkily.

"He most likely hates me. I'll be back before you have chance to miss me."

She got out of the car and made her way to the check-in desk, nervous at the fact she was right. Brenda had been keeping her informed about things that were happening in the factory, but what Brenda didn't know was that all her conversations were being recorded. Noah had his suspicions she was keeping Gabriel informed and had her phone tapped, as well as her computer hacked, so he could have access to all her emails. It seemed there were no secrets between them and his instincts that there was an inside enemy were correct.

That following Monday morning, he walked into his office and saw Brenda sat at her desk in her own office with a woman sitting opposite her. It was Gabriel. He felt nothing but anger towards her as bile rose in his throat at the thought that he'd once believed he was in love with this woman who now sat there, smiling and drinking coffee with Brenda. As he walked past Brenda's open office door, he stopped and stared at Gabriel. Brenda had seen him approach and stopped talking, making Gabriel turn around to see why.

"What are you doing here?" he asked in a gruff tone.

She stood up and walked towards him. "I had to come back to collect some stuff from my house," she said. "And I needed to see what was happening here."

"I thought you'd already know what was happening here," he said, glancing at Brenda, who looked away sheepishly.

"I also want to apologise to you about what happened."

She waited a few moments, looking Noah directly in the eyes, trying to gauge his mood.

"Go on then, I'm listening," he said.

Gabriel turned around and looked at Brenda then turned back to Noah. "Er, can we talk in private?" she asked.

"Why? Brenda knows everything there is to know, so why leave her out? I'm sure she'd like to hear your explanation, too." He then looked at Brenda. "Well?" Brenda bit down on her bottom lip, realising she'd been rumbled.

"Noah, please, at least can we just go to your office?"

He shrugged and walked away, then opened his own office door and switched on the light before throwing his briefcase on the desk and making himself comfortable in his executive leather chair.

"I'm busy," he said. "Make this worth my while."

Gabriel sat down opposite him and crossed her legs and Noah couldn't help but notice how attractive she looked dressed in a tight skirt as it rode a little, revealing the tops of her stockings. But he swallowed down his thoughts. He was disgusted with her and the image of her dressed looking like a prostitute that Friday night suddenly entered his head again.

"I wasn't expecting my ex to turn up at my parents' villa. It was out of the blue. But he wanted to see the kids and they were thrilled to see him. I couldn't turn him away."

Noah knew she was lying, of course, he now knew she was so good at this it was something she obviously did as a way of life and up to now, she'd got away with it. He let her carry on, looking at his watch as though he was bored already.

"I'd been having a few drinks with Mum and Dad when he turned up, so I just agreed to have a drink in one of the local bars for old times' sake."

"So, you always dress like a whore when you're having a drink with your mum and dad?" Noah said, his eyes roaming her up and down. This was a side of him she had never seen, and she didn't like it.

"I got changed before we went out, if you must know. I was in jeans and a t-shirt when he turned up."

"Which means you got dressed up that way for him? Keep going, Gabriel, the shovel's over there when you need it."

"Shovel?"

"The hole you're digging, you stupid bitch, dig any further and you'll end up in fucking Australia."

"There's no need for language," she said. "I'm just trying to explain what happened."

"You're a lying bitch who dresses like a whore." Noah's voice was eerily calm as Gabriel sat and stared at him in shock. "I trusted you, thought we had something special going on, and I wanted to spend your birthday with you, show you how much I wanted you to be a part of my life, you and the kids. His fucking kids that I was willing to take on. I know you've been talking to that cow in the other office, I've seen her on the phone, glancing over at me, obviously hoping I hadn't realised she was filling you in on everything going on here. You're pathetic and you've been found out."

At that point, the door opened and in walked Brian. Gabriel forgot for the moment she wasn't the boss and in a dismissive tone said, "Brian, give us a minute, will you."

But before he could leave, Noah said, "No, Brian, stay. What I've got to say you need to hear."

Brian walked into the office and closed the door before sitting down in the seat next to Gabriel, a little awkwardly, as he knew what was coming.

"So, first of all, Gabriel, you mistook my acts of kindness as acts of weakness, and that was where you began to trip up." He let that statement sink in for a moment. "You've been lying to me about your husband, Alfonso Sanchez. He was jailed for six years for supplying drugs, wasn't he. You never divorced him." Gabriel looked away, an embarrassed expression now clouding her attractive features. "If you'd told me the truth, I could have run with it, and we could have just had a working relationship. Instead, I developed feelings for you and decided I wanted to spend the rest of my life with you, help you bring up your kids and maybe even have one of our own. That's why I went to Spain."

"What do you mean, that's why you went to Spain?" Gabriel asked, glancing at Brian to see if he knew anything. Noah opened the top drawer in his desk and took out the navy-blue ring box, placing it on the desk before he sat back in his chair. He pushed it a few inches away from him, towards Gabriel.

"Open it," he said.

She took it in her hands and lifted her eyes to meet his, now aware of how much she'd hurt him. Upon opening the box, she gasped at the beautiful, platinum, diamond solitaire engagement ring.

"What's this?"

"It was for you, I intended proposing to you on your birthday and then taking your family out for a slap-up meal to celebrate. For some stupid reason, I thought you'd say yes straight away. If I'd have known you were already married to that fucking greasy Spanish bastard, I could have saved myself the bother."

"Jesus, Noah, I had no idea you were planning this."

"Of course, you didn't. You've been playing me, using me for sex and someone to help you entertain your kids, who, by the way, I took to and was prepared to treat like they were my own once we were married."

He then opened the drawer again and took out a large brochure, placing it on the desk next to the ring. "This was going to be our home. I bought the biggest plot on a new estate; detached, five bedrooms, plenty room for us all if we had another kid together. It was all going to be a surprise, and I had every intention of letting you choose the kitchen fittings, the carpets, and sort out a swanky interior designer to come and design the interior." Noah shook his head then and put the brochure back in the drawer then closed the ring box and replaced that, too. "And just like that, it's all gone. Boom! You've ruined it all with your lies and deceit and thinking you can cheat me into believing you wanted to be with me."

Tears were streaming down her face now and she looked at Noah whilst Brian sat in his seat, shuffling about uncomfortably. "Noah, I'm so sorry," she said.

"Too late for apologies," he replied. "What's done is done." Then he turned to Brian and said, "Would you mind asking Brenda to come in?"

Grateful for the chance to leave the atmosphere for a few moments, Brian scurried through the door and went to tell Brenda she was needed in Noah's office. Meanwhile, Noah and Gabriel sat in silence. Noah had already decided not to let her and Brenda think he knew anything about the new competition they were starting up in Spain and when Brian came back into his office with Brenda in tow, he asked, "I need to know where you two stand now Gabriel has moved on."

Gabriel looked at Brenda, quite sure that Noah only assumed they'd been talking about Gabriel and her husband and how she'd fooled Noah, and this was nothing to do with them helping set up the business abroad. Neither of them, of course, had any idea that Brian had been the one to tell Noah.

"I've worked here for most of my working life," Brenda said. "I've no reason to change that." Nodding his head, Noah turned to Brian.

"Same. I'm happy here," was all he said.

Gabriel was, by now, assuming he knew nothing about the new development as Noah seemed to accept Brenda's plea to stay.

"I guess that finishes what needs to be said," Noah announced, looking at Gabriel. "I've got work to do as I'm sure you have. Didn't you say you needed to get some things from your house?"

Brian stood up again and went to the door, Brenda following swiftly behind him.

"If that's all," Brian said, "I'd better be getting on."

"Sure," Noah said, nodding before looking at Gabriel. "Well?"

"I'm so sorry, Noah. I really am." She stood up and hesitated for a few moments, before running her fingers through her hair and leaving his office, and Noah looked down at the desk then opened the bottom drawer and took out a hip flask filled with whisky.

He took a large gulp before putting it back and banging his fist on the desk.

"Fucking Bitch!" he exclaimed, not loud enough for her to hear. He felt humiliated and hurt; he'd been in love with her and had to accept she was someone he couldn't have.

Noah arranged to meet Franco that afternoon to get an update on what was happening in Spain, and he was more than impressed by the way he'd handled the task set for him when he filled Noah in on what he'd found out.

"Everything's in place. My contacts have told me most of the machinery has been installed and the factory opening will take place the first week in June."

"What happens next?" Noah asked.

"It's up to you. Do you want termination, demolition, or both?"

The way Franco spoke was so matter of fact that it scared Noah. He was talking about killing people here, not just frightening them. Noah had had enough. He'd been screwed over by Gabriel and her family, and he wasn't about to walk away with his tail between his legs. "Demolished," he said in an adamant tone. "I want them to suffer and be left with nothing."

"Does that include the villa they live in?" Franco asked.

Noah nodded. "Yes. Remove the lot of them, the bastards."

"I'll get onto it," Franco said. "I also need to ask something else. Do you know a crew that work for your distribution that go by the name of the Bennett brothers?"

"I know of them, but I don't know them personally. I think they're somewhere down the line of distribution. I never get involved at that level. Why, is there a problem?"

"Yes, they've been flashing the cash and have come to the attention of the police. They're going to be raided in the next twenty-four hours. They're too far gone to save, so don't consider warning them, you'd only be putting yourself in the pot."

"How come you're so sure?"

"Money talks, my friend. Even the police have people who are on the take."

"So," Noah said, "how much is this job going to cost me in Spain?"

Franco thought for a moment then said, "For something that big, I'd say usually four hundred thousand, two up front and two when the job's been done. But I'll tell my contacts they'll be getting two hundred, and I'll keep one hundred for myself."

"Three hundred grand, then?"

"Yeah. I'll make sure it's done properly with no problems." He then took a notepad out of his briefcase along with a pen and started to write some numbers down, before he tore it out and passed it Noah. "This is the bank account you need to transfer the money to. It's a Spanish account and the quicker you make the transfer, the quicker the job will be carried out."

"I take it you know the contacts you'll be using, like you've used them before?"

Franco nodded but didn't say anything further.

"I don't want any casualties," Noah said.

Franco stared at him. "If that's how you want it, there will be no dead bodies. Destruction to buildings and materials only."

"Right, good." Noah put the piece of paper in his pocket. "I'll arrange for the transfer this afternoon."

After his meeting with Franco, Noah rang around the others and called a meeting with them, instructing them all to be at the Hanover pub in Hanover Street at 8pm that evening. He wanted to change the routine so they would mix with the locals who would be watching the match on TV. It wasn't something Noah did to call an urgent meeting for the same day, so the lads knew something was possibly going down.

"Who knows the Bennett family?" he asked, looking around at their faces to see if there was any recognition. The only one nodding was Archie. He was taken aback at the sternness in Noah's voice.

"I hope for fuck's sake they don't know you."

"Why?" Archie asked.

"Because they and all their associates are due to be arrested first thing in the morning. They're on top of the Merseyside police hit list. They've been putting it around that they're the biggest dealers in the city, and they've let everybody know, the fucking dickheads."

Looking at Archie, he knew what was going through his mind, so he told him, "And no, Archie, you can't warn them, it's much too late. Who have you got that supplies them?"

"Three, possibly four suppliers. I've never met them but have heard of them."

"Good. The chances are they'll spill the beans, so expect to lose one or more of your chains."

Archie was not too happy.

"How do you know all this and why couldn't you have given me more warning?"

"The thing is, Archie, it's *we*, not *me*. We're a team; all for one and one for all."

"How come you get all the information?"

"Well, you should thank me because if the powers-that-be get close to us, who do you think will be first to disappear? Me, and believe me when I tell you they'll know well before we do, so you should be saying thank you that I have kept you all out of the picture. These people have no value of life; killing people is their only way."

"How did you find out what was going to happen?" Archie asked, still pissed at the fact Noah seemed to always be first to hear any news that affected everyone else.

"Franco has connections high up in the police force. He only found out himself yesterday, and that's another reason we can't warn anybody. Franco would know it was me and he would never trust me again."

Archie shrugged and sat back in his chair, taking a long swig of his pint. He knew not to bother arguing anymore with Noah. Everything was in hand and at least Noah was keeping them all updated with anything they needed to know.

"I've got a few things in Spain to sort out," Noah continued. "So, I won't be around for about three weeks. If you need me for anything, ring my mobile. But only if it's urgent."

Sure enough, at dawn the next day, twelve homes in and around Liverpool were raided all at the same time, and over twenty people were taken into custody. A large amount of cash was seized along with a large quantity of cocaine, and the front page of the local Echo had the raid as its leading story headline. The police had made sure the Echo newspaper was on hand to witness the arrests, which was their way of letting the public know they were in charge.

CHAPTER THIRTEEN

Hitman and expert destroyer of buildings, Ancle Rodriguez, had been to check on the factory on the outskirts of Benidorm and was happy that as it was a new development not yet completed, it had no security cameras fitted, which made things easier. And at five-thirty the following Monday morning, there was a series of massive explosions at the new engineering factory belonging to Thomas Hobart and everything was destroyed, including all the new machinery.

Parked in the road where the Hobarts' villa was situated were the four men who had been busy all night in the factory, planting the explosives that had been set on timers. A call was then made to Mr Hobart's residence informing him his new factory was on fire. Some twenty minutes later, he and his wife were in their car making their way to the factory and the minute they were out of sight, the four men broke into the villa and dosed the place with petrol after checking nobody else was at home. They then left a detonator to go off five minutes after they left.

Just as the Hobarts were pulling up at their now-destroyed factory, the fire in their home was in full flames, destroying their villa and all its contents so it would not be habitable for a very long time. Noah got a phone call off Franco telling him to check his email, as there was a very interesting video of two fires that had recently taken place in the Costa Blanca. When he looked at the video, he was impressed with the job that had been done on his behalf.

Brenda was in his office when Noah arrived at the factory, talking with Lydia.

"Brenda has just given two months' notice," Lydia said, as Brenda began to walk away when she saw Noah approaching them.

"Have you spoken to Gabriel?" he asked Brenda, causing her to turn around and face him.

"No, not recently."

"It's a shame what happened to her dad's new factory, don't you think?"

Brenda was confused. "What do you mean?" she asked.

"I thought you'd have been the first to know, Brenda. Someone blew it up. It's no longer there!"

Shocked, Brenda said, "When?"

"Last night, I believe."

She threw her hand to her mouth and hurried into her office, picking up her phone and dialling Gabriel's number.

"Is it true? Has the factory in Spain been destroyed?" she asked when Gabriel answered the phone.

"Yes," was Gabriel's answer, and she added, "along with my parents' villa. Everything's been burnt to the ground. I was going to ring you. How did you find out?"

"I've just heard it from Noah. He said it happened last night."

There was silence for a few moments before Gabriel asked, "How did he know that it happened last night? How the fuck did he find out?"

"I don't know, he's only just told me."

"Is he in the factory now?"

"Yes, he's in his office," Brenda said, and the line went dead. It was just thirty minutes later when Gabriel stormed into the factory and burst into Noah's office.

"You bastard!" she screamed. "You destroyed my parents' villa and factory, didn't you. I know it was you, don't bother denying it."

Noah sat with an amused look on his face, grinning at Gabriel as she stood in the middle of his office dressed in jeans and a jumper and a pair of trainers, looking dowdy and not at all how she'd looked when he saw her in Benidorm that fateful Friday night.

"Is that the same factory that was going to undercut this business to supply Vauxhall Motors with bearings?" Noah asked.

Gabriel couldn't speak. She turned to look at Brenda, who was standing in the doorway.

Noah continued. "The guy who sold this factory to me because his wife had health problems and needed to relocate to a warmer climate? Not to mention the huge grant he was getting from the Spanish government to relocate his engineering company to Spain."

"Did you have anything to do with the factory blowing up?" Gabriel asked, ready to hit the man whom she now despised. The smirk on Noah's face was driving her crazy. He was laughing at her.

But then, as he changed his expression to one of utmost seriousness, he leaned close to her and said, "You and your dad should have done your homework and found out who you were doing business with. He's lucky. Some people would have just put a bullet in his head, that would have been much cheaper."

Gabriel took a step closer to Noah, now almost on the verge of smacking him across the face, but thinking better of it, worried she would probably end up dead. Noah then turned his attention to Brenda.

"You'd better make your mind up what you're going to do. It looks as if there's no job or accommodation for you in Spain after all."

Both women knew there was no point in denying it now; they were aware they'd been outsmarted by Noah or whoever his associates were, as they now understood he was quite obviously not working on his own.

"And you should know, Brenda," he carried on, "Eric Holden had no intention of transferring the order for bearings for Vauxhall Motors to Spain. When he was showed a video of your so called sister and him at the Moat House doing the horizonal tango, well, let's just say it made him have second thoughts." Giving it some thought he asked, "So, how much did the escort charge? She looked rather fit."

"You've been spying on me?"

Noah nodded and grinned from ear to ear. "Yes, you and everyone else in management when I found out Thomas Hobart had done a number on me." Turning to Gabriel, he then said, "And no, I didn't blow up Daddy's factory or set Mummy's villa on fire."

By now, Lydia had joined them too, wanting to know what the hell was going on. She was frozen by the doorway, scared by Noah's casual approach and the way his behaviour had changed so much from the Noah she'd known for many years as her brother-in-law.

"Gabriel, you played me, and I was taken in hook, line and sinker, but I suppose it runs in the family, like father, like daughter. You didn't think you'd get away with what you did to me, did you? Are you really that stupid? While I admit that my feelings for you were strong once, now I look at you and all I see is that dressed-up whore parading herself around Benidorm thinking she'd got one over on Noah Burgess. Well, fuck you!" He then looked between Gabriel and Brenda and added, "Now, get the fuck out of my office before I throw you out."

Gabriel pointed her finger at him. "You won't get away with it," she said. "I'll go to the police and tell them and when my dad hears this was your doing, your problems will escalate. He won't let you get away with this."

Noah sniggered and huffed at her. "Just make sure he's well insured. He'll need to be."

There was nothing more to say and Gabriel and Brenda left the office, leaving Lydia to walk towards Noah, who sat in his chair still smiling.

"What the fuck?" Lydia said. "What just happened there?"

"Look, I'm sorry you had to hear that, Lydia," Noah replied, "but you were right about her all along. She used me. I was going to ask her to marry me, like I told you and Bram, but it was a set up from the beginning and I had no idea until I caught her in Benidorm with the husband, who she'd told me was her ex."

"So, she wasn't divorced?" Lydia asked, sitting down now, not really shocked at his revelation.

"No. They're still married. He got a six-year sentence, went down for dealing cocaine. Hobart had another factory built in Spain, brand new machinery, same as this one, and planned to eventually put us out of business by selling bearings at a much cheaper cost. Once things had got up and running, the plan was that Gabriel would move there, join her husband and set up their new home together. Meanwhile, we'd be shut down because they intended stealing all our top clients."

"Jesus, Noah. I knew there was something not right, but I just thought she didn't love you, not the way you loved her. Both me and Bram were concerned that you were smitten, wanted to take on her kids. I know you wanted to have one of your own one day, but we honestly just didn't trust her. I had no idea she'd been deceiving you to this extent."

"Yeah, well, she had, and I feel like a fool to have allowed it to happen for so long. But no more. Karma can be a right bitch, don't you think?"

"Did you blow up the new factory and her parents' villa?"

He thought for a while before answering, as she would know if he was lying. "Thomas Hobart crossed a lot of people both here and in Spain," he said. "He made a lot of enemies." Then he sighed. "But no, I didn't blow up his factory or his villa."

It was, of course, the truth, he hadn't done the deed himself. Lydia, however, wasn't too sure if he had told her the truth, but she decided to let it go and changed the subject.

"Okay," she said, "I'll accept what you're saying. I just hope you get over her quickly, Noah. She isn't worth you brooding over."

"Ha!" he said with a snort. "I won't be brooding over her or anyone. No one tramples over me like that and walks away scot-free."

This was another side of Noah that Lydia wasn't used to. He was her husband's baby brother and she'd known him a long time, but perhaps she had to give him the benefit of the doubt and move on.

"I've received good references for the last two apartments," she said, changing the subject. "That means all ten are now let at six hundred a month, so it should bring in a tidy monthly income." It was her way of letting him know that if he wanted to, he could pull back from his other business interests.

"That's good news," he replied. And with that, Lydia stood up and left his office, leaving Noah to contemplate the last half an hour of what had been a life-changing conversation with Gabriel.

Gabriel and Brenda, meanwhile, were in the car park talking about what had just taken place.

"My dad and Alfonso will kill him," Gabriel said, still filled with anger. "They won't let him away get away with it. They'll make him pay big time."

Brenda listened, now realising that Noah wasn't your average day-to-day businessman and not someone to be played.

"Noah is almost certainly part of a much bigger organisation who have a lot of clout, and not the type you want to mix with," she said, hoping to deter Gabriel from doing something she might regret.

Gabriel gave it some thought before saying, "I need a drink, let's go to the pub." Brenda agreed, and they both got into their own cars and drove out of the car park, watched by Noah who was looking out of his office window.

Later that day, Noah got a phone call from Degsy.

"Get an Echo," he said. "The front page has photographs of ten people who have been jailed for ten to thirteen years."

"Were the Bennett brothers amongst them?"

"Yes, they were described as the main suppliers. They got thirteen years each. I think we should start looking at pulling out, like you suggested."

Degsy was nervous. The length of these jail sentences was a shock to the system, and this was no laughing matter anymore. The money was always welcome, of course, but at the expense of their freedom. No, this was getting too heavy as far as Degsy and Noah were concerned.

They met the following day after Noah rang everyone and called an urgent meeting. The tension around the table was palpable as solemn expressions and worried thoughts took the place of their normal handshakes and ordering beers. Everybody was waiting for Noah to talk first and eventually he turned his attention to Archie.

"How many layers of dealers do you have between you and the Bennett brothers?"

"Three," Archie replied. "But they only deliver the goods. Payment is collected separately."

"How do you get paid?"

"The money is handed over on a Saturday night when the town's very busy and there's loads of people about. We use different locations in and around Lime Street Station."

"The reason I'm asking just you, Archie, is that out of twenty dealers taken into custody, only seven were charged. Three were arrested when they got off the plane at Liverpool Airport."

Noah paused for a moment, then added, "Somebody must have tipped off the police, and you can bet your bottom dollar it was one that had been taken into custody."

Everybody went quiet. They all knew what Noah was saying was true.

"We can't be too careful," Noah continued. "The police will be working hard now to find out who else is dealing in the city. So, Archie, you need to cut all ties with the dealers you now supply, not all at once, but starting with the ones that knew the Bennetts. You can guarantee the police have enough leads and informants to give it their full attention, that eventually could lead to us if we haven't taken the right precautions."

Everyone nodded before Noah gave them further instructions to hopefully avoid a jail sentence.

"What we all need to do is get your number one to start changing the ones they supply and give them another supplier contact. Tell them you're pulling out of the business. If we do that, we might break the chains that could lead the authorities to us."

Everybody agreed.

"The cartel has hired the top computer programmers in the world, and they've come up with a programme that's developed the most advanced banking system ever been invented so far," Noah said. "The way it works is if there's an emergency, and you need to move the money from your overseas account so it can't be traced back to you, this online banking app enables you to transfer your money to twenty different banks on five continents. It's a sophisticated way of transferring all your funds and keeping tabs on every penny you own. The bank accounts will be in different names, and you'll set it all up in your own banking app. It's a case of pressing 'Transfer All' and it's sorted.

"Once the money's transferred, the original bank account you've transferred it from will be instantly closed so there's no comeback and no trace of what you've done. You'll be the only one to access these accounts, you'll hold the passwords, and it'll be securely protected.

"My suggestion is we all do this anyway, even if there isn't an emergency. The thought of having the cops on our tail now worries me and we need to start taking this seriously."

Archie wasn't happy, though. "I'm not sure about this. What if one of these accounts wasn't legit? What if none of them are? Who are these people the cartel's hired, anyway? How do you know we can trust them that this app is above board and isn't just a way for us all to be ripped off?"

"Look," Noah said, frustrated with Archie's lack of trust in him. "It's just an option and I'll be taking advantage of it. I won't be waiting until there's an emergency. If you don't want to go ahead that's up to you. But I'll be carrying out the transfer within days of it being set up."

"Count me out," Archie said, "I'll do things my way, thank you."

Unfortunately, George agreed with Archie.

"Is there a charge for this app?" Stuart asked. "Surely they need a fee from people who use it."

"One hundred grand per head," Noah replied.

"Has anyone used it so far, that you know of?" Archie asked, shaking his head and once more infuriating Noah with his questions.

"For fuck's sake, Archie, get real. In this business you don't get references. If these programmers stole money, they'd be signing their own death warrants, there wouldn't be a place in the world they could hide from the cartel, so it's highly unlikely it's a scam. You need to trust me on this. We all know what the cartel are capable of, and if they were putting their hard earned in the hands of a bunch of amateur scammers, I'd be damned sure the scammers wouldn't see daylight again."

Archie shrugged. He knew Noah was right, but he also knew this wasn't something he would feel comfortable doing. Noah called an end to the meeting, unable to reason with him anymore, and not wanting to fall out with him.

As they left the room, Stuart pulled Noah to one side.

"Have you got a minute, mate?" he said. "I need to talk to you about something."

Noah nodded and led him towards the bar area where he ordered a couple of pints for them both. The others waved and left the hotel.

"What's up, Stuart?" Noah asked, taking a sip of the pint the barman had just placed on the bar in front of him. "I'll get right to the point," Stuart began. "I'm selling up and moving abroad."

Noah put his glass down and wiped his mouth with the back of his hand. "Where abroad?"

"Spain. One of the Costas. Somewhere sunny where we can mingle in with the crowd and give the kids a decent life. I've got a wife and four kids, Noah, I can't take the chance of losing everything. When the Bennett brothers got thirteen years inside it put the shits up me with our involvement; we'd get at least twenty."

"I agree," Noah said, nodding. "Once we get this new banking system in place, I'll be calling it a day not long after."

"I got that impression," Stuart said. "Have you told any of the others?"

"No, I'd prefer to keep it between the two of us until nearer the time. I'd advise you not to tell anybody other than close family where you're moving to, either. And don't say Spain when they all ask!"

Both men started laughing, knowing half the wanted villains in the UK moved to Spain.

"What about you?" Stuart asked. "You got any plans?"

"No, the factory is squeaky clean, the ten apartments in Tarbuck Road are all legit. Bram and Lydia sorted that out from day one, so no problem there."

"What about the house you bought from my building company?"

"Angela Rylan, Bram's solicitor, as you know, works in the grey area of conveyancing, but she's pushed it as far as she can. She made me take out a mortgage, and it looks as if she has pushed her luck to the limit."

"What's going to happen to the business, then?"

"She'll sell it for a lot less than it's worth, move to Australia with her husband, or that's what she'll tell everyone, at any rate I doubt if that's the truth."

"Your house is progressing really well," Stuart said, changing the subject. "Have you been over there recently?"

"Yeah, I plan on going again tomorrow. Will you be there?"

"I can be. We can grab a pint if you come over at lunchtime. I'll take you over the road to that trendy bar that'll be your local." Noah nodded and finished the pint in front of him, before slapping Stuart on the back.

"It'll work out," he said, and Stuart smiled, knowing his friend was completely on his side.

The following day, Stuart was standing outside Noah's new house when Noah drew up in his car, accompanied by Lydia, who'd asked if she could go with him for a nosey around. Stuart held out his hand and Noah shook it, then he shook Lydia's hand too, before opening the front door and standing aside so they could both go in. It was quite impressive with its huge hallway and sweeping staircase, several doors leading off into rooms on the ground floor, including a downstairs loo, an understairs cupboard, a lounge, a study, and the kitchen. Lydia was taken aback when she went into the kitchen, inspired by the units and the expense that obviously hadn't been spared. Large patio doors led out on to the back garden, which still had to be landscaped. It was when Stuart took them into the utility room and pointed out a switch on the wall to Noah that Lydia thought seemed a bit cloak and dagger.

"Press that switch," Stuart said, standing back to allow Noah to step forward. He pressed it and what seemed like an invisible door in the wall, slowly swung open to reveal a small room beyond. Lydia peered in and looked around. It was empty, just a few shelves having been fixed to the far wall. Noah nodded and then moved back into the utility room and pressed the switch again, allowing the secret door to close with a click. *Mysterious,* Lydia thought, wondering what on earth it could be used for.

It was equally as impressive on the first floor with three huge bedrooms and two small ones, two of the bedrooms being en suite with luxurious walk-in showers and corner baths, and the main bathroom having another walk-in shower and a large claw-footed bath.

Lydia couldn't help but feel envious. The garden was a huge expanse of soil and a high fence bordering it from next door.

"What do you plan on doing with the garden?" she asked, as she peered out of the window from one of the bedrooms.

"I'll have most of it turned into a nice lawn, but I want a decent-sized patio and a rockery, probably have a few trees planted at the bottom, too. I'll have that done just before I move in.

"It's very impressive," Lydia said. "I need to get Bram to sort our garden out. Let me know who you use to do the landscaping and I'll get them round for a quote."

The tour was then wrapped up and they went back downstairs and through the front door, and then all three of them walked across the road and had a lunchtime drink.

That night, Bram and Lydia were having their evening meal in what Bram felt was an awkward atmosphere. Lydia had hardly spoken to him all evening and he'd even told the kids to go to their rooms and make a start on their homework so he could be alone with his wife and hopefully get to the bottom of her mood.

"Are you okay," he asked. "You seem out of sorts. Is something bothering you?"

Lydia put down her knife and fork. "Not as such," she said.

"Then what is it? You've been in a funny mood since I got in."

"You know I went to see Noah's new house in Southport this afternoon?"

"Yes, you said you were going." Bram put his cutlery down too and smiled at Lydia. "Don't tell me you want to move now."

"No, not at all. That place is far too upmarket for us. The kids would wreck it in five minutes!"

"So, what, then?"

"Well, when Stuart was showing us around, something got my attention. He pointed to a switch on the wall in the utility room, flicked it up, and suddenly, a door opened in the wall. Until it started to open, I hadn't even realised there was a door there. It was like some kind of storage cupboard, about four feet by ten feet. There were shelves attached to one of the walls, but I just couldn't work out what it would be used for, why it's even there."

Bram shrugged and picked up his fork, stabbing a piece of chicken and popping it into his mouth. "Well," he said, "it's probably a safe. You need to have a secure place to keep your valuables and cash in when you run your own business."

"I'm not so sure," Lydia said, shaking her head.

"You're reading too much into it, love. Noah has a lot of money, he probably has a lot of valuable items, too. I'm sure he's just using it as a safe."

"Noah's changed," Lydia pointed out, making Bram pay attention. "He's become more assertive and more aggressive. The way he put Gabriel in her place when she came to work, accusing him of burning down her dad's factory was very strange. He denied it, of course, but the look on his face said he knew who'd done it to me. I've known him long enough to know when he's not being entirely honest."

"She and her dad played not just Noah but me as well," Bram said with a sigh. "Thomas Hobart lied through his teeth to me and on what he said, I convinced Noah to invest his life savings and take on a large commercial mortgage." Bram put his fork down again, his appetite now lost. "What her dad didn't tell me was that he had a deal in place with the Spanish government to relocate the engineering company from the UK to Spain. They were given a purpose-built factory rent free for five years and a huge European grant to buy the most up-to-date engineering equipment. Their plan was in place for Vauxhall Motors to change suppliers once the factory was up and running."

"Sure, I get that, you already told me," Lydia replied. "But something's telling me there's a bigger picture going on here. At first, I thought it was because Gabriel didn't want to marry him, but to burn the factory down, there must have been more to it than meets the eye. Noah has some clout behind him."

"The Hobart family don't give a shit for anyone bar themselves," Bram said, a little frustrated now that his meal seemed to have come to an end. "Part of the plan was to keep Gabriel here to keep tabs on things, work out if Noah had a clue as to what was going on. She was even sleeping with him, as you know. You didn't trust her, did you, you knew there was something dodgy about her from that first day you met her."

Not convinced, Lydia gathered up their plates and took them to the sink.

"It's not just Noah," she said, turning around to face Bram again. "It's the rest of his mates. Something's not right."

Bram had no intention of telling Lydia about Noah and his friends' illegal activities, knowing she'd never approve. He didn't either, but having been sucked into it all through Noah, he knew he needed to convince him it was time they got out. But Lydia hadn't finished, much to Bram's annoyance.

"It's not just the factory," Lydia continued, filling their wine glasses up. "The other day I was in the hairdresser's when Archie's wife, Terry, walked in. She didn't see me as I was sat at the opposite side of the reception area, but I nearly choked when she gave her name as Tereza Griffin. Tereza, I ask you! But the thing that stood out was the amount of jewellery she was wearing. Expensive gold chains and diamond rings, she just looked like a gangster's moll. I mean, who wears that amount of jewellery at two in the afternoon?"

Bram nearly spat his tea out. Lydia was right. If Terry was acting like that in the middle of the day, what was Archie acting like? Bram had only met him on a few occasions as they moved in different circles, but what Lydia told him next got his blood boiling.

"She even pulled up outside the hairdresser's in a brand new golden-coloured Porsche, got me thinking she must have married a rich man. The young hairdresser who did my hair later told me that Terry was a stay-at-home mum and came in every Saturday, leaving a tip of twenty quid every time."

Bram was thinking he needed to talk to Noah urgently. His friends were on a slippery slope and the only ending he could foresee for any of them was a stint behind bars.

CHAPTER FOURTEEN

The next day, Bram contacted Noah and filled him in on what Lydia had told him about Archie's wife seemingly splashing the cash. Noah then rang Stuart and Degsy. That afternoon, the three of them travelled in Noah's car to the new estate where they knew George and Archie had recently moved to and drove around several cul-de-sacs until they spotted the one with the biggest houses and huge front gardens. But what really drew their attention were the expensive high-end cars in the driveways: brand new Porches, a new Jaguar, and a new E-class Mercedes with blacked-out windows. They were sick to their stomachs, realising what this meant.

At first, Stuart wanted to call in at Archie's house, but Noah told him to hold fire.

"He could have family in there," he said. "We need to call an urgent meeting. This is just fucking ridiculous."

And so, that following night, Noah rang George and then Archie, and ordered them to be at the White Swan not too far away from the exclusive estate, where he pretended he wanted to just buy them a pint. Stuart and Noah were sitting in a quiet part of the pub when George, Archie and Degsy turned up together. They sat down, a pint each in front of them, and Noah took out a brown folder and opened it to reveal a bunch of photographs. Eight, in total, of the houses on the estate where Archie and George lived.

"Spot the drug dealers," he said, as Archie and George looked at the photographs.

Everybody stayed silent, until Archie looked up and stared straight at Noah.

"What's going on?" he asked.

"You tell me," Noah said.

"Why have you been taking photos of our houses?"

"Two Porsche sports cars and a Mercedes, for fuck's sake," he said, looking at Archie before averting his eyes to George. "A jag? For fuck's sake. All with private number plates, too. Archie, your name is Archie Carmichael, not Richard-fucking-Branson."

"What difference does that make?" Archie said. "I'm a successful businessman!"

Noah had planned on telling the group about cutting ties, but not now. It would, however, be the beginning of the end as far as he was concerned.

"Multi-millionaires have successful businesses, not what you and George have. What is it again, a string of sunbed shops and a landscaping business?"

"They both show a profit," George said, starting to feel very uncomfortable now.

"Get fucking real, both of you," Noah scoffed. "Over a hundred grand's worth of cars on the driveway outside houses that are worth hundreds of thousands. That's way more than the average businessman can afford. You two have lost the basics we started with five years ago. That we must keep a low profile, or don't you remember that rule?"

"We have, apart from the cars," Archie said.

"Archie, when your wife walks into her hairdresser's with around twenty grands' worth of jewellery hanging around her neck and wrists, it stands out. This isn't a fucking game we're playing."

Nobody said anything, Noah was waiting for some sort of response but got none.

"There's only one reason I'm sitting here. We're a team and I don't want to be standing in the dock one day, getting a guilty verdict and a fucking jail sentence of ten to twenty years. That goes for all of you. Right now…" he looked at Archie and George in turn, "You two are the weakest link to us all getting caught. What part of that don't you understand?"

"Me and George have ten sun-tanning salons as well as a very successful landscaping business. The cars are company vehicles that we deserve to have and that shows we mean business."

Noah shook his head and looked around to each of his associates. "Look," he said, "when we landed on our feet all those years ago, none of us expected to be in a position we're all now in, but the things we were told not to do was flashing the cash, drawing attention to ourselves, or to the money we've made. You two aren't just flashing it, you're shoving it up people's fucking noses!"

Archie glared at Noah and pointed his finger aggressively towards him.

"You might not drive a flash car," he said, "but you have a fucking factory and ten apartments worth ten times more than what my cars cost."

"You still don't get it, do you," Noah replied. "No one, other than us in this room, knows that. All my investments have been bought with commercial mortgages and would stand up to any police investigation as being legal. How did you buy your cars, your houses?"

Neither George nor Archie bothered to answer. Noah decided to change tack, not wanting to give away anymore of his personal business information that he already had.

"And tell me this," he said, "who the fuck drives around Liverpool in a gold-coloured Bentley? A fucking Bentley, I ask, what the fuck?"

Everybody knew who he was talking about: Archie's number one, a flash bastard called Curtis Harris.

"You do realise that half of fucking Liverpool know who Curtis is, don't you? It's not *if* he gets caught, it's *when.* He'll bring everybody down with him. He's already known to the police. He stands for everything that we don't want, and I'm telling you, Archie, you'd better tell him to get rid of the fucking Bentley or there's going to be problems."

"What do you mean, problems?" Archie asked, a little more worried now, and somehow less argumentative.

"When he gets pulled for dealing drugs, whose name is he going to throw into the mix to avoid a big jail sentence?" Noah asked. Archie shrugged. "Yours, you stupid prick," Noah said.

For the first time, Archie was stuck for words, realising that what Noah was saying was true. He would have to handle the Curtis Harris situation before it got out of hand, if it wasn't already too late.

"Okay, what do you suggest I do?" Archie asked.

"How many times do you have to be told it's *we* not *me*? You are the link to everybody in this room."

"Okay, so what do you want me to do?" Archie repeated.

"Replace him with somebody lower key."

"How do you suggest I get rid of Curtis? He's worked his way up from being a street dealer. He's my main distributor now."

"Already taken care of," Noah said, finishing his pint. "Have someone ready to take his place by the end of the month."

Noah's words, *taken care of,* played on everyone's mind as he drew the meeting to a close, saying he needed to get home.

It was a month later, when this statement was fully understood after Curtis Harris's body was found on wasteland on the outskirts of the city, slumped in the driver's seat of his infamous gold-coloured Bentley, with a single gunshot to his head. Noah's call to Franco, the day before that meeting, informed him that the police knew all about Curtis Harris and his daily activities as a drug dealer, and that he was one of the most wanted men in Liverpool. Franco and Noah agreed that he had to be 'taken care of' as quickly and as swiftly as possible.

Archie had a lucky escape. It would have been him who'd been killed had Noah not spoken to Franco, but Noah's promise to keep Archie in line had proved to save his life. Within a week of Curtis Harris's body being found, Archie privately sold both his Porsches and bought two salons, both of which lined the high street in a much more inconspicuous way. Not only that, but Terry removed all the expensive jewellery and put it into a safe, making sure whenever she left the house, she blended in with the other women who used the hairdresser's and wandered around the city's shops. The cartel took no prisoners, and this had put the fear of God into Archie. He'd had a stark reminder of exactly who they were dealing with.

Noah was happy with the way things were being run at his factory, having left Lydia in charge and deciding to keep Brenda on for the time being. It was a sign of trust on his part, though he didn't know if trusting Brenda would backfire on him at some point. It was a Thursday morning when Lydia and Brenda were closing their daily briefing, with Brian leaving the office to start his day.

"So, what are your plans?" Lydia asked. "Are you still moving on or are you staying here?"

Brenda had started to trust Lydia but missed working with Gabriel. She and her husband had been looking forward to moving to Spain, but her heart wasn't in the job anymore. The contact at Vauxhall Motors, Eric, had been moved on and replaced by a younger, sharper man, so even that enjoyment had been taken away. She missed the monthly meetings with him and blamed it all on one person: Noah Burgess.

"I'm glad you've come on board," Brenda said. "I don't think I could feel comfortable working with Noah after everything that happened."

"He's not that bad. It hit him hard after he found out what Gabriel and her dad had done. They played him good and proper. With you and Brian intending to jump ship and taking the best part of the order book with you, he might have had no choice but to close the factory down and made over sixty workers redundant. The Hobart family didn't give a single thought about the workforce they were throwing on the scrap heap. Only you and Brian would have been looked after, but they picked on the wrong person. Noah's well-connected." She paused for a moment as she watched the expression on Brenda's face turn from disgust to inquisitiveness. "Did you know the real reason he went to Spain?" Brenda shook her head. "He was going to ask Gabriel to marry him. He'd fallen in love with her. He showed me and Bram the solitaire diamond ring he bought, and he had this plan to ask her on her birthday. He was gutted, absolutely heart broken when he found out she was still married and still with her husband. I've known Noah a long time and I knew that affected him badly."

"Gabriel didn't discuss her private life with me," Brenda said. "I just knew she was on her own and I presumed she'd split from her husband. I think if she'd known Noah was going to propose, she'd have said something to me. We were friends, though not particularly close. Just close in business, I guess."

"If you get on Noah's good side, he's an okay kind of guy. He wouldn't have burned down Hobart's factory in Spain. Thomas Hobart got on the wrong side of several Spanish engineering companies who felt they should have been the ones to receive the government grants, not a company from England. Chances are it was one of them that burnt down the factory, it makes more sense."

Brenda gave that some thought before saying, "Well, I'd better make sure I get on his good side by getting down to working hard and bringing in more orders."

She was beginning to realise that this factory was in good hands and not at all how Gabriel had made out. She'd trusted Gabriel, listened to her and gone along with the plans to move the factory to Spain, closing this one down and putting many good people out of work. Glad of this new-found working relationship she seemed to have built up with Lydia, she decided to tell her about a contract she'd managed to secure that was sure to improve turnover for them.

"I've been given a chance at submitting a quote to make the bearings for the new Nissan cars to be built in the North East. Their buyers are due in the country next month and will probably want to come to the factory before they let us even put in a tender."

That's when Lydia surprised Brenda as she pulled out a set of plans showing that planning permission had been granted to build a huge extension to the factory, giving the chance to double if not treble their production.

Brenda looked at the plans with a confused expression. "Nobody mentioned anything about extending the factory. Does Brian know?"

"No," Lydia said. "Noah told him he was thinking of expanding but hadn't told him how advanced his plans were."

"When do you think work will start on the extension?"

"It starts in two weeks," Lydia confirmed. "Should be finished in six months and operational not long after."

What Brenda asked next didn't really surprise Lydia. "When is Noah in next?"

Looking out to the car park, Lydia knew he was due in at any time now.

"That's him, pulling up in the car park," she said.

Brenda looked nervous, but she knew she had to bite the bullet and make her mind up where her future lay. Both women greeted Noah when he entered the office.

"Good morning, ladies, how are you today?"

He then smiled at them both, which they both returned.

"Can I have a word?" Brenda asked, pottering after him as he made his way to his office.

Lydia took this as her chance to leave the two of them alone. "I'm going to show Brian the plans for the new extension. I'll be twenty minutes or so."

Noah opened the door to his office and Brenda followed, waiting for him to put his briefcase on the floor and sit down before she, too, sat down in the seat opposite him.

"Noah, we got off to a bad start," she said, watching her boss lean back into his chair with a slight smile on his face.

"I was given the impression that you bought the factory as some sort of tax scam and wasn't really interested in its future. I was told that anybody who wanted to relocate for a brand new way of life in Spain would be taken care of, but I now know that wasn't true." Noah continued to smile, noticing how awkward this was for her and quite enjoying the attention she seemed to be giving him. "I was very close to Gabriel, but she played me, too. The only reason she and her dad wanted me on board was the fact I brought in all the big orders, mainly the Vauxhall Motors one, that I won by whatever means I used to get it."

Noah put his hands on the desk and turned his mobile phone over a few times, averting his gaze from her to the phone and then back to her again.

"Look, Brenda, I'm not an entrepreneur or a seasoned businessman, I just landed on a decent sized inheritance left to me by my grandparents. My brother, Bram, being somewhat older than me, waited for a good business opportunity to come along to invest in on my behalf, and here we are," he said, turning his palms over in a gesture.

"Is that Bram the accountant?"

"Yes, and Lydia is his wife. It was just a slice of luck that I found out about the engineering factory in Spain. We had an email from Nissan asking about the new development over there and funnily enough, it was you who told them about it. They wanted to install their manufacturing machines in Spain, and they wanted to know if the company would be able to supply their new Nissan factory that was being built in the north-east of England."

Brenda now realised Noah and his family were a lot more professional than the Hobart family had thought. They thought he was naïve and inexperienced, but she knew now that was not the case, just the opposite, in fact. Her decision was made; from that day onwards, Brenda planned on a future career with the Kirby Engineering Company.

"So, have you been in contact with Gabriel?" Noah asked.

Brenda nodded. "Yes, she still thinks you were behind the factory explosion, but I've told her that I'll be re-evaluating my plans due to what's happened, and I'll now be telling her that my future lies here with Kirby Engineering."

Noah sighed and smiled. He was happy. Two of the key players were on board, and he knew he had a good management team in the company.

All he had to do now was get out of the drugs business and leave that life behind him. Possibly, even, start looking for a wife. He was now thirty and felt it was time for him to take the more traditional way of life.

CHAPTER FIFTEEN

Stuart had sold his house and was ready to emigrate. He didn't want to be involved with the drugs industry anymore. His four children and loyal wife knew nothing about his business dealings with the others, and the fact the amount of cash that was now coming in every month to their joint account was increasing, it was getting to a point where it was harder to get rid of the money. So, at the next meeting, he told the boys what he had already told Noah, that he was calling it a day, had sold up and was moving to Spain next month.

Noah, Degsy and George thought it a shame to lose one of the crew, but all Archie could think of was who was going to take his place in the supply chain. To him, it meant even more money in the pot. He voiced that he would take on Stuart's supply chain when he moved on, but then Noah put a burner phone on the table and looked at everyone in turn.

"I renew this every month and give my contact the new number on the last day of the month, so how you divide up the dealings with my contact distributor is up to you. As of now, I'm out as well."

Three of the five partners were taken aback by this chain of events. Greed drives a lot of people forward, but Stuart and Noah were looking at things differently. They had both made huge amounts of money, and both had taken advantage of the cartel's banking facility, giving them substantial amounts of legitimate money to work with.

It was agreed that Archie would take on Stuart's supply chain, which would mean a substantial increase in his income. Noah was happy there hadn't been any objections to Stuart leaving but he knew it was going to be harder for him, not so much as his connection to the boys, but his connection to the cartel's main man in Europe: Franco. That was a completely different story, and he knew the cartel would not be too happy to end the top-class relationship they now had going.

Noah arranged to meet with Franco the following day to let him know he was going to have some time out and he took Archie with him to re-introduce them. But Franco had an announcement of his own to make. He would be relocating to New York soon and had his own replacement to introduce Noah to. Brendan Foster was a sophisticated man, a lot older than Noah and Archie, in his mid-sixties.

They all shook hands, and it was agreed there would be a few more meetings between them all before trust could be gained, but in this business that was paramount.

After the meeting, Noah and Archie met up with the others at the Adelphi for an evening meal and he noticed that George seemed a bit perplexed.

"Are you sure you want out of all of this?" George asked him.

Noah nodded. "You're all in solid relationships with children, you've got good partners and you must all be sitting on between four and five million pounds worth of assets. How much money can you spend in one lifetime?"

"But surely you'll miss the large amount of cash we all receive every month?"

"Not really," Noah replied. "I use my debit card to pay for most things and the build-up of cash becomes a liability."

Archie, listening to the conversation, joined in. "I have over twenty accounts with different banks. Each has money deposited on a weekly basis alongside the accounts set up by Shelley in the Cayman Islands. That account has over two million in and it's making interest at five per cent, which is paid into my personal account in the Isle of man."

Noah was thinking it would only be a matter of time before they tracked down all the accounts, they had people who specialised in that sort of thing. So, taking the piss, he took them all by surprise when he jokingly told them he had buried over a million pounds in cash, in his garden at his new address in Southport.

At first, they all thought he was having them on, but then decided he was telling the truth when he went into more detail.

"You can fit five thousand pounds into a freezer bag used for storing food, which would then be placed into a bin bag. Each bin bag will hold two hundred and fifty thousand, and I've got four bags in total buried."

"What if you forget where you buried it when everything starts growing over?" Archie asked.

"Well, it gets buried dead centre of the lawn."

There were smiles all round as everyone envisioned Noah digging his lawn up and placing bin bags in a hole, then covering it up again and having it landscaped. He'd always remembered what Shelley told him when all this first started; never keep drugs in your home and never keep large amounts of cash under any circumstances, and he had done everything by the book. Noah knew Stuart had got it right, thinking of his family and putting them first when cutting all ties with the group. Another thing Shelley told him was to put out there as much false information about where you keep your cash, the money in the garden being one such idea.

Things had settled down, back into what looked as if it was an orderly routine. Archie had expanded his take in the business and had learned his lesson about not flashing the cash. He'd also bought George's landscape gardening business to make it look as if that was where his cash came from. George, in the meantime, had decided to invest in mobility shops, something he felt were very much needed in and around Merseyside. Archie had changed the name of the landscape business to *'The Lawn Ranger'* and had it printed on vans and merchandise that his employees used, still not understanding the meaning of keeping a low profile.

Brian and Brenda were lost for words when Noah asked them to join him and Lydia for lunch in a local restaurant one Monday afternoon. As they sat down to a glass of wine it was Lydia who took control and started the conversation.

"As you both know," she said, looking from Brian to Brenda, "the new extension to the factory is near to completion, therefore we'll have a bigger capacity to increase our manufacturing output." Both nodded, wondering what all this was about, and Lydia continued. "In order to expand the company, we need two new directors to join me and Noah; a marketing director and an engineering director."

Giving both Brian and Brenda time to take in what she had just told them, Noah then intervened, putting two documents on the table in front of them.

"The two new directors we want to enlist are you two," he said. "Brenda, I'd like you to become the marketing director and Brian, you the production director."

Both were speechless, and Noah couldn't help but smile.

"When and if you sign the directorship documents in front of you," Lydia said, "your basic salary will increase by twenty-five per cent, plus you will receive an annual director's dividend, which, as things currently stand, would be in the five-figure bracket."

Brenda couldn't believe what she was hearing. "Why?" was all she asked.

"I don't think you two realise how important to this company you are. The high quality of the finished product is down to you, Brian, and the order book being continuously full is your doing, Brenda, so who better to bring on board than you two?"

Brian pushed the papers back towards Noah and said, "I don't need to read the documents. I accept your offer."

"Me too," Brenda added. Their hard work was finally being rewarded, and this was proof enough to them both that what they did for Noah's factory was more than appreciated. It also proved to Brenda that she had been forgiven for the part she played in Gabriel's deceit, something she thought would eventually ruin her career.

There was no doubt to Lydia and Noah that these two were the best at the job they did and two key players to keep if the company was going to expand.

After all the documents had been signed, Noah called the waiter over.

"We're celebrating," he said. "Could you bring a bottle of Dom Perignon to the table, please." The waiter scurried off and returned moments later with the bottle in a silver ice bucket, before taking it out and popping the cork.

"To new beginnings," Noah said, raising his glass as the others did the same.

Having got that sorted, Noah felt he had a huge gap in his life, especially when Degsy asked him to be Godfather to his fourth child. It was something Noah wanted; a family of his own, but without a woman in his life it was highly unlikely it would ever happen. He often thought about Carol, his first girlfriend, and how she had lied to him. He'd think back to that time when he caught her with her boss walking out of the Holiday Inn. At the time, it had been loving as far as he was concerned. But he was naïve back then and thought he had it all when she announced she was pregnant. Finding out the baby wasn't his almost destroyed him; it certainly destroyed his self-esteem for a while, not that he allowed anyone to notice. But here he was, in his thirties now with more money than he knew what to do with, a nice suburban house, decent car, good friends, yet no one to share it all with.

Even the thought of taking on a ready-made family had appealed to him when Gabriel came on the scene along with her two children. Once again, he'd thought it was true love, the luck people find when they meet the love of their lives.

He was sure she'd have said yes to his marriage proposal if things had been different and if she hadn't already been married. But she'd deceived him and now he knew that wasn't real love, just a relationship borne out of convenience on her part. He wanted to experience the kind of love that his friends had with their partners; the kind where you think about only the woman lying beside you before you go to sleep at night, and then again when you wake up the next morning. The kind that would give him a lifetime of memories and happy occasions, children and grandchildren and all the responsibilities that came with having a family. He was ready. More than ready. But it wasn't happening for him, and the sadness he felt daily was starting to leave him bitter and resentful whenever he saw happy couples wandering about the city or checking into hotels when he was having a lonely drink at the bar.

The monthly meetings that had once taken place at different locations had stopped, and now the meetings were taking place in one of the lads' homes, which meant their meetings were not as private as they once were. One nosey wife was one too many, and they knew they were making a rod for their own backs.

Noah had put his second-in-command, Jackie Harper, in contact with George who would now take his place in supplying her with the product. He advised George to keep the system he had in place, which was simple but effective, having set up a string of safety deposit boxes throughout the city and the surrounding areas. Once a month he would give Jackie the address and box number of two safety deposit boxes. In one she would deposit the cash she had collected that month and put it into the box at one bank then go to a different bank or train station where she would collect a kilo of cocaine.

After Jackie picked up the cocaine, she would make her way to one of ten apartments that Noah owned in the city centre. There, the cocaine was divided into smaller amounts with additives added. These smaller parcels would then be passed on to distributors all around the Merseyside area by Jackie's one and only contact Brendan. He, in turn, would pass it on to his dealers.

This system had worked successfully for years, with no links to Noah as far as he was concerned. The same system was used by all four of his partners, each of them having a safety deposit box in banks in areas all over Lancashire where they would place the money that was due to the cartel.

Jackie Harper was a pillar of the community. Where she lived, she had never been associated with any type of criminal activity. She was a successful businesswoman who worked for the Chamber of Commerce at Liverpool City Council and had a successful garage that her husband ran. He knew nothing of her extra activities with Noah.

It had been fortunate that she had hooked up with Noah. It had happened by chance at his factory's first Christmas party. Noah had been pointed out by Brenda as the guy who had bought the factory and Gabriel had told Jackie that Noah must have connections as he had paid a large amount of the purchase price under the counter to avoid paying tax on any profit her father would have made. As luck would have it, her husband had bought a run-down garage that needed a complete revamp at a cost they simply couldn't afford, so the cash she earned was duly sank into the garage, which added to their long-term income.

Although Noah and Stuart had moved on, Noah had kept in contact with Franco, giving him his latest burner-phone number, which was just as well as one day Franco rang him.

"Do you know a Jackie Harper, or do any of your connections have any dealings with her?" Franco asked.

"She's my number one, my second-in-command. Why?"

"Somebody has put her name in the frame for supplying. My contact in the police told me today that she's being investigated. You need to get shut as soon as possible."

Noah didn't like what Franco was saying, knowing what his interpretation of 'get shut' meant. The first thing he did was to call Jackie and arrange to meet her. She'd just been given the codes to two safety deposit boxes and Noah told her that under no circumstances was she to go to them until she had met him. This worried her, of course, knowing of Noah's connections and what he might be capable of. In all the years she'd known him, they'd only actually met in person a couple of times.

It was a strange place to meet but you could be invisible shopping in an Aldi supermarket, and so Noah told her to grab a trolley and meet him in the dairy aisle. She was standing there when he walked in, pushing his own trolley with a couple of shopping bags inside, and after being convinced she wasn't being followed, he made his way to her.

A couple of shoppers opened the fridges and grabbed what they needed while Jackie pretended to peruse the butter just as Noah approached and opened the fridge himself.

"You're known to the cops," Noah said quietly as he pulled out a tub of butter and placed it in his trolley. "You need to cut all ties with your dealers straight away."

"None of my dealers know my name, so I doubt anyone's grassed me up," she said, as Noah began to move away. She followed him and grabbed a carton of apple juice to add to the few items she already had in her trolley.

"If that's the case," he said, "someone higher up has put you in the frame. Whoever that is will know you're connected to me, and we need to put a stop to that."

Jackie looked at him, knowing exactly what he meant. If names had been leaked and it was someone with direct connections to the cartel, it was inevitable that lives were in danger, not least Jackie's and Noah's. The powers-that-be didn't take kindly to the police being involved in their discretions and wouldn't hesitate to get them out of the way.

Jackie abandoned her trolley and left the store, rushing home where she destroyed anything that would connect her to Noah and the organisation. She was in a panic; her whole life would come crashing down around her if she was arrested in connection with drug dealing.

Noah needed to inform the others and called an emergency meeting, telling Archie this one wouldn't be held at his house but at the Hilton Hotel instead. They needed privacy, no earwigging from nosey wives or kids. Archie wasn't too happy with this, but went along with it anyway, knowing there was no point arguing with Noah when he was in this frame of mind.

"So," Noah began as everyone arrived and ordered a beer before sitting at their table in the corner where they couldn't be overheard. "I had a call from Franco the other day and it's not great news…"

"How come Franco called you and not me?" Archie asked, interrupting Noah.

Noah looked over at Archie and sighed. "He thinks I'm still involved, albeit on a much smaller scale. We had a good working relationship and he's kept in contact."

Judging by Archie's expression, Noah could tell he had a problem with this and before he could continue telling the others about his contact being investigated, Archie asked, "How come you handed over your share of the business to George and not me?"

Noah was frustrated now. "Jesus, Archie, all I did was pass my connection on to George, how you shared it out was not my problem, which brings me to the reason why I called this meeting. Do you mind if I carry on?" He glared at Archie and got a shrug in response. "Somebody has put my old connection's name in the frame, and she's being investigated by the drug squad."

Realising he'd just revealed that his connection was female, he could have kicked himself. It was the first time he'd let anybody know it was a woman, apart from George.

"What I'm saying is that for her to be in the frame means someone is talking to the fuzz. It could be someone from her side, so I've taken the decision to remove her from my circle."

Everybody went quiet for a moment, assuming Noah meant he'd had her killed. To them, when someone was 'removed', it meant they'd been killed.

"I, like all of us, have been making sure people down the line of dealers have not got any names, which means they also won't have ours. Right?" All nodded in agreement. "So, the only other weak link could be family and friends."

Everyone nodded with a look of dread on their faces, each having their own individual thoughts about any family members or friends that could have leaked information about their business dealings. The house meetings had been a risk and one at Degsy's had resulted in him having to tell his wife to take the kids out to the park because they kept disturbing their conversation.

"We all need to make sure we have nothing in our homes that might link us to the people we deal with, that means anything. I have a burner phone for each of you here. Each one contains our numbers only and must never contain any other number. You need to make sure you dispose of this after this weekend and then get another, and every week after that. From now on, you don't use any of the phones you've been using to do business with your dealers. Is that understood?"

Noah then reached into his briefcase and took out three mobile phones, pushing each one towards his team.

"Nobody but me has the number of these phones. They are for us only. We communicate to each other using these and subsequent ones from now on. Okay?"

Everybody nodded in agreement.

"We've discussed this numerous times, but it's more important than ever right now that you don't keep any large amounts of cash in your homes or at work."

"What about the bin bags buried in your garden?" George asked.

"They're safe, and I suggest you do something similar." He chose not to mention that his story about the buried bin bags was simply that, a 'story'. It had been a wind up that he never dreamed they'd take seriously.

Noah called an end to the meeting, glad he'd managed to get through to the rest of the team and made them understand how important using those burner phones would be over the coming months. There was no telling what would happen to Jackie Harper, and if she did get arrested, whether she'd grass Noah up. It was, of course, the worst thing for any drug dealer to do, but under pressure, who knew what someone else could reveal.

Jackie had since closed all her bank accounts apart from one, which her salary was paid into, and had placed all her expensive jewellery along with a substantial amount of money into her sister's safety deposit box in her hometown of Cardiff. Six months went by, and it seemed like things had quietened down. The lads continued to change their burner phones every week like Noah had instructed, and money was no longer being kept at their houses in safes but in a different location that only they knew about. Jackie hadn't been arrested, but she was quite sure she had been followed on many occasions. It could have been her imagination. After all, she was on constant high alert these days. But she was relieved to get out of the drugs trade. It had served its purpose and made her a huge amount of money that set her up for many years to come. She knew it would just have been greed to have stayed any longer.

Just as things seemed to be settling down and the lads were getting on with family life, living day-to-day with the knowledge of not being caught, the local news reported that over twenty homes in the Merseyside area had been subjected to a dawn raid and there had been numerous arrests made. As no names had been given out there was a lot of nervous people in and around the city, and it was expected that more arrests would happen as some of those now in custody would most likely become informants.

Archie, George and Degsy met in their local pub when the news broke, all in agreement that their connection in the business had hardly been affected. It was a relief all round when the names of the ones arrested started to filter through, knowing they weren't known to anyone. This, however, gave them a false sense of security and it wasn't long before they resumed their meetings at Archie's house.

Noah felt he was well out of it. Bram, happy to see his brother cut ties with the drug scene, congratulated him on the success the factory had become. Planning permission had been granted to extend again for storage and this only meant it would give the company a more legitimate feel. Noah felt safe. Enough time had passed to keep him out of the loop and portray himself as the professional businessman.

When further news broke about the raids and the people arrested, it came as no surprise to them all that the latest group of dealers were handed sentences ranging from ten to twenty years, and George was also wondering if he should have got out. Foolishly, however, he was talked into staying and giving the business at least another few years by Archie.

The whole drug scene had changed, not only in Merseyside but Europe, too. Cocaine was now the in-product and would be for the foreseeable future. It was making a lot of people very rich, generating huge amounts of unaccountable money. The whole of Europe was hooked on making money, and this was only the start of it.

CHAPTER SIXTEEN

It had been over a year since the police had carried out any major raids in the city of Liverpool and most of the dealers were starting to relax again, none more than Archie, who had invested in a purpose-built villa in Spain. He was under the false impression that the Spanish authorities turned a blind eye to people spending cash, and to an extent they did. But when somebody tipped them off that a major drug dealer was moving into their country, they made enquires with the UK police and discovered that Archie had been in trouble with the law when he was a teenager, albeit twenty years ago.

He had been brought to the attention of the Merseyside police on more than one occasion, so they had decided to keep a close surveillance on him, and it wasn't long before they had a reason to arrest him. His arrogance shone through as they discovered he'd been taking huge amounts of cash over to Spain once a month to make payments to the builder who was constructing his villa. It was at John Lennon Airport that he and his wife, Terry, were stopped for a routine search, which had been set up by the Merseyside police.

When asked if they were they carrying cash, Archie told the officer that he had the legal amount of ten thousand pounds on him. He felt like choking Terry when the officer asked her the same question and she answered the same as Archie had. They were then marched to a side office where they were ordered to produce the cash they had on them. Unfortunately, the amount of notes far exceeded the legal limit and the officer asked how much cash they each had in their wallets. When they told the officers they both had cash on them, they were asked how much and both acted dumb, saying they didn't know. But when Archie's wallet was taken off him and searched, the officer discovered it contained over a thousand pounds, which took the amount way over the top of what they could legally take out of the country. And until they could prove where it came from and what it was for, the majority of it was confiscated.

Archie just hadn't learnt his lesson. Of all the times that Noah had drilled into him the importance of being extra cautious, not carrying huge amounts of cash around, not drawing attention to himself, it seemed it had all been a waste of time. Terry was once again dripping in gold jewellery and wore several diamond rings and other precious stones that the officer was quite sure hadn't been bought with hard-earned wages. The couple turned up at their holiday destination with just a small amount of cash to pay the taxi driver. But they had their debit cards and didn't realise the confiscated money was just another piece of the jigsaw as far as the police ongoing investigation was concerned.

Archie's next mistake was to accept that he probably wouldn't get the confiscated money back. He no longer had any value for money and losing twenty grand plus at the airport was like a drop in the ocean. It was too much like hard work finding a number for the customs office at the airport and having to go through the proper channels of demanding the return of his money. It was nearly a month later when the police called at his house to ask him to account for the money he'd had taken off him and Terry.

They knew he was lying when he told them it was from clients for landscaping work he'd carried out, and when they asked him for a list of names and addresses of those clients, Archie's response was that he'd had a fire in his office block and what information he still had, he would get over to the police station first thing in the morning because they were at his old burnt-out office.

After the police officers left, Terry said, "Don't you think you should go and get those contact details now? I don't want to be in any more trouble than we're already in."

"Nah," Archie said, reaching for a beer from the fridge. "They won't come back, and there's no way they'll go to the yard. They've got better things to do than chase the likes of us, love." But Terry wasn't so sure.

"I'll come with you, if you like?" she said, going up to him and kissing his neck, trying to seduce him. They'd often used his desk for sex and had been all through the yard and buildings when no one had been about.

"Forget it," Archie said, pushing her away. "I need a few beers tonight and then I'll take you shopping tomorrow afternoon and treat you to that necklace you saw the other week."

This pleased Terry. Her materialistic attitude was too important to her and even though she intended seducing her husband later instead, when they went to bed, she was quite happy to know that by the weekend, she'd have another diamond to add to her extravagant collection.

Unfortunately, the police were one step ahead. They'd already applied for and obtained a warrant to search Archie's office and yard, quite sure they would find something illegal.

The following morning when he arrived at the yard, Archie got out of the car and unlocked the gates, failing to notice the two police vans parked around the corner and obviously out of sight. As soon as he unbolted the padlock, both vans screeched around towards the yard and came to an abrupt stop, leaving Archie shocked and frozen to the spot.

They gave him no time to hide his clients' details or move cash to a secret place. His desk was filled with envelopes stuffed with money, and the safe was bulging at the seams.

Knowing there was nothing he could do, he cursed his wife for only being interested in receiving another piece of jewellery and muttered under his breath how this was her fault for opening her big mouth at the airport. They could have walked away had she not said anything, but no, she stood there, covered in expensive jewellery and wearing designer clothes, showing off a Positano tote bag. *Stupid cow,* he thought, as eight officers rushed past him and made their way to the office.

Archie had that much cash in his safe he couldn't even tell them how much there was, and this gave the police a good reason to detain him and take him and the contents of the safe to the local police station. The stuffed envelopes had also been seized from his desk drawers, along with clients' files from his filing cabinet.

Chief Inspector Alan Conboy was over the moon, as Archie's name was one that had been popping up time after time, along with George Carmichael and a bloke known locally as Degsy, whose real name was Derek Owens. Those three names had been given up every time one or more of their dealers got caught, but they had never been able to prove anything against any of them for too long now, and

Conboy rubbed his hands together as he realised this could be the breakthrough he needed.

When all the cash was counted it was no surprise that it totalled over one hundred thousand pounds. It was way too much for Archie to account for, so the police applied for and got a search warrant to raid his home address. Once again, Archie hadn't been careful enough and had, over the years, been supplying his wife's sister with cocaine. Terry had kept a supply in the house as her sister would often turn up out of the blue, and when the place was raided, there was enough white powder in the property to give Chief Inspector Conboy plenty of evidence to charge Archie with supplying a banned substance.

Terry was also arrested and charged with possession with intent to supply.

It didn't take long before the news got back to Noah, and his concern was that he didn't know if Archie would spill the beans by giving everybody up to save his own neck.

Both Archie and Terry spent a week in police custody until eventually, their lawyer managed to plead their case and get the pair out on bail.

"What the fuck?" George said when he and Degsy went to the police station to pick them both up.

"We haven't been charged with anything yet, but we're still under investigation."

"How much cash did you have in the house?" Degsy asked.

"Fuck knows," Archie replied. "But there was a shit load in my office at the yard, that's why they raided the house." He then turned to Terry who sat next to him in the back seat of Degsy's car. "I told you to find a good hiding place for the money," he said, shaking his head then feeling guilty as his wife began to cry. He took hold of her hand. "It's going to be okay, babe. We'll get this sorted and you'll have your diamond necklace back before you know it."

"I don't want the fucking diamond necklace," Terry spat, disgusted that he even mentioned it after their week behind bars. "I want to live a normal life, Archie, and not live in fear of being put away for ten fucking years for dealing."

Archie had already told Terry not to mention the stash of cocaine the police had discovered in their home as that was the diamond rule – no drugs in your home or on your person.

What Archie or the others didn't know was that the Chief Constable of Merseyside Police had significantly increased his budget to wheedle out the drug dealers in the city, something that was having a big impact on the drugs trade.

His network, led by Chief Inspector Alan Conboy, used some underhanded methods to get results and they were well on their way of getting to the main men at the top. He wrongly thought, however, that if he got to them then it would stop most of the dealing in the city and completely misunderstood that if there was a demand then there would always be a supplier.

Because of the trouble Archie had caused, Noah and Bram went over the accounts and all the finances that were connected with the purchase of the factory and Noah's ten apartments. Fortunately, everything seemed pretty much watertight. The bank had financed the building of the huge extension to the factory, and Brenda had nailed her colours to the mast by bringing in a huge order from the new Nissan plant in the north-east of the country for the firm to supply the suspension units for the latest cars. That order alone was worth millions.

When Noah tried to contact Angela Rylan, who had done all the conveyancing to his purchases, he was happy when he was told she had recently moved to America, but that all his records and files were kept on site. He informed her replacement that he'd probably need to see them for tax purposes, and they agreed he was welcome to call in anytime and take photocopies. He had a similar result when he tried unsuccessfully to track down Jackie Harper. She and her husband had sold the garage and disappeared to God-knows-where. No one knew. Of course, Noah assumed it was probably Spain where all the rogues disappeared to in a hurry and this was good news, as it meant it was only the lads that could tie him to anything now.

The last thing Noah thought was that one of their own might grass them up, but facing the possibility of being sent to prison for a ten-to-twenty-year-stretch, most people would sell their souls if not their grandmother to get out of it.

Unfortunately, there was a traitor in the camp and that person was Archie. The police had already offered him a deal if he were to give up his two present colleagues and his two from the past, and promised they would make sure he got a suspended sentence, telling him he would be allowed to keep hold of his assets but not the cocaine or cash.

When they told him that Terry had already mentioned the names of his partners, he knew he had one chance and one chance only. Terry was scared, he knew that. But he was still furious with her for grassing them up. He began to realise arranging meetings at the house was probably the worst thing he could have done, especially as Terry's sister was often there, making eyes at Degsy after she'd snorted a stash of cocaine in their back bedroom. And so, he took the deal. He knew he'd have to hide at least one million of the cash he had stashed away all in used notes, plus if they were all going to go down, he wanted to make sure he had a good bundle to greet him when he got out. And he thought he knew just where there was a million waiting to be claimed: Noah's back garden, right in the centre.

Chief Inspector Alan Conboy was grinning from ear to ear when he was praised by the Chief Constable for being the one to cut off a huge supply line. His name would go down as the one who took out the drug barons of Liverpool. It was a huge feather in his cap, as he had done what all his previous chief constables had failed to do: He had busted the biggest drugs cartel in England, if not Europe.

Two things happened in the next couple of weeks that made Noah realise for definite that Archie had betrayed them. The first thing was the timber yard, once having been the main importer of pure cocaine, had been raided, but it was only Noah who knew that its location had, in fact, been changed.

Noah phoned George and asked him to meet without telling Archie or Degsy. He agreed and went to the Hilton Hotel that night and sat at the bar waiting for George to arrive. It was a surprise when George wheeled himself into the bar area, followed closely by his wife, Wendy. No pleasantries were exchanged as Noah was too annoyed that George hadn't come alone.

"How much does she know about the business?" Noah asked, glancing at Wendy.

Before George could answer, Wendy said, "Everything."

"What do you mean, everything? I thought you were coming on your own, George?"

George shrugged and looked at his wife, who was now staring at Noah with an expression of disgust. "I know the ins and outs of everything that has happened since you lot came back from Belize," she said, in a threatening manner. But when Noah gave her his warning glare, she realised she wasn't dealing with the likes of Archie or Degsy, and she backed off slightly.

"Be careful, love," Noah said. "The last three people that knew the ins and outs of my business are all dead."

He didn't need to say anything else. Neither George nor Wendy spoke, and the silence hung in the air for a few moments.

"If we don't make sure all our backs are covered, Franco is coming back to Liverpool," Noah added.

George knew what that meant. His face went white as he knew somebody would probably end up dead and it wouldn't just be Archie, either. Anybody that could lead back to Franco, or his replacement, would be removed completely. George asked the question both him and Noah had been thinking.

"Do you think Archie has turned?"

Noah had to be choosey with what he told George, or anyone for that matter.

"Well, it was only two weeks after Archie was arrested that the timber factory in Widnes was raided. The police found nothing though, as the whole operation had been moved over a year ago. I never told anybody, so it wasn't so much lucky but good management."

"Do we need to be worried?" George asked.

"The thing I'm worried about is mine or Stuart's names being put to the top of the most-wanted list. Yeah, I do think we need to be worried. But we keep a low profile and I'll see what happens."

"So, what do we do about Archie?"

Noah pursed his lips as he thought about the snake in the grass that could very well blow their whole operation and identify each and every one of them, landing them a hefty jail term.

"That's the thing," Noah said. "I heard that Archie's up in front of a magistrate, charged with supplying drugs."

"But drugs charges go to crown court, surely?" Wendy pointed out.

"Yeah, they do, which means he's turned."

It was the following week when the news travelled that Archie had received his sentence in the magistrate's court, a sentence of two years suspended. It was obvious by then that he'd become a police informant.

Over the next few months, Noah got an inkling that he was being investigated. Simple things, like an unfamiliar face in his local bar who would sit at a table in the corner with one drink lasting at least an hour, a drink that looked like either water or lemonade. When he was having a mid-week pint in the Everyman pub in town, which was normally quiet at that time, Noah ordered his usual pint of Guinness and sat at the bar chatting to the barmaid, Jess. He couldn't help but notice a well-dressed lady walk in and approach him before Jess turned to her and asked what she wanted.

"A double gin and tonic," she replied in what seemed like a posh accent. She then took one mouthful of her drink and replaced the glass on the bar.

"I needed that," she said, turning to look at Noah.

He found her to be quite an attractive lady, surmising her to be in her late thirties or early forties perhaps, but what looked odd to him was the shopping bag she was holding. It was dark green with *Harrods* written across it, certainly not a common bag seen in and around Liverpool. He knew she must have passed at least a dozen pubs to get to this one, so he thought he would humour himself and start a conversation with her.

"I didn't know there was a Harrods in Liverpool?"

She smiled at him before answering. "Oh no,' she said, "I've just got off the train from London."

Noah wasn't sure what to think and decided to be on his guard, wondering if she could be an undercover copper.

"Must have a few bob, love," he said, taking a gulp of his pint. "I couldn't even afford the bag you're holding!"

He then replaced his glass on the bar and stood up from the stool before he turned and walked out of the pub, half expecting her to follow him or at least an accomplice to.

He'd been told that most female undercover officers worked in twos, so he thought if she was a copper, she would have a partner. Noah knew in his heart and soul that trouble was coming his way, that George and Degsy would be next on the hit list then him, and his thoughts went once more to selling up and leaving the country. Even though he'd once craved spending his life with a good woman and having a family of his own, this was no longer a priority to him. After spending a long time thinking about his life logically, he had no excess baggage to worry about, no wife and kids, which meant he was free to just up and leave.

Bram came to the factory the following day to do the annual accounts and once again Kirby Engineering showed a healthy profit. The directors, who now included Brenda and Brian, received their well-earned dividend bonuses. The new extension to the factory meant the company could employ an extra twenty workers, which was all good for the image Noah wanted to give out. He was now a successful businessman, but it would not be long for this image to be tested to the full.

He was left in the dark as to what was happening in the drugs trade and the contact number he had for Franco was now out of service. He still didn't know for sure whether he was being investigated, but the news about Archie's lenient sentence, and especially him not going to crown court, was still prominent in Noah's mind. It would only take one slip of the tongue for Archie to grass everyone up.

When Noah's new house had been coming to completion, he'd paid an extra twenty thousand pounds to have top-of-the-range surveillance cameras fitted to the front, back, and sides. These cameras were movement activated and recorded any activities all around the property, including his back garden. All four sides of his house had separate recording devices which had a sophisticated unit fitted that flashed if it recorded any movement. He was used to the camera at the front of the house flashing every day with people walking past, but the ones at the sides and the one that covered the back rarely went off unless a bird caught them.

It was one night, just as Noah was going to bed, that the light flashed on in his back garden and he peered through the window, not expecting to see much. But then a figure appeared through the darkness, holding what looked like a small torch. And then, much to his surprise, he recognised the figure as Archie. As well as the torch in one hand, Archie had a spade in the other and began to sink it into the lawn. The centre of the lawn, to be precise, and Noah smiled, realising Archie still believed there was a million pounds buried beneath the grass.

One of Archie's tasks as a police informant was to give them a clue as to where Noah kept his money and in order to keep himself out of jail, he'd already told them about the cash buried in the garden. But Archie was here to make sure it was still there before the police raided Noah's house. He needed to be sure he wasn't sending the police on a wild goose chase, otherwise it could result in him being questioned on his loyalty and even put back under the police radar, which would result in him going down.

Noah decided to leave Archie to it, knowing he wouldn't find any bin bags. But he was even more surprised when two days later, Archie was in his garden again, digging the hole that he'd neatly covered over previously, and placing what looked like a large black bin bag into it. This meant only one thing: Noah was being set up for a raid on his home. Archie knew the chances of Noah having anything incriminating in his house would be nil, and all the information he had been giving to Conboy was just hearsay. He had made out that Noah was the top man, with solid connections to the cartel, and as he'd always taken his orders from him, he needed something concrete on Noah to implicate him.

It might have looked comical to see Archie digging a hole in the dark in Noah's lawn, but in truth, it was now getting serious. It was time he hired a criminal lawyer, knowing an arrest was probably on the horizon. And so, after a discussion with Bram and Lydia, they decided together that the best person for the job was a very experienced and respected lawyer called Karen Veitch, known as one of the best in Liverpool and throughout the North West.

He walked into her office the following week and couldn't help but see how young she looked, probably mid-thirties .She looked like a graduate who'd just been let out into the big bad world and he sat down in the chair opposite her and wondered if this was a huge mistake. But it didn't take long for him to realise that she was well-organised and extremely professional, and within a few minutes of her shuffling papers around on her desk and Noah nervously contemplating whether he should just leave, she got straight to the point and fired her first question at him.

"You are one of three named drug dealers, Noah," she said. "Are you into drugs? Do you deal?"

She'd put Noah on the back foot, and they both knew it, but she wanted to know where she stood and if she could help him before deciding whether to take on his case. Noah wasn't sure if it was wiser to tell the truth or give her a watered-down version, but before he could say anything, she continued.

"Look, it's no good defending you if you lie to me. It only makes the case to defend you harder. If the police have got evidence about your activities and criminal events that have happened, they will prove it in court and your story won't add up, meaning pleading your case with a 'not guilty' plea will be a waste of time."

Noah nodded, realising there was no point in sitting here and telling this woman a pack of lies that would most probably land him in more trouble than he could already be in.

And so, he decided to tell her the truth, albeit slightly amended.

"When I left the army and came home, the cocaine industry was really starting to get going in the UK. It was talked about, and people were dealing, but not on the scale they are today. We didn't understand what we were getting into, but the demand for cocaine just grew and grew. We started off with five members of our small group, four of us that came out of the army at the same time after a tour of duty in Belize and our close friend, who had been badly injured when we worked down the coal mines."

Karen listened intently, all the time thinking about her friend, Jackie Harper, who had confessed to her a year previously about her own dealings with the drugs business. Karen was aware that someone had told Jackie to get out and move away and she now wondered if that person was Noah.

"Who was your second-in-command," she asked him. "Could they have information that could harm your case?"

"No," Noah said, shaking his head. "She got out of the business not long before me. She's happily married, has a good job, and no need to get back into the drugs trade."

This made Karen happy as her mate was still not too sure if she would get a knock on her door, so she asked Noah a question which could have grave consequences in her friend's life.

"A woman, then. What was her name?" Karen asked, quite sure her theory was correct.

Without hesitation, he answered her. "That's something on a need-to-know basis. She's out of the business now and is in a good place in life. She wouldn't grass on anyone, and I want her name kept completely out of this."

Noah then slid a memory stick containing evidence of Archie planting a bin bag full of money in his back garden.

"This should help," he said. "It proves corruption. Look at it and tell me you agree."

Karen lifted the memory stick from the table and inserted it into the back of her desktop computer, then clicked the 'play' button.

"This needs to be clear enough to give us a way out," she said.

She stared at the screen, gobsmacked. She knew the police were under pressure to bring drug dealers down, but this was a new low.

"Who is it?" she asked.

"Archie Carmichael." Noah replied. "One of our fellow soldiers on tour in Belize. He was one of the original five. I didn't trust him from the start, but he grew on me over time.

I always felt like something was off about him, he was often aggressive and argumentative, never felt like a team player."

"So, what's driven him to do this?"

"He was arrested, him and his wife. They were caught trying to take twenty-odd grand through John Lennon Airport on their way to Spain, and it got confiscated. The police turned up questioning why they hadn't bothered to retrieve the money and ended up with a search warrant for Archie's work's premises along with his home. They found coke and money, stashed just about everywhere."

"I did hear about the arrest," Karen said, still watching the man in the middle of Noah's lawn fumbling about with a black bin bag and trying to shove it into the hole he'd dug.

"Next thing we hear, he's up in front of a magistrate and gets a two-year suspended sentence. That is iffy, don't you think?" Karen nodded and Noah continued. "We reckon he's been blabbing to the cops, his get-out-of-jail-free card, and they've offered him a deal. So now, he's working for them to keep his freedom, and this is one of the ways he's obviously needing to stay out."

"By setting you up," Karen said, matter-of-factly as she pulled the memory stick out of the USB socket and put it on the desk in front of her.

"Exactly. I should have gone with my initial instinct and not trusted the snivelling little shit."

Karen then opened the folder on her desk and took out a form, pushing it towards Noah. "You'll need to fill this in, give me some details and then sign it. I will accept you as my client, you'll probably need us. This company will represent you."

She handed him a pen and he took it from her then started to fill in the form. It was just a formality, which was necessary, and he signed it then popped the lid back on the pen and handed it back to her.

"So, what now?" he said.

"Well, Mr Burgess, we may be in touch, depending on what transpires."

Although satisfied to have found what appeared to be good representation should the shit hit the fan, Noah couldn't help but feel saddened at how the others had never truly understood the rules of drug dealing. Archie had shown off his wealth and allowed his wife to do the same, whilst George and Degsy had followed closely behind in the last couple of years that Noah had been out of the business. He was glad Stuart had got out when he did and even more glad he'd chosen to take that path, too. He got back into his car and leant back into the seat, sighing heavily before he put the key in the ignition and turned over the engine. Then he put the gear stick into reverse and manoeuvred out of his parking space before driving onto the main road. Karen watched him from her office window, not sure whether to feel sympathy for the fact he was now probably under investigation, or frustration at yet another drug dealer who thought he could get away with being a criminal in a world where evidence was now much easier to get hold of than it was even just ten years ago.

CHAPTER SEVENTEEN

Noah was giving the possibility of emigrating to Australia or Canada serious consideration. He couldn't make up his mind whether it was in his best interest to just leave for good or stick it out in the UK and face what might come his way. There was over three million pounds in his Zurich bank account, which he could withdraw and live off quite happily. But running away didn't appeal to him. It had been at the back of his mind to do it after Stuart had left to live in Spain, but he was on his own, he didn't have a wife and family to protect and so he decided for the time being to hang fire and carry on in the UK.

It was less than a month after Noah had hired the services of Karen Veitch that he got a strange phone call from a woman he didn't know.

"The police plan to carry out a raid on your home at 7am sharp tomorrow morning," she said.

"Who is this?" Noah asked, perplexed as he stood frozen to the spot in his hallway.

But the phone went dead. The woman had hung up, leaving Noah utterly baffled. He dialled Karen's number and told her about the call, and she informed him it sounded like a police informant who was most likely on his side but keeping herself out of prison.

"Probably someone you've dealt with in the past, maybe inadvertently, but someone who's now most likely under police radar," she said.

"Am I going to be arrested?" he asked.

"Do you have anything in your house that could lead them to arrest you?"

"Nothing," he answered. "I'm clean."

"Then you should have nothing to worry about. Hang tight," Karen said, and hung up.

Noah then tried to ring Degsy, but the number was no longer available. When the same thing happened with George, he realised he now had no way of warning them. If he was being followed, which was probable, there was no way he could go round to their houses as he'd be followed there and create even more evidence to the prosecution, should it go to court, that they were hiding something.

Noah knew common sense would mean that the lads should have nothing incriminating in their homes, but lately, common sense had gone out of the window. None of them had thought Archie would drop them in it, but unfortunately, George and Degsy had other incriminating evidence in their properties apart from money. They had kept hold of stolen goods; items that had been used to pay for drugs they'd sold to people who had no ready cash available. TVs and computers and expensive cameras, along with stashes of jewellery and gemstones were amongst those items, which meant another nail in their coffin.

The raid happened, just as the mystery woman had said, at 7am the following morning, but Noah's house wasn't touched. Chief Inspector Alan Conboy and a team of over sixty police officers entered ten houses around Merseyside and arrested a total of twenty-five men and women, including George and Degsy. The raids made the local morning news and Noah sat watching his TV in shock as he saw his two friends being carted off in handcuffs and shoved into the back of police vans.

He called Karen at 9am, who was surprised to hear from him, assuming he'd have been one of the people arrested a couple of hours ago. She'd been driving to work with the intention of visiting him in a police cell later that morning, not hearing his voice on the other end of her phone.

"Where are you?" she asked.

"I'm at home. I don't know what happened. They arrested my friends, but no one turned up here or my factory. What does that mean?"

"Could mean a lot of things," Karen said, "but more than likely they decided they didn't have enough evidence against you to raid your house after all. That's something they'll try to get from those they've arrested."

"I doubt whether Degsy or George would drop me in it," Noah said, which Karen thought sounded quite naïve. "We've been through a lot together."

"Noah, I hate to burst your bubble, but in my experience it's quite common for someone who's been arrested and looking at a lengthy jail sentence if they don't cough up some information, to affect their way of thinking and give out a few names. They'll be under immense pressure and the police will have found enough evidence to make those arrests." She sighed. "Can you make it into my office this morning?"

"Yeah, I'll be there in an hour," he said, then hung up. Just as he was walking into the kitchen to make himself a strong coffee, the phone rang, and he raced back to answer it.

"You're at home, thank god for that." It was Bram, relieved that his brother hadn't been arrested along with the others.

"Yeah, I'm here. Guess I've got you to thank for that," Noah said.

"Me? Why's that, then?"

"If you hadn't talked me into getting out of the business when you did, I might have still been involved and then I would have been locked up with the rest of the poor bastards."

"I'm just glad you did get out. You made the right decision."

An hour later, Noah sat opposite Karen in her office cradling another strong coffee.

He hadn't slept much over the last twenty-four hours and wasn't sure if he needed caffeine or a few pints in the local pub. As he was sat in a lawyer's office, he settled for the coffee.

"I've been asked to represent Samuel and Laura Mills, a husband and wife team," Karen said. "Do you know them?"

Noah thought for a moment then shook his head. "No, never heard of them."

"I'm glad, because they knew George and Archie, as well as Derek, or Degsy as you know him. They haven't mentioned your name, though. When I asked who they got their supply from, they said three men were the main suppliers who supplied the people who supplied them. Obviously, I couldn't ask them if they knew you but the way they were talking made me think they wanted to grass everyone up. They obviously want to cooperate fully with the police."

This angered Noah. Those three idiots had thrown out the rules that had been set out at the very beginning by Shelley, having emphasised time and time again to let nobody outside the industry know your business. Having just one right-hand man each was all they needed and to keep everything under wraps, including their luxurious lifestyles, something none of them had done properly.

Karen had done her homework and had been digging around.

"It seems your mates, George and Degsy, have hired top criminal lawyer, Rex Makin," she told Noah.

"I've heard of him. He's the one with the reputation for getting people off, even though the evidence is stacked against them."

"Yes," Karen agreed. "And if he doesn't get them off, he nearly always manages to get them the minimum sentence so long as they agree to cooperate with the police. Everyone arrested this morning will remain in police custody while the police carry out their investigations."

"I need to keep a low profile," Noah said.

"Well, I'd advise you to run your factory and carry on as normal. Don't draw any attention to yourself and make yourself look guilty. If your name does get out, it won't be long before you're joining them all."

Noah stood up and thanked Karen for her advice, before leaving the office.

She liked him, but she worried for him at the same time.

Chief Inspector Alan Conboy was over the moon. All the arrests that had been made were near the top of the chain of the most wanted drug dealers in Merseyside, and all the information he had been given pointed to Noah Burgess as being the main man connected to the cartel.

It came to his attention that Noah was amongst the first to start importing cocaine, which had led to a multi-million-pound business leaving Noah and his associates very wealthy indeed.

Over the next three to four weeks, things in Liverpool and Manchester were heating up as arrests were being made all over both cities. But the trend was going down the scale to street and local traders and not up to some of the main importers.

It had been a month since George's arrest, so it was a total surprise to Noah when he got a call to his office address from Wendy, George's wife, asking if he could meet her as she needed his help.

He invited her to his office that afternoon and when she turned up, Noah noticed immediately the stress etched across her face. She seemed to have aged, even though it hadn't been that long since he'd last seen her, and when he opened his arms up in a gesture to give her a hug, she seemed to fall into them like a feather.

"It's good to see you," he said, pulling away and going to the coffee percolator to pour them both a cup. "I'm so sorry about what has happened to George." He placed a mug of coffee in front of her then sat back down in his chair. "How are you?" he asked, knowing she was quite obviously not okay by the amount of weight she'd lost and the drawn expression she wore.

She took a sip of her drink. "I wish George had taken your advice and got out of the drugs business when you did. We wouldn't be in this mess now."

Noah picked up a pen and wrote something down on a sheet of paper in his notebook, then turned it around to face her.

Are you wired?

Tears began to roll down her face and she nodded. Noah stood up and went round the desk towards her, then hugged her again. This told him she'd been forced to come here to try and get him to talk, incriminating himself and giving the police sufficient evidence they were still missing in order to arrest him. But it was something she just couldn't do. Noah had been nothing but a good friend to her and George, apart from which he was even a Godfather to one of her children, so when he started talking rubbish she just smiled.

"Well, you know when Archie talked George into the drugs business, I wanted nothing to do with it. That's why I distanced myself from all of them. It's simply not my scene."

Wendy gave Noah a thumbs-up sign then rolled her hands, encouraging him to carry on. "So, Wendy, how can I help you?"

She reached for a tissue out of her handbag and blew her nose before taking another sip of the coffee, replacing the cup on Noah's desk.

"The police have confiscated all our cash and frozen our bank accounts. They even took my jewellery to check if it was stolen. I bought most of it myself and of course George was always treating me. But they said it was evidence. I went to the Citizen's Advice Bureau to see what I should do, and they told me to go to the DSS to try and make some sort of claim. But they told me the best they could do was to put my kids into care."

She sniffed loudly and looked at Noah.

"They're my children, Noah, I can't let that happen. That's why I'm here; I need your help."

"It's not a problem, I'll sort something out." Noah reached for the notebook again and picked up a pen. "Do you have a bank account?"

"No, it's been frozen," she said, then took the pen from Noah and wrote in the notebook, *my mum has.*

Noah nodded. "Okay," he said, before picking up the phone and ringing through to Lydia in her office.

"Lydia, can you bring me a business cheque in for the amount of five thousand pounds made payable to cash, please."

Lydia had met Wendy on a few occasions and was wondering what Noah was up to, but she did as she was told and brought the cheque to him. Noah signalled a zip motion across his mouth as she opened his office door before she had chance to ask any questions.

"Put this down as an advance against my director's dividend due the month after next," he said to Lydia as she handed him the cheque. "and can you call the bank and let them know them one of our employees has been awarded a cheque for the five thousand pounds."

For the sake of the wire, and the fact the police had instructed her to get as much cash from Noah as she could, Wendy said, "I really appreciate this, but haven't you got any cash. I am desperate."

Noah smiled and Lydia left the office, closing the door quietly. "I don't deal in cash at all," he said. "I use my debit card all the time, or company cheques."

Wendy had been told to ask for cash in the hope Noah would take a decent amount from one of his safe places, a place that the police would be expecting to hear about from her when she got back to them with the recording. But he would come across as a squeaky-clean businessman, which was exactly what he needed to do. Nonetheless, he took his wallet out of his suit pocket and opened it, taking out four ten-pound notes and handing them to her.

"Sorry, love, this is all the cash I have on me. Make sure you keep in touch, and don't you ever get yourself into this position again," he said with a smile. "I will always be here for you, okay?"

Wendy nodded, tears appearing in her eyes again, then she stood up and walked towards his side of the desk, kissed him on his cheek and whispered into his ear, "Thank you." She'd hated being put in this position, but the police had told her and George that if he wanted to have any chance of a reduced sentence, they would have to give them as much information on Noah as possible. Every angle they'd tried had come to a dead end as all his business dealings were totally above board and documented.

Noah stood up and put his hands on Wendy's arms. "How is Degsy's wife faring?"

Wendy shook her head exaggeratedly and said, "She's gone back to Scotland, back to her parents."

Then she silently mouthed, "Isle of Man." Noah nodded. "She knew nothing about the drugs," Wendy added, speaking out loud this time. "She was anti-drugs."

In the police van parked around the corner from Noah's factory, two police officers were listening to the conversation taking place between Noah and Wendy, both feeling extremely disappointed that Noah hadn't incriminated himself. They knew he could afford to give her a one-off gift of five thousand pounds from the salary he was earning. They'd done their homework.

After Wendy left, Noah took a call from Karen Veitch, asking him to meet her at her office that afternoon. When he arrived, she was sat behind her desk with a few folders opened up, and Noah caught the name George Collins at the top of a sheet of paper inside one of them.

"The crown prosecution is trying to set a date for George and Degsy's trials. I have it on good authority that if they do a deal with the police, they're most likely going to receive much shorter, lenient sentences. But we have a problem so far as that's concerned."

Noah thought as much and beckoned for her to continue.

"In order to get their sentences reduced they will have to give evidence against you, and that will lead to your arrest and conviction. However, once they're sentenced, they can withdraw their information about you, say they got it wrong, and their sentences won't be increased. They might get a conviction for perverting the course of justice, but it won't add time onto their sentence.

"The good thing is that Rex Makin is pushing for an early trial, and he carries a lot of clout in the city, but that's not the main reason I have asked you to come in. I wanted to suggest that you go away for say a month or two. The reason being that if you're out of the country you can't be arrested, as you haven't been charged with any offence and have no criminal background."

Noah thought about it for a moment then said, "I've just landed a new contract to supply Nissan Motors with bearings for their new factory in Sunderland over the next ten years. The contract's worth the best part of ten million plus, and that's ongoing."

Karen's ears pricked up. "Will that mean you'll be taking on more staff?"

"We should be employing around another sixty to a hundred people, maybe more."

This was good news to Karen as it all added up to Noah being a pillar of society. He would be viewed in a different light to the everyday criminal, especially being ex-military, too. This contract could be the turning point and the best way to keep him out of jail. She smiled and looked down at the desk, feeling glad that she'd decided to represent him.

"Nissan have asked for my engineers to go over to Japan and learn how they manufacture the parts, so they're in sync with their UK factory."

"How long will that take?"

"It's not been decided yet, but it could be a month or so. I could go with them and even if the engineers need to get back home, I can take an extended holiday."

"Sounds like a good plan," Karen said.

"I'll set the ball rolling when I get back to the factory, make the arrangements and call a meeting to decide which engineers to send. And I'll get myself some plane tickets and book a hotel."

"Will you take your wife with you?"

"I don't have one, or a girlfriend," Noah said with a shrug. "I travel light."

Thoughts were racing through Karen's head as she envisioned getting on the plane with him and leaving her husband and kids at home. But it was just a daydream. She'd become quite fond of Noah since they'd started working together, and couldn't help fantasise a little about how a trip to the far east with him could be particularly enjoyable. Before he left Karen's office, he gave her his new contact number in case she needed to get in touch, and he also gave her Bram's number.

Things happened fast over the next few days and Noah managed to sort out a group of engineers, which included Brian, to go to the Nissan factory in Japan, getting Lydia to book their tickets and hotel room, and he went ahead and booked a separate hotel for himself, travelling on a different plane first class. He was happy to leave Lydia and Brenda in charge; they were on top of everything and knew what to do if there was an emergency. And Bram would keep him updated with news and any updates on the police's investigation. It was when Noah arrived at his hotel when Bram messaged him to say the trial dates had been set for George and Degsy in a month's time, and he should stay away for the time being.

Chief Inspector Alan Conboy wanted the trial of all of those arrested to be put back at least three months. He was not a happy man. He had no solid evidence to arrest Noah, and that infuriated him, so he decided to take a chance and get a warrant to raid Noah's home. He'd already tried to speak to Noah by visiting the factory and being told he was in Japan on a business trip, and so he thought this could perhaps be his lucky break. There was a very high chance he would find something that would finally be the incriminating evidence to convict his most-wanted subject.

Noah had a cleaner who went in two days a week and before he'd gone away, he'd asked her and her husband if they could housesit while he was away. They were only too happy, especially when he left her a chunk of cash in an envelope for essentials and told them to help themselves to his drink's cabinet! He hadn't mentioned anything about the possibility that the place could be raided as he wanted their innocence to shine through when or if it happened. They knew nothing about his past and he knew they would totally cooperate with the police, so he gave them Bram's contact details and told them to ring him if they had any problems.

Noah had been in contact with Lydia as to what was happening with the Nissan contract and was very pleased that Brian had met their engineers at the factory in Japan and they'd agreed to what type of machinery they would have to install in the new extension in the UK. It turned out the engineers only needed to stay in Japan for a week, which Noah was happy about as it meant they could get back to work in his factory and he wouldn't need to fork out on extortionate hotel costs, not to mention meals and drinks. He'd told his engineers they could put everything on the company account, and he knew they'd take full advantage. Who wouldn't! His plans were going in the right direction as far as the factory was concerned. What his engineers did not know, however, was that when they returned to the factory, Noah had gone to Portugal to lie low for a few weeks until the trial and sentencing of George and Degsy was complete. Bram, Lydia and Brenda were the only ones who knew where he was, and were sworn to secrecy, instructed to tell anyone who asked that he was still in Japan sorting out arrangements and all the finer details.

Unfortunately, after the engineers returned to the UK factory, the final contract had to be signed off by him and that would mean him having to return to the UK to face the possibility of being arrested. But he couldn't go back yet, not until after George and Degsy's trials were over.

To Noah's surprise, however, Brenda volunteered to bring the contracts out to him to sign in a local notary as neither Bram nor Lydia could do it. Grateful to her, he booked her a room for three nights in the hotel where he was staying.

Brenda was a plain type of woman, always had her dark-brown hair tied back, and always wore business suits. On the morning she was due to arrive, Noah waited in the hotel reception to greet her, expecting her to turn up in one of the suits with her usual hairstyle, probably carrying an official-looking briefcase and wearing no makeup.

But the Brenda who walked through the entrance surprised him somewhat, as she approached him wearing denim jeans and a cream-coloured blouse and ankle boots with a small heel. She was even wearing a bit of makeup and had her hair down, subtle waves gently resting against her shoulders. She looked so much younger than he'd ever seen her at work, younger even, than her thirty-five years.

When he walked towards her and offered to take her suitcase, she leant towards him and brushed his cheek, feeling relaxed and flattered at the way he'd looked her up and down when he first saw her. She'd remembered him looking at Gabriel that way, and she smiled to herself. The first part of her plan was working.

The second part was when she told Noah she was in no rush to go home as she had told her husband she would be away for a week or more.

"I'm due some holiday," she said, as they went to the reception desk so she could check in. "Plus, I haven't had any proper time to myself in ten years and I intend to chill out for a bit while I'm here."

Noah took no time realising that Brenda was on a mission and the mission was him. At first, he was concerned, knowing she was married with two school-aged children, so he decided to just wait and see how it played out. He'd met her husband a few times and had never liked him; a bloke, in Noah's opinion, who thought the world worked around him. Noah was quite sure he wouldn't feel at all guilty about taking Brenda to bed, but he would let her make all the moves.

Once checked in, Brenda went up to her room and unpacked, grabbing herself a miniature bottle of wine from the minibar and gulping it down before she went back to join Noah in reception. They then made their way to the local notary to get the contracts signed and notarised before getting a courier to take them to the Nissan factory a few miles away.

"That was easier than I expected," Brenda commented, as they got in a taxi and went back to the hotel. It was mid-afternoon and they headed straight to the bar where Noah ordered them a bottle of white wine before finding a table for two.

The waiter brought the wine over in an ice bucket and Noah poured it into two glasses, then handed one to Brenda and clinked his glass against hers.

"Cheers!" he said. "So, what are you intending to do with your week off?"

Brenda took a sip and smiled. "Well, now that's done, I intend to take the rest of the week to relax. I haven't had a decent holiday in years."

Noah was no fool. She wanted to have a fling and as far as he was concerned, she was a grown woman who knew what she was doing. His love life had been non-existent in the last twelve months, and he knew it wouldn't affect their working relationship. If that was what she wanted he would oblige. But first, a little flirting was in order.

"I didn't recognise you when you arrived at the hotel earlier," Noah said.

"Sometimes I think it's good to dress up. I get bored wearing a suit all the time."

"Sure, but you always look good at work, too."

That made Brenda blush. "I try to look professional," she said, as Noah stared into her eyes. "I think it's important to give the right impression, don't you?"

"I do. I used to think Gabriel always gave the right impression, but I guess I was wrong about her."

"You liked her, didn't you?" Brenda asked, not sure if she wanted to know the answer.

He nodded. "Yeah, I guess I did. I thought we had a future, but I misjudged our relationship. Big time." He took a large swig of the wine and pulled the bottle from the ice bucket, filling up their glasses.

"I used to be jealous at the way you looked at her," Brenda suddenly blurted out. The wine was going to her head and making her relax more.

"Jealous? Why would you be jealous? You have a husband and kids at home."

"I know, but I'm still a woman, I have needs, and I know a good man when I see one."

"I don't mean to be personal, but is everything okay at home, with your husband, I mean?"

"It's always a little frosty. The kids are at school, and I have my job, but he doesn't excite me anymore." She then put her glass on the table and touched Noah's hand. "You do, though."

Noah watched as she circled his hand with her finger. "What do you mean?"

"I'm on holiday, I want to enjoy myself. If something were to happen here, between us, it wouldn't need to go any further, no one would need to know. And I can assure you it wouldn't affect our working relationship in any way whatsoever."

Noah moved his hand and grabbed the glass in front of him. "I'm flattered, Brenda, truly I am. But let's take it easy and see how it goes. You're here for a week. Maybe we can get to know each other better, outside the workplace."

She smiled; happy he hadn't knocked her back as such. She had thought that tonight she might share his bed, but maybe that was a little premature. There was something about him that excited her. In her eyes, he was a dominant man, however much Gabriel had tried to make a fool of him. She thought he had been naïve back then, weak and an embarrassment. But she now knew she was wrong. He was a winner, the opposite of her husband who she still loved, but the tingle she was feeling just being with Noah right now and sitting so close to him was making her want him.

"Maybe we could explore the area tomorrow," she said. "Unless you have other plans?"

"No, I've no plans tomorrow. We can have lunch somewhere nice, there's a good steak restaurant a few blocks away." He then turned towards the bar and beckoned the waiter to bring them another bottle of wine. "I assume you want a top up?"

Brenda nodded. "I'd love a top up. Though wine goes straight to my head, which is why I just embarrassed myself."

"You didn't embarrass yourself, Brenda. I've never been the type of man who just sleeps with someone as a one-off, and I want you to be sure it's really what you want if anything were to happen between us. I don't want you regretting it when we get home and you're lying in bed with your husband thinking about me."

Not only was he a good man, but he also cared about her feelings, and that made Brenda want him even more. "Thank you," she said, as the waiter returned with a fresh bottle of wine, pouring what was left from the first bottle into their glasses and putting the new bottle in the ice bucket.

They spent another two hours in the bar and got through a third bottle of expensive white wine, and eventually, Noah stood up and held out his hand.

"Come on," he said. "Let me walk you back to your room. I've got a table booked for dinner tonight at eight, and it's already six now."

Brenda stood up, unsteadily, and pointed to her jeans. "I need a shower first," she said. "I need to change out of these clothes and put something more suitable on..." She let that statement hang in the air and thoughts raced around Noah's head.

Dinner was a pleasant occasion, and Noah had ordered a bottle of champagne to their table when they sat down, much to Brenda's satisfaction. She did indeed look stunning in a navy-blue tightly fitted dress that clung to her curves and showed off the cleavage that Noah hadn't noticed before. He struggled to take his eyes off her all through the meal, as did many of the other men in the restaurant, and when they'd finished, he led her back to his room where he offered to pour her a nightcap and finish the evening off in private.

They'd both had a lot to drink, and it was inevitable that Brenda wouldn't need to wait much longer for Noah to make a pass at her, as he passed her a glass of Courvoisier brandy and they sat at the small table on the balcony overlooking the golden sands and beautiful turquoise ocean, waves gently lapping on the shoreline. When he stood up and held out his hand towards Brenda, she looked at it and took it in hers. Then she stood up, placing the glass on the table, and allowed him to take her in his arms, softly and gently, slowly caressing the back of her neck with his other hand, running his fingers through her hair.

He then led her back inside the bedroom and began to undress her, peeling down the zip at the back of her dress before it shimmered to the floor, landing in a heap as she now stood in her lacey underwear and high-heeled shoes. She was beautiful, everything Noah wanted in a woman. Curves in all the right places and a black bra giving her breasts an even shape. Her long legs were slim and tanned and he was taken away by the way she now stood before him, pushing herself into his erection as he began kissing her with a passion she hadn't experienced for a long time.

They made love into the early hours, and the following morning Noah led Brenda into the shower where they washed one another and made love beneath the water as it cascaded over their aroused, naked bodies. All thoughts of this being a one-night stand went out of Brenda's head. She was having the experience of a lifetime, one she never thought could ever happen to her. She couldn't think about her husband right now, couldn't envisage being back at home and sharing a bed with him. She wanted to continue sharing a bed with Noah, and she wanted this fling to become something more permanent.

That afternoon as they were walking into a local bar, she got a feeling like she'd never had before. She was getting looked at, admired, noticed. People thought they were a couple, and it felt incredible.

Brenda stayed at the hotel with Noah for nearly two weeks. She rang her husband after a few days and told him she was needed there as things weren't going quite to plan. He wasn't bothered, he was enjoying having some time to himself also, and he'd been asking his parents to look after the kids so that he could spend plenty time at the golf course and then in the pub with his friends, something he rarely did. Brenda was having mind-blowing sex with the man of her dreams, but she knew it had to come to an end at some point.

The time came when she had to leave, and a taxi waited outside the hotel to take her to the airport. Noah carried her suitcase and placed it in the boot, then kissed her softly on her cheek.

"Thank you for an amazing time," he said.

"You have no idea how amazing," she replied.

"Will you be okay?"

"I'd rather not have to leave now, and I wish you were coming with me, but yes, I'll be okay." She got into the back of the car and Noah closed the door gently, before she wound the window down. "When will you be back?"

"I don't know. Soon. I'll keep in touch while I'm here," he said, as the cab began to pull away.

CHAPTER EIGHTEEN

George and Degsy both pleaded guilty and both received a six-year jail sentence. It was a lot less than any of the others had received, of course, except Archie, and that only meant one thing: they'd dobbed Noah in. Chief Inspector Alan Conboy was now more confident than ever that he had the main man in his sights, and it was only a matter of time before he also had him in handcuffs.

But what Conboy wasn't yet aware of was that war had broken out in Merseyside between the main drug dealers who were all trying to take the place of Archie, George and Degsy. One dealer, Warren Curtis, had taking things into his own hands by choosing to bypass all the middlemen and going to the main cartel in Columbia to do a deal with them directly. Warren's plan was to have any dealers that didn't want to join him be removed from the scene, and that was when the gangland war started.

Hardly a week went by without shootings taking place and the government gave the incidents top priority to ensure a clamping down on the drug cartels in Liverpool, which were now supplying all of Europe.

Noah phoned Karen to ask if it was safe to come home yet as the police hadn't raided his home or his factory. But when she told him the chances were it could happen within days of him returning if they didn't collar him at the airport, it made Noah wonder if it would be safer to fly to Dublin and go over the border to Belfast, where there were no passport checks, and then get the overnight ferry to Liverpool.

One thing that was making things harder for him was the fact he'd had no contact with the cartel since Franco and Shelley had moved on and he had handed the reigns over to Archie. He didn't know there was a battle going on in the city as he was now completely off the scene.

He made up his mind and called Wendy to see how she was bearing up since George had been jailed.

"I'm so sorry, Noah," she said. "He's put you in the frame in exchange for a shorter sentence."

Noah sighed. "I know," he said. "I had a feeling it would happen. But I understand why he did it, Wendy. He has you to think about. He's been through enough with his disability. Perhaps he'll be treated leniently in there and be out well before his sentence is up. How are things with you, money-wise?"

"I'm okay. George left his mother a substantial amount that she told me about after the trial. It's enough to keep us going for at least three years."

"And are you able to stay in the house?"

"Yes. The police say we don't have to move out, so we're staying put."

"I have a different number for you to contact me on," Noah said, reeling it off to her. It was a test more than anything, to work out if Wendy really was remorseful and on his side. If someone else rang him on that number, he would know she'd given it away as no one else had it, and then he would have to destroy the phone and cut all ties with her and George.

He couldn't have been happier when Wendy called him a week later and told him that George and Degsy had planned to go to court to testify against him, but in reality, they would be testifying *for* him in a back-door way. He didn't quite understand why, but it made him feel better as it would give him a better chance at not getting convicted.

Noah got a flight to France and spent a few days there before getting a flight to Dublin, where he also stayed for a few nights, before taking the train to Belfast. His next journey was the midnight ferry to Liverpool, but instead of staying in his home, he stayed in a city centre hotel where he met up with his brother and a day later, Karen Veitch.

"Seems we have a snake in the grass," Karen said when she met up with Noah in the hotel bar. "A couple called Samuel and Laura Mills. I defended them and they got a suspended sentence on a plea bargain. They were told they'd need to testify against the top dog in the Liverpool drugs scene if they didn't want to go to prison, to which they agreed."

"I remember you mentioning them. And who's the top dog, then?" Noah asked with a smirk.

"You are! And I remember you saying you didn't know the Mills couple. Have you met them since?"

"Nope, like I said, I don't know them." Noah replied, which made Karen realise her suspicions about Chief Inspector Conboy were correct. He was corrupt, trying anything and using anyone he could to nail Noah and have him sent to prison.

"They didn't mention your name at first, but then they must have realised that to keep on Conboy's good side, they'd need to grass you up as well. When I spoke to them, they were quite convincing, even I wondered whether to believe them. I even asked about which car you used to meet them and where that took place, and they told me a car park just outside the city and that you always turned up in a blue jag."

"Bastards," Noah spat.

"According to them, you've been supplying them for the past four years."

"They're lying. I never met any drug dealers whatsoever. We had three or four layers of staff who handled the distribution. The last time I even laid my eyes on cocaine was seven years ago when we emptied George's garage out where he'd been storing it. At that time, we didn't have any idea what we were dealing with."

"So, you never came in contact with any dealers yourself?"

"No, I only had one that picked up the product and passed it on to four or five dealers that only she knew. I didn't know them, and they didn't know me."

"She?" Karen said. "A woman was the main distributor?" He nodded. "Are you still in contact with her?"

"No, she got out of the business about the same time as me."

This tied in with what Karen already knew, that Noah had pulled out of the business just about the same time as her friend got out of the industry.

"I think we can keep on top of this," she said. "Keep a low profile, as you have been doing, and maybe buy a different car. Your blue jag has been mentioned a couple of times now, so it looks like someone's desperate to stitch you up." Karen felt confident now that if Noah was arrested, she would be able to get him acquitted.

After Karen left, he made his way to his factory to meet his staff and catch up on everything that had been happening during his absence. On entering his office, he saw that Lydia was in a meeting with Brenda and Brian. They all looked up when he walked by, seeming happy and surprised to see him. He hadn't forewarned them he was coming back, though of course Lydia knew because Bram had told her. The one thing that caught Noah's attention was Brenda's appearance. She looked like a totally different person.

Gone was the drab hairstyle, replaced by a short blonde bob, which knocked years off her. Also gone was the tired-looking trouser suit she wore all the time, replaced by a smart pin-striped suit, and she was also wearing makeup, albeit not much.

The other reason they were all so happy was it had just been confirmed that Nissan would be supplying all the new machinery in the factory extension at no cost to the company. It didn't go unnoticed by Lydia the exchange of looks between Brenda and Noah, not to mention his demeanour towards her. He normally acted as though he didn't want to be around her and was glad to get away from her, but now he was expressing how good it was to see her, looking at the others as though extending that sentiment to them all. But Lydia wasn't stupid, she'd noticed the change in Brenda too, especially since she came back from her extended so called 'business' trip to Portugal.

Noah sat himself down in his office and tried to get hold of the contact he'd introduced to Archie when he moved on, but the phone number was unobtainable. That afternoon, a woman called the office asking to speak to him, and Lydia answered, taking a message as Noah was on another call.

He dialled the number as soon as he'd finished, noticing that Lydia had written *Urgent* across the top of the piece of paper that also contained the phone number, and was pleasantly surprised to hear Shelley's voice on the other end.

"Is that you, Noah?" she asked.

"Yes. Shelley, God, it's good to hear your voice," he said with a sigh of relief.

"Noah, this isn't a social call. You're in trouble. We need to meet today."

"Okaay," Noah said, stringing the word out. "I'm staying at the Adelphi for a few nights. What time do you want to meet?"

"I'll be there at three. Meet me in the hotel bar," she replied, then abruptly hung up.

Judging by the expression on Shelley's face when Noah saw her waiting for him near the bar an hour later, he was quite sure she was angry about something.

"Do you want a drink?" he asked.

She shook her head. "No, but you might need one. There's a table over there, I'll grab it while you get yourself something."

He bought himself a pint of Guinness then hurried to the corner table in an alcove where Shelley sat, still looking annoyed. "What the fuck's happened?" he asked.

"You tell me," she said, making him feel like he was being scolded for being naughty. "What's been going on with Archie? I hear he got caught at the airport, that he had over the limit of cash to take out of the country, and then he ends up with a two-year suspended sentence."

Noah wasn't sure what to say, so he decided to just sup his pint and say nothing.

"How the fuck did you let things get into this mess?" she asked.

"I haven't been involved in the business for a while now. Franco knows everything, but yeah, it's all gone tits up recently."

Shelley sat and listened, then said, "We've managed to replace our contact in the Merseyside police force, but they've tightened up the way they do things. The drug squad don't share their information with anyone in the force like they used to. Do you know where Archie is staying? Is he in a police safe house?"

Noah shook his head, wondering if he should disclose any information. Even though Archie had set him up good and proper, he knew he could be contributing to his death sentence if he told Shelley. But, figuring she'd find out eventually from another source, he decided to tell her. "He's living with his in-laws in Shrewsbury."

"Do you have his address? You must know by now that he's turned on you, that he's a police informant?"

He nodded and opened his briefcase, taking out a notebook and pen then wrote the address of Terry's parents' house down. In this industry, it was kill or be killed and as he was happy to have the cartel on his side in the form of Shelley, he tore the piece of paper out of the notebook and pushed it towards her without saying a word.

"Do you have a burner phone number so I can keep in contact with you?" Shelley asked.

Noah gave her the number of one of several phones he had and told her it would only be used between the two of them. She gave him her number in return, then stood up.

"I'll stay in touch, probably contact you in the next couple of days," she said. "Change hotels before we next meet," she added, before strolling off and leaving the hotel.

Noah was once again in two minds, wondering if he should just disappear and set up a new life with a new identity somewhere else like Stuart had, and within half an hour, he checked out of the Adelphi and booked a top-floor suite at the Hilton Hotel instead.

Later that day, he met up with Bram for a pint in the hotel bar, after ringing him and letting his brother know he'd moved to a different location.

"I want to sign ownership of the factory over to you and Lydia," he said, as they sat down with a pint each.

"Why?" Bram asked, surprised at this sudden announcement.

"I just think I'm ready to jump ship, move abroad and start a new life."

"I can understand that bro," Bram replied. "I'll get the papers drawn up in the next day or so, if you're sure?"

Noah nodded. "Shelley's back in Liverpool, we met up this morning, that's why I've moved to a different hotel."

"Aren't you going back home?"

"Not yet. I want to stay away from the house for a bit longer, keep the police away."

"So, what did Shelley want?"

"Mainly to find out what the fuck's going on. She wanted to know Archie's whereabouts."

"Did you tell her?"

"Yeah, I did. He dropped me in the shit when he turned informant. I don't owe him anything anymore." Noah sighed and took a large gulp of his drink, leaning back in his chair and feeling a bit saddened again at the way their team had split up the way it had.

"You know what this means, don't you?"

Noah nodded. "Yeah, I've just signed Archie's death warrant, and Terry's too, if she's with him when they get caught. They leave no witnesses."

Bram knew this bothered his brother; he wasn't a killer, but it was how things worked and he had to accept it.

CHAPTER NINETEEN

Noah was getting a bit concerned. Shelley hadn't been back in contact with him during the last three days and he was beginning to think something had gone wrong. Wondering what she was doing, he decided it was safer to change hotels again; the last thing he wanted was for the police to find him now. He went to the Holiday Inn, not out of choice so much, as it always brought back memories of his first girlfriend, Carol. But because it was cheaper than the others he'd recently stayed at and it most likely wouldn't be a place the not-so-friendly Chief Inspector Conboy would look for him. Bram had offered for him to stay at his place, but he chose not to. He had no intention of dragging Bram and his family into this. Trouble could be just around the corner, and it would mean Lydia and the kids would go the same way as he and Bram would.

Instead of wearing his usual business attire of smart suit and tie, he started wearing denim jeans and casual shirts, with baseball caps and trainers. It had the desired effect as he looked totally different to the suited and booted businessman seen all over the city. Noah was trying to make up his mind about moving back home as it had been two months now and so far, no police had been to his house. But one thing he knew was that it would only be a matter of time before he got a visit from the police in connection with his past dealings in the drugs industry.

He phoned Karen for advice, and she told him Chief Inspector Alan Conboy was on a mission to dig up as much information as he could, and that he had been joined by other senior officers who seemed hell bent on nailing Noah.

"Do you have anyone that could be keeping him informed of your whereabouts?" she asked.

"No, the only ones who know I'm not living at home are Bram and Lydia."

"What about your house sitter? You told me you had someone looking after your house?"

"They still think I'm working away."

"Hmm," Karen said, "maybe that's the reason they haven't called at your home."

Noah was quite sure it was the reason they hadn't been there, but Shelley seemed to be insinuating someone did know where he was and was keeping tabs on him. He had to get away, just for a short while to clear his head, and so he decided to pop to a pub he hadn't been to for a while, the Old Rope.

He had just finished his pint and was about to order another when a female voice from behind him said, "Buy a girl a drink." He turned to look at the woman whom he assumed was chatting him up and was surprised to see it was Shelley.

How had she found him in an old part of town in an out-of-the-way bar like the Old Rope?

"How did you know I would be here?" he asked.

"I was going past in a taxi, and I saw you coming in."

Noah didn't believe her, but he ordered a gin and tonic and they found a table.

"So, what's happening?" he asked.

"Franco has been encouraged to come out of retirement. He'll be in England in the next seven days."

Noah didn't like the sound of this. Franco was a hitman, so he asked, "What's he coming over here for?"

Shelley saw the fear in Noah's eyes. "Don't worry, it's not for you," she reassured him. "But I think your friend should be worried. We've confirmed where he's living, and yes, he has done a deal with the filth. He's willing to testify against you when you get arrested."

There was a silence for quite a while before Shelley got up and made her way to the bar for another round of drinks.

"Penny for them?" she asked when she returned.

"Do I have to worry that Franco is coming back?"

She smiled before saying, "Do you think I would be telling you if you were on the list of things to be done? No, he's here for one reason: Archie. He's told them everything and he's mentioned me as well as Franco. What Archie doesn't know is that we have a new man in the police force giving us information."

Even though Archie had done the dirty on him, the fact that he was going to be neutralised made Noah feel a bit guilty,

"What hotel are you staying in?" she asked.

"The Holiday Inn."

He was surprised when she leaned into him and whispered in his ear, "Book the executive suite at the Adelphi, and you might just get lucky tonight."

This inevitably caused Noah to develop the biggest erection he'd had in a long time. He could never forget the times he'd spent with her and how much she turned him on. She was a woman who knew what she wanted and enjoyed every moment to the full. Noah started to relax. If the cartel were going to have him killed, it would surely have happened by now.

"Call me when you've booked in," Shelley told him, swigging the rest of her drink. Then she stood up and walked out of the pub.

He made his way back to the Holiday Inn and packed his bag, which hadn't even been fully unpacked, as he knew he wouldn't be staying long. Before leaving his room, he made a call first to the factory to get an update on everything that was happening, of which Lydia told him there was no need to worry as everything was in place for the opening of the new extension to the factory on time, and they should be starting production in the next two months. And the next call was to Emma, his cleaner and house sitter, and he wasn't too surprised when she told him that two police detectives had called to the house and said they wanted to talk with him.

"They wouldn't tell me what it was about; they said it was personal."

"When was that?" Noah asked.

"Two weeks ago," was her reply. Noah thanked her before telling her he didn't have a date when he would be back as he was still tied up with business abroad.

He then called Karen Veitch to inform her about the police visit and she asked him when he was thinking of moving back.

"I'm in no hurry," he said, looking forward to a few nights in an executive suite at the Adelphi, hopefully with Shelley.

"Okay. You're doing well under the circumstances," she said, hanging up and hoping she could keep it that way.

As he was leaving the Hilton Hotel, it hit him again how Shelley had come into the pub when she did, knowing it was a place off the beaten track. The phone she'd given him probably had a tracker fitted to it, though he didn't know for certain. He also didn't know if it was a good or a bad thing, but he'd have to give it some thought before he just vanished.

Noah called Shelley when he got to his suite at the Adelphi, telling her he'd booked in and was waiting for her if she wanted to join him. She turned up within the hour, carrying a small holdall and looking stunning. In fact, she spent the next three days and nights with him in that suite, where they made love at every opportunity, had room service each night, and drank the mini-bar dry, having to order replenishments several times. For the first time since he'd been with Gabriel, he felt he was getting close to someone again and on their third night together, whilst they lay on the sofa together listening to music, he asked her about her personal life.

"Don't you have someone special in your life?"

Shelley sat up, causing Noah to readjust himself as she turned to face him. "There is someone, yes," she said, much to his dismay. "He has no idea what type of work I used to do, and right now he thinks I'm back in Liverpool on holiday with my mother and sister. I thought I'd left all this behind when I moved in with him three years ago, but it's almost impossible to cut all your ties with the cartel." Noah understood that perfectly and put his hand on hers. "What about you," she asked, "anyone special in your life?"

"There was," he replied, "and I was going to ask her to marry me, bought the ring and everything. I was going to surprise her and propose to her in Spain on her birthday, but she had a bigger surprise for me."

"Oh?"

"She'd told me she was divorced but she'd lied. Her husband had been inside for drug dealing, and they were still very much together. He lived in Spain near her parents."

"Sounds to me like you had a lucky break."

"Yeah, well, I guess I'm a shit judge of character when it comes to women. I believe them no matter what line they shoot me."

The truth being ever since he had a lucky escape in his teens, he had always kept clear of getting into a proper relationship and the one time he *had* let his guard down, he'd been played yet again.

That third night was special to Noah as they went to bed and fell asleep in each other's arms. But when she packed her case the following morning and announced she would be leaving to go back to New York in a few days' time, after spending some time with her mother, disappointment overwhelmed him, and it took all his strength to walk her down to the waiting taxi at the hotel entrance.

What she hadn't told Noah before she left, however, was that she'd spoken to Franco the previous day and he'd informed her that Archie had been taken care of. It had been her mission to make sure he was removed and therefore could no longer testify.

She'd grown fond of Noah and if she hadn't got a man in America, she'd have been tempted to take him back with her, offer him a new life. He ticked every box.

After discussing with Karen about the fact the police had been round to his address, she advised him to move back in the following Monday. It was time to let things take the path they were going to and handle it as it happened. Noah hated the feeling he had, waiting for a possible arrest, maybe even a bullet, and he made his mind up that one way or another he wanted it finished and over with.

What Emma didn't know was that Noah had secret cameras installed all over his property, so no matter where he was in the world, he knew that nobody, but she and her husband had lived in his house all the time he was away. He went through hours of tape recordings, checking out that nothing had been planted in his absence. Shelley had warned him that Chief Inspector Conboy was known not to hesitate when it came to carrying out underhanded moves to get a conviction. But he was happy finding that nothing was out of order.

He moved back home the following Monday on Karen's advice. Unfortunately, first thing Tuesday his home was raided, and he was arrested on suspicion of supplying illegal drugs. The one phone call he was allowed to make was to Karen to tell her of his arrest, and she told him to say nothing until she got to the police station.

The information that she was given by the desk sergeant was that the police had searched his house after obtaining a search warrant and he would be held in police custody while they undertook their investigations. It was a week before she was able to get his case before a magistrate and get him out on bail, and he was subsequently charged with supplying illegal drugs worth over five million pounds.

Noah was now convinced he should have just moved to another country like Stuart and Shelley had done. They seemed to be living the life, and apart from Bram and Lydia, he never really had any ties to keep him in the UK. Now he'd been charged, and his passport confiscated, it obviously made it harder for him to get away.

CHAPTER TWENTY

Although Noah had only spent a week in custody, it was something he did not want to do again and even though Karen had told the magistrate that the prosecution had no evidence against her client but only the word of three convicted drug dealers, finding a bin bag buried in his garden containing a huge amount of cash was, of course, incriminating evidence that would swing things in the prosecution's favour.

No matter how much Karen told Noah that he would not be convicted on the evidence that the prosecution had, and if he had nothing hidden away that might come back to cause new problems, Noah was now wishing more and more he'd just done one and started a new life abroad. Besides having the factory and the flats, he had several million pounds in various banks all around the world, and he also had several contacts who could get him a fake passport and identification, which he had already been looking into.

Noah had forgotten about the mobile phone Shelley had given to him and hadn't realised the importance until she told him it was Archie's connection to the police. She told him to keep it in a safe place, not his home and not the factory. He'd left it in his brother's house for safe keeping away from the police, so was surprised when Bram called him and told him there was a message on it from someone telling him Noah had been arrested and he should make himself ready to testify in a month's time.

Not wanting to scare his brother more than he already was, Noah told Bram that Archie had done a runner and was living in Australia, unable to voice his true concerns that it was more probable he'd been killed.

He then got in contact with Wendy, George's wife, and asked her to meet him at his factory the following day.

"Get the bus," he said. "Don't use your car in case you're followed."

She agreed, even though she felt he was being somewhat paranoid.

She looked so much more relaxed when she arrived at his office, and he asked how she was getting on.

"They've transferred George to HMP Kirkham, it's an open prison. I can visit him every weekend and take him out between nine and five. I've been travelling there for the past four weeks since he was moved."

"That's great news," Noah said. "He'll be a lot more relaxed there. Are they looking after him well?"

"Yeah, most of the prison is on one level, so it's much easier for him to get around. Obviously, it's not ideal him being away, but we're getting through as best we can. Most of the inmates have jobs and are allowed to buy their own food in the canteen. They have a large building where they gather as well, and they take it in turns to cook meals for everyone."

"I didn't want to ask over the phone in case the police are listening in, but firstly, are you okay for money?"

She nodded. "I'm all right. As I told you George put a lot of cash into his mother's care but she's in no rush to part with it. She told me she was holding it for when he gets out of prison, but I have enough to get by on for now."

Reaching into his draw, Noah took out an envelope and pushed it over to her.

"What's this?" she asked.

"Ten grand. Don't let anybody know you've got it or where you got it from. There's more where that came from, so you won't go short, okay?"

She stood up and threw her arms around him. "Noah, you're a good man, thank you so much."

What Wendy didn't know was that Noah had heard it through the grapevine that Wendy was now living on welfare as George had hidden his cash in banks only. He had wrongly thought that the money he'd left with his mother would be handed over to Wendy when he was serving his sentence.

Noah was thinking that maybe he could catch up with George on one of his Saturdays out of the prison, so he did his homework and found out the only thing the prison officers were interested in when checking everyone back inside was the head count. So long as that tallied up, anyone could have stayed inside that prison.

And so, two weeks' later, on a Saturday, Noah arranged for George's brother, who looked very much like him, to hire a wheelchair and take his place for a week while he got George, Wendy and their kids to Butlins for a much needed break away. Andrew was happy to go along with it, especially as Noah offered him ten thousand pounds in cash to do it, though he wasn't too happy about being locked up for a week, but it went quickly and before he knew it, George swapped places again in the local pub and with Wendy in tow he was taken back to the open prison. The ploy had worked a treat, a ploy that would be repeated a few times during the prison sentence George was serving.

Looking at the pure love that surrounded George and his family made Noah understand that something was missing in his life, something that would make him much richer than having all the millions in the bank and the valuable assets he owned. He wanted that love, to share what George and Wendy had, and it made him realise that his life could have travelled along a much different pathway had he just found the right woman to be with. It made him resent Carol and then Gabriel even more, as he sat in his lounge after dropping Wendy back at home and then taking Andrew back to his flat, poring over his thoughts in great detail.

A date for his trial had been set and the following Monday morning he was sat in Karen's office, going over every aspect of what was going to happen. It made him feel a lot better when Karen told him that on the lack of evidence the prosecution had, she was positive of an acquittal.

"As long as there are not going to be any last-minute surprises or something you haven't told me about?" she said.

"I've told you everything," Noah replied. "If there are any surprises, it'll be something I'm not aware of."

Karen continued. "I have it on good authority that Archie has left the country on forged documents and won't turn up for the trial, and Degsy has let it be known that he's not going to give evidence the way the prosecution is expecting him to. You haven't been in contact with him, have you?" Karen had concern in her voice and Noah just shook his head.

"No. Elaine, Degsy's wife, still goes out with Wendy, George's wife. But they've both been told by their husbands that the police have been trying to get them to say I was more involved right up to when they arrested me. They said they'd just tell the truth with a bit of embellishment."

"Don't take that for gospel," Karen warned him. "We deal with facts. The police are not doing that with regards to Mr and Mrs Mills, who are prepared to purge themselves, which is a criminal offence."

"Meaning?" Noah said.

"We need to keep things simple, not complicate it with falsehoods. I've got proof that the evidence the Mills are going to divulge is false and I've given my information to the barrister. It'll be revealed at the trial along with the recording of Archie burying that bin bag in your garden if necessary."

Fortunately for Noah, what the police were counting on was the fact Archie would be in court to testify to the fact that Noah was top dog for the north-west of England.

There was a couple of weeks to go, and Noah was still in two minds as to what to do. He had many contacts in the city and now had two passports and two drivers' licences, one in his own name and one under a false name just in case he decided to do a runner. The thought of spending ten to twenty years behind bars terrified him to no end.

The week before the trial, Karen had arranged for Noah to meet the barrister who would be representing him, and he was introduced to a rather attractive and smartly dressed woman who seemed like she spent her whole life at work.

"I am Esther Epstein," she said, as she shook his hand and tried to put him at ease. As she was used to now, she noticed a look of disappointment cloud her client's expression as he'd obviously assumed his barrister would be an older man with years of experience defending high-end criminals.

"Don't look so worried, I've been defending criminal cases for thirty-five years and I win a lot more than I lose."

Noah was not so convinced until just about an hour later when the meeting was over. It was obvious to him that she knew her way around the legal system and almost promised him that he would walk away having been found not guilty. This barrister had a personal score to settle with Chief Inspector Alan Conboy as, in her opinion, he'd fitted up a lot of known criminals for crimes they had not committed.

"So, how do you know the main witness who's going to be testifying against you might not turn up," she asked, meaning Archie.

"His wife came back to Liverpool to renew her passport so she could join him in Benidorm, but I imagine he'll be nowhere near Benidorm now. I think it'll be a long time till they come back." Noah was lying, of course, knowing that Terry had indeed been seen near the passport office, but that Archie had disappeared off the face of the earth and most likely wasn't sunning himself in Spain.

"That doesn't mean he will not come back by any means," Esther pointed out. "Unless there's something you know that I don't?" She glared at Noah, giving him a stern look to make sure he knew she meant business. "Well, is there?" She knew there was something he wasn't telling her. At this stage, she didn't really want to know, having a fair idea Archie had been paid off to relocate and do a disappearing act. But Noah was now convinced the disappearing act everyone thought he'd made was to a shallow grave rather than Benidorm!

Esther took a liking to Noah. He didn't seem like a lot of the types she defended, but her biggest pet hate was bent coppers and Alan Conboy fitted into that category to the hilt.

Over the years, she had come across more than a few convictions to which Conboy was involved and for a reason, she knew in her heart that Archie Carmichael was not going to turn up for the trial, which indicated to her that there was more to Noah Burgess than met the eye.

Noah spent more time in the factory in the weeks leading up to the trial, happy that the Nissan contract was starting to work as they continued making bearings for the factory in Sunderland. Bram had managed to get huge government grants towards the recruitment and training for over one hundred engineers, including labourers and apprentices.

Noah had also continued to notice that Brenda was dressing a lot sharper than she had before their fling in Portugal and she was starting to appear very attractive and a world away from the woman that once worked at the factory when he took over ownership. Although they had agreed that what had happened between them would stay in Portugal, Noah decided it best not to go there again, unless he was asked.

Lydia couldn't help but see the looks Noah and Brenda gave one another and she was now quite sure something had gone on between them when they'd been away.

Brenda had been down in the dumps when Noah was away in police custody, and when he returned, she developed a sudden spring in her step. Lydia couldn't hold back any longer and made two coffees that she took into Noah's office, placing them on the desk and plonking herself down in the chair opposite him.

"I don't know what happened to Brenda when she met you in Portugal, but she came back a changed woman," she said.

As soon as she looked at Noah, she realised she'd hit the nail on the head. He smiled and shook his head, unable to speak, and it put a huge smile on Lydia's face confirming what she had suspected. It was at that moment that Brenda walked in, and Noah's face turned a crimson red. The silence was deafening and told Brenda that they'd been talking about her.

"What's going on?" she asked.

"Nothing, why?" Lydia replied, trying hard to disguise her grin.

Brenda's eyes knitted together. "What's he been saying?"

"He never said a word," Lydia said.

"Hmm, are you sure?" asked Brenda.

"Okay," Lydia confessed. "So, I kind of suspected something had happened between you two in Portugal, and he certainly wasn't going to deny it."

Now it was Brenda's turn to blush. She didn't know what to say and just shook her head before leaving the office. And Lydia knew she'd been right all along!

It had been part of the plan to tell everybody that Noah had been in Japan when in fact he had been in Portugal. If there was anyone close who was giving the police information, it would be false. The only ones that knew different were Bram, Lydia and Brenda.

CHAPTER TWENTY-ONE

Noah gave Shelley a call to let her know the date of his trial, telling her he was in two minds whether it would be best to just do a runner. But Shelley put a stop to that straight away, telling him to put such thoughts out of his head.

"You do that, and you'll be on the run for the rest of your life, and when they do catch up with you, it'll be a much longer sentence than any drug dealer has ever been handed out."

"Yeah, I know you're right," he said. "But I should have got away long ago. I shouldn't have let this happen. What a fucking mess."

"Look, just promise me you're going to turn up in court. Promise me, yeah?"

Noah sighed. "I promise," was all he said before hanging up, wishing he had the confidence that everyone around him had, assuming he would be acquitted.

The court date was almost upon him – 1st of May – and by now he just wanted to get it over with. He was making less visits to the factory and was, in fact, avoiding Brenda after Lydia had spoken to him again, but this time in a more serious tone, making him feel guilty about the fact Brenda was married with kids. But the truth was that if she offered herself to him again, he wasn't too sure he could turn her down.

Bram invited Noah to join him in the pub that Friday after work and they were just starting on their first pint when in walked Lydia, followed closely by Brenda. Noah had a feeling he'd been set up but wasn't sure as Lydia seemed to have been warning him off, so perhaps it was just an innocent and friendly drink, letting their hair down after work, so to speak.

"That's good timing, girls," Bram said, standing up and giving his wife a peck on her cheek. "What are you drinking?"

If it wasn't for the fact Noah had a full pint in front of him, he would have made his excuses and left, but he was trapped. He didn't understand why he felt this way, and he knew that if Lydia knew about him sleeping with Brenda, then Bram would have found out from her.

At first, it was small talk, a conversation about the progress the factory had made since Noah had taken over, and then they started talking about some of the new engineers who'd recently joined the team, good workers who put the hours in and were an asset to the company. When they were coming to the end of their drinks, Noah got up to go to the bar, asking if everyone wanted the same again.

"I'll give you a hand," Brenda said, getting up too, and following him.

Standing at the bar waiting for service, she punched him in a playful manor on his arm and said, "What's the matter with you? You haven't spoken a word to me since I came in. Is it because of what happened when we were away, and the fact they know?"

He stayed quiet and just shook his head.

"Then what is it?"

He let the question hang in the air for a few moments as their drinks were prepared, then said, "I don't like people knowing my personal business. Did you tell Lydia we slept together?"

The barman placed four drinks in front of them and Noah gave him a twenty-pound note, telling him to keep the change. "No, I didn't, but I think she must have guessed by the colour you turned when she insinuated it."

Bram and Lydia were watching the pair talking, both having an idea what the conversation would be about, and when they returned with the drinks, the atmosphere was a lot lighter. It was plain to see that the couple had cleared their differences.

It was when they'd finished their second round that Bram stood up and offered to buy them all another, and Lydia went off to the ladies. Brenda turned to Noah and asked if he'd mind if she attended his trial, and although he would have preferred her not to as he didn't want the trial to become a huge spectacle, he reluctantly agreed. He'd already arranged to stay in the Hilton Hotel for the duration of it, which was the closest hotel to the court, and as it was expected to last around seven or eight days, it gave Brenda an idea. She could tell her husband she had to go away again and stay with Noah, keep him company and share his bed for a week.

"So, what do you think?" she said, after she'd told him her plan.

"Okay. But be discreet. I don't want any comeback with your husband. I could be in enough trouble as it is."

Noah booked into his top-floor suite at the Hilton and met up with Esther shortly after, who informed him she would convince the judge that he had no criminal convictions, had surrendered his passport, and the case against him was a circumstantial one based on no hard evidence.

Brenda told Lydia that she was taking the week off so she could attend Noah's trial but asked her to keep it to herself as she'd told her husband she was away on business again. Lydia didn't want to have to lie, but chances were he wouldn't ring her anyway.

She had an idea what was going on but decided not to say anything. It was going to be a difficult enough week for Noah as it was without her trying to stop him having at least a bit of fun, and company, of course, when he got back from court each day.

Brenda checked in that evening and met Noah in the bar, where they shared a bottle of wine before going up to the suite and spending the night together. It was like old times. Noah had thought it might not happen again, but as he rolled off her after passionately making love to her, and panted by her side, he was glad of the distraction of having her there. It would make the trial more bearable, at least.

The following day, the first day of the trial, Noah had to attend the court an hour before the proceedings were due to begin. On arrival he was led to a private waiting room where he once again wished he'd done a runner instead of having to sit in this small depressing space with a desk and a chair and a window too high up that he couldn't see through. The forty-five minutes they made him wait there felt like the longest of his life, and he made his mind up that for the rest of the days he would have to attend court for this godforsaken trial, he would turn up at best a half-hour before and not the hour they'd instructed him to. He never wanted to be in this situation again. It was soul-destroying, and he suddenly felt very sorry for George and Degsy, who had already been here before him.

It was a relief when an officer opened the door and told him to follow on, leading him along a dreary corridor and towards the courtroom, which led him into the dock where he was then instructed to sit. The thing that hit him the most was the closeness of everybody as he looked around at the people who obviously had a morbid fascination at seeing someone go through a trial, whether they were guilty or innocent. He suspected some of the faces here were just nosey bastards, come for a look at the man who was dubbed as Liverpool's top dog in the drug dealing business. But when he saw Bram and then Brenda, he felt slightly better, and as he continued to look around, he was suddenly approached by Karen.

"Remember what we discussed," she said quietly. "When they ask how you plea, you look straight at the jury and say with determination, 'not guilty'."

Noah nodded and then watched as twelve members of the jury were led to their seats, every one of them looking at him as though he was already guilty, which made him feel uncomfortable.

Things were happening fast now, as the clerk of the court said, "All rise," when the judge entered and took his seat, then the charges were read out.

"Noah Burgess, you have been charged with the importation and distribution of a Class A drug. How do you plea?"

Looking straight at the jury in a raised and determined voice, he said, "Not guilty."

The prosecution barrister, Nigel Harrison, then stood up and approached the jury, glancing at Noah as he seemed to stroll casually towards them.

"Members of the jury," he said, the smug look on his face already beginning to annoy Noah, "we have a strong case that will prove beyond a doubt that the accused, Noah Burgess, is the main importer and distributor of cocaine and cannabis on behalf of the Columbian cartel. The evidence I will present to you will leave you in no doubt of his guilt." He then turned and sat back down, as Esther Epstein stood up and also walked towards where the jury sat.

"Ladies and gentlemen of the jury," she began, "the prosecution say they have a strong case against my client, which is so far from the truth as the truth can be. In my thirty-five years of working for the Crown, I have never come across a single case where nearly every single prosecution witness is a convicted drug dealer. My client has worked from the day he left school, moving on to serve Queen and country for over four years and gaining an award with distinction while on a tour of duty in Cyprus. He has never ever had any problems with the law, not even a parking ticket."

Shaking her head, she returned to her seat next to Karen.

The prosecution then called their first witness, Chief Inspector Alan Conboy, who took to the stand and introduced himself to the court, swearing his oath on the Bible that was given to him by the clerk.

Nigel Harrison looked like he would be better off in the Old Bailey rather than Liverpool Crown Court. His plummy English accent was bound not to go down well with a Liverpool jury as far as Karen and Esther were concerned.

"Chief Inspector Conboy, were you the arresting officer of the accused?"

"Yes," Conboy said with a pronounced nod.

"And what were the circumstances of his arrest, Chief Inspector?"

"After a successful police operation against the top drug dealers in the Merseyside area, we were successful in arresting a lot of the top dealers who were supplying most of Liverpool."

"So, was the defendant arrested at that time?"

"No, sir, it was after the arrests were made that the name of Noah Burgess kept coming up as the main supplier and importer of cocaine and cannabis."

"Did you have him checked out to see if he had a criminal record?"

"Yes, he had no criminal convictions, but that does not necessary mean that he was not involved. As I'm sure you are aware, sir, these cartel mafia types have lots of people to take the fall on behalf of them."

Esther was happy. Conboy was trying to make Noah out to be a big-time gangster, a drugs baron with dangerous connections, and so far, all of what he was saying was complete hearsay. He had nothing to incriminate Noah, and she couldn't wait to rip into what she thought was a shyster blagging his way through life. If he thought he could do this in a court of law, he had another thing coming. Conboy was used to railroading his way through the court system with cases that he knew would put the accused behind bars for a long time.

"Can you tell me, Chief Inspector, what made your mind up to raid Noah Burgess's home?" Nigel Harrison asked.

"Yes," Conboy began. "We had a tip off from a reliable source that Mr Burgess had a substantial amount of drugs money hidden at his home address in Southport."

Esther stood up. "Objection, My Lord, how does the witness know the cash found was so-called drugs money?"

"Objection sustained," the judge said.

Unless he knows more than he is telling the court, Esther thought, as she sat back down.

"So," Harrison continued, changing tack slightly. "When you raided Mr Burgess's home, what did you find?"

"Half a million pounds in used notes," Conboy replied, matter-of-factly.

This brought a gasp from around the court room and influenced the jury, much to the annoyance of Noah. The prosecuting barrister repeated what he had just heard in a very loud voice.

"Half a million pounds in used notes? So, what conclusion did you come up with, Chief Inspector?"

"It was a typical drug suppliers set up," he said. "They have money coming out of their ears, and because of how tight it is now to put money through the banking system, many choose to hide cash in all sorts of places."

Looking around the court, Conboy now had a smug look on his face, as did his lawyer and back-up team. Nigel Harrison then returned to his seat saying, "No further questions for this witness, My Lord."

The judge looked at Esther. "Mrs Epstein, would you like to cross-examine the witness?"

Esther rose to her feet and approached Conboy, shaking her head and looking down at the floor.

"Mr Conboy," she said, deliberately leaving out his official police title, "that's a very interesting statement you have just made. Please would you mind telling the jury exactly what you witnessed that could be incriminating against my client?"

"Sorry, I'm not sure what you mean," was Conboy's answer, rattled at the fact Esther hadn't addressed him formally.

"What are you here for, Mr Conboy, apart from passing on hearsay you have gathered from a gang of low life convicted drug dealers?"

Alan Conboy stood there not knowing how to reply.

"Well?" Esther asked again.

Clearly uncomfortable now, he said, "We found half a million pounds in used money in his house."

Esther sighed. He'd just walked into her trap, and she had the pleasure of making him squirm even more.

"In his house, you say. You found half a million pounds in his house?"

Now fumbling to find the right words, Alan Conboy looked around the court room and rested his eyes on Nigel Harrison, who wasn't even looking up from the paperwork in front of him.

"Well," Conboy began, "not exactly in his house. It was buried in his back garden."

"In his back garden," Esther repeated back to him before glancing at the jury. "How big would you say the rear garden of my client's home is?"

Conboy shrugged. "I don't know," was his reply.

"Well, if you went to my client's home, and perused the area where this money was buried, you must have some idea how big it is." She then looked around and waved her arm about. "Would you say it was as big as this room, twice the size, perhaps, maybe three times as big. Come on, Mr Conboy, you must have some idea?"

"It's Chief Inspector Conboy," he replied gruffly. "I am a chief inspector with the Merseyside police force."

But Esther was having none of it. "In this court, Mr Conboy, you are a witness no matter what you might call yourself and bound by the same rules to tell the truth, nothing more and nothing less. Do you understand?" She then turned to the judge. "My Lord, may I introduce, in evidence, exhibit NB-zero-one, a security video taken at the rear of my client's home some six months after he moved into the property?"

"Objection!" Nigel Harrison stood up in protest.

"On what grounds is your objection based, Mr Harrison?" the judge asked.

"The prosecution has not had time to look at this tape to see what it contains, My Lord."

Turning to Esther, the judge said, "Mrs Epstein?"

"My Lord, the prosecution were given copies of security tapes taken overlooking the rear and front of my client's home. I have here a receipt from the prosecution stating they had received the recordings."

Pulling a receipt out of her files and making a big thing out of trying to read the signature, she added, "As you can see, My Lord, the receipt was signed by Chief Inspector Alan Conboy some four months ago. If he never passed it on to the prosecution it is simply not our problem." Turning towards the jury, she then emphasised, "Had he allowed the prosecution to view this footage, then we might not be here today."

This instinctively had the jury wondering what was on that tape.

"Fair enough," the judge said. "I will need to view this tape during lunch, but I will allow it to be shown to the jury."

Nigel Harrison was furious. He had not been given the tape showing Archie burying the cash in Noah's garden and this didn't look good for his prosecution case at all. The tape not only showed Archie digging the hole in Noah's garden and burying the bin bag, but she'd also added onto it the footage of him arriving a few nights previously to dig up the garden in the first place, believing Noah had left four bin bags there.

Chief Inspector Conboy had only been given the second tape, and the fact he had not given any tapes to the prosecution lawyers meant he couldn't deny that he had been shown the first tape revealing Archie looking the place over, then digging the hole, and the second tape showing him turning up again and planting the money.

An adjournment was announced for an hour's lunchbreak and the judge left the court room as everyone rose from their seats once more.

Noah was taken back to the little depressing room, where he was served with a tuna sandwich, a bag of crisps, and a cup of tea, and Esther and Karen joined him to let him know things were going well.

"Conboy is a fool," Esther said. "I've come across him often and I've known him to plant evidence, too. I won't let him get away with it this time." Suffice to say, Noah managed to enjoy his sandwich before it was announced that the hearing was about to commence as the officer came to fetch him and led him back to the dock.

Everyone took their seats again, including the judge, and then Esther stood up and approached the bench.

"If it pleases you, My Lord, I would like to bring into evidence tapes one and two, showing a convicted drug dealer planting a bag that turned out to be the cash, according to the prosecution."

A TV and VHS player on a stand was then pushed into the courtroom and Esther passed the video to the usher, who inserted it into the VHS player. There was Archie, looking around the garden, holding a torch in one hand and a spade in the other, before he started digging, hoping to find the hidden money. When he didn't find any, he could be seen shaking his head and walking quickly away, back towards the driveway where he disappeared onto the street and out of view. Then the next footage showed him returning with a large bin bag under his arm, once again digging up the lawn, before he placed the bin bag into the hole. The bin bag was bulging.

"Members of the jury," Esther began, "you can plainly see that the person placing the so-called drugs money was a wanted man and a convicted drugs dealer known as Archie Carmichael, whose company, The Lawn Ranger, did all the garden maintenance on the estate where my client lived."

Turning to Conboy, who had returned to the witness box after the hearing had resumed having not been discharged from the witness box, Esther then asked, "Did you check for fingerprints on the plastic bag?"

"No," was his reply.

"No, Mr Conboy? Are you telling this court that you never checked for fingerprints which could prove who was the responsible party in planting the bag of cash in the rear garden of Mr Burgess's property?"

A bemused Chief Inspector Conboy looked embarrassed as he shook his head and repeated, "No."

"So, you have nothing to connect my client to this money hidden on his property to make him look like a dealer?" Conboy shrugged. "Well," Esther shouted, "Let's face it, Mr Conboy, if you had just one fingerprint from my client, you would have been waving it around the court today, isn't that true? I find it hard to believe the police force never looked for fingerprints on the planted money."

Esther, shaking her head, looked around the court and rested her eyes on a few members of the jury. "Of course, you would not have to look for prints if you knew that my client had not been anywhere near the bag, is that not true, Mr Conboy?"

"No," was all he said again.

Esther then pressed play on the remote control again, to show further footage of police officers surrounding the hole and lifting the bag from it.

"Can you tell me why you and the other officers are wearing gloves in the video I have just shown?"

"We were wearing gloves as to not contaminate evidence," he replied.

"Contaminate evidence? Contaminate evidence? What was the point if you did not even check for fingerprints?" Esther turned to the jury again, shaking her head, before saying, "That's if you are to be believed, of course. It is more than possible that the bag you took from the defendant's garden was tested and nothing was found connecting it to the defendant." She then made her way back to her seat where she sat down, still shaking her head. "No further questions for this witness," she said.

"Your next witness, Mr Harrison?" the judge asked as the prosecution barrister stood up.

"I call Mrs Laura Mills," he said.

After the formalities had taken place, Nigel Harrison began. "Mrs Mills, how do you know the defendant?"

Her answer brought a gasp to the courtroom. "He was the one who supplied me and my husband on a regular basis."

"Supplied you with what?" Harrison asked.

"Cocaine and cannabis."

Nigel Harrison looked towards the jury members and then back to Laura Mills. "Can you tell the court how and when this all took place, please?"

"We'd call the contact number we were given; place our order and they would call us back. Then we were given a meeting place to collect what we'd ordered. That's when we would meet up with Noah, er, Mr Burgess," she said, nodding her head in Noah's direction.

"What would happen then?"

"We would give him the cash and he would give us the gear."

"Over what period of time did this take place?"

"It was a long time. Four to five years at least," was her reply.

"Four or five years, Mrs Mills, as long as that? And was the defendant the person that you always delt with?"

"Yes, he would be parked up mostly in different pub car parks all around the city."

"Did you know what type of car the defendant was in at the time?"

"He had a very distinctive blue Jaguar," she said, a little too confidently.

Nigel Harrison turned on his heels and made his way back to his seat. "No more questions for this witness," he said, as he sat down.

Esther stood up then and approached Laura Mills. "A blue Jaguar, Mrs Mills."

It wasn't meant to be a question, but Mills nodded and said *yes*.

"Was that not a bit odd considering you wanted to be as discreet as possible?"

"No, he always wanted to look flash, and the exchange only took seconds to make."

"You keep saying 'we', Mrs Mills. Who was the other part of *we*?"

"My husband."

"Your husband, Mr Samuel Mills, who is currently serving a suspended jail sentence for dealing drugs?"

"Objection," the prosecution barrister shouted out.

"On what grounds?" Esther asked, looking at the judge in hope he would overrule it.

"On the grounds that what Mrs Mills' husband has done has nothing to do with these proceedings here today."

Esther replied in a raised voice, "It has got everything to do with this case, Mr Harrison. Mr and Mrs Mills are two convicted drug dealers."

Esther once again looked towards the jury, making sure they had all understood what they were hearing. Then she looked at the judge who said, "Objection overruled."

"Thank you, My Lord. So, Mrs Mills, you say that you have been dealing with my client for four to five years?"

"Yes," was her reply.

"And he was the one that you dealt with in all that time?"

"Yes."

"In his nice blue Jaguar?"

Laura Mills now looked towards her solicitor, who was sat behind Nigel Harrison. "Yes," she replied.

Turning to the judge, Esther then asked, "My Lord, may I refer to Exhibit NB-zero-five, a document showing that the car my client drives is indeed a blue jaguar, but is, in fact, a company registered vehicle that is less than one year old. Mrs Mills is plainly not telling the truth here. This is the type of car that does indeed stand out and therefore the last type of car any known criminal would wish to be seen in."

After the bill of sale had been taken into evidence showing the jaguar was only twelve months old, Esther then tore into the witness in a raised voice. "Do you know committing perjury is a criminal offence and you could be jailed for lying to the court?"

Trying to cover for being caught out lying she said, "He had another blue jag before that one. You must have paperwork for that, too."

"My Lord, I would like to introduce to the court the logbook of the previous car my client drove in the previous three years. It shows my client's previous car was a brown Rover, not, as Mrs Mills claims, a blue Jaguar. This witness is obviously lying. I have no further questions for this witness, My Lord."

The prosecution then called their next witness, Degsy.

"Could you tell us your real name, please?" Nigel Harrison asked him after he'd sworn to tell the truth whilst his hand rested on the Bible being held by the clerk.

"My name is Derek Owens, but most people called me Degsy," he said.

"Mr Owens, do you know the accused here today?"

"Yes, we went to the same school before working down the mine. Then we joined the army together."

"How long were you in the army?"

"Four years or more," Degsy said.

"And could you tell us where you were stationed, please?"

"Our first tour of duty was to Cyprus, then we were moved to Belize before being discharged."

"And could you also tell us, Mr Owens, when you were stationed in Belize, was this your introduction to the cocaine industry?"

"Yes," he said.

"Was that the first time you used cocaine?"

Degsy was shocked at the question. "I have never ever used cocaine or any other drugs," he said in a voice louder than he intended.

"I shall rephrase that question," Harrison said. "When did you first encounter cocaine?"

"When we were sent into the jungle to destroy cocaine plants on several farms. But it was a publicity stunt, thought up by the British and American governments. We realised after a while it'd take a lifetime and a million men to make any impression."

"So, when did you and your friends start importing drugs into the country?"

"I didn't," Degsy replied, indignantly. "It was the sergeant major in charge. He organised it all. We just provided a place to store the product when it was brought into the country."

"Did the accused get involved with the storing of cocaine when it arrived in Liverpool?"

Degsy glanced towards Noah, who was staring straight at him. "Noah? No, he didn't want to get involved in any way. All he was interested in was destroying the cocaine fields, he never once got involved."

Degsy's answer took Nigel Harrison totally by surprise. He had been told that this witness would implicate Noah as being one of the main men on the importation of the drugs, and the fact that one of their own witnesses had said that Noah was not involved would go right against their case.

Degsy looked to Noah again and curled his lips up slightly. They both knew he'd just given Noah a big chance of an acquittal.

"No further questions for this witness," Harrison said, now confused as he walked briskly back to his seat and started scribbling something on a piece of paper.

Esther approached Degsy now, smiling as she walked towards him standing in the witness box.

"Mr Owens, you said you have been a very close friend of my client for how many years?"

"Since we were at school. At least twenty years."

"Have you recently been jailed for dealing drugs, Mr Owens?"

Degsy nodded and looked at the floor. "Yes, I'm serving a six-year sentence."

"Did Noah Burgess ever deal or get involved in the supply of drugs into this country?"

Shaking his head, Degsy said, "No, it was not his thing. He always said it's not *if* you get caught, it's *when* you get caught. He wasn't interested in it whatsoever."

"So, let me get this right, Noah Burgess never was a drug dealer?"

"No, never," Degsy replied, looking at the jury now. "He had his inheritance and his partnership with his brother in an engineering factory."

The prosecution was furious. This witness was on the side of the defence. Esther then took her seat, confirming she had no further questions.

Nigel Harrison then stood up and asked the judge if he would grant a short recess before calling his next witness, to which the judge agreed. But things only got worse for the prosecution when they found out that their main witness, Archie Carmichael, had still not turned up and now looked like he'd gone missing, probably even fled the country.

That left two witnesses, Samuel Mills and George Collins. The lawyers were at a loss for what to do. Should they put Samuel Mills into the witness box knowing that his wife had shown to be lying when she was giving evidence, or bring George in. It was obvious Laura Mills' evidence was questionable, and Esther would probably rip Samuel apart like she had done his wife, and so, Nigel Harrison decided to call George, who waited for the door to be held open so he could wheel himself into the courtroom. That got the court's full attention as all eyes turned to him. Realising he wouldn't be able to climb the couple of steps into the witness box, he was allowed to sit in front of the bench, where he swore on the Bible and gave his name to the court.

Unfortunately, Nigel Harrison hadn't been briefed fully on who exactly George was, and he turned to the judge in order to ask for another recess. But the judge looked up from the desk through his little oblong spectacles perched on his nose and glared at the prosecution barrister.

"Could we continue, Mr Harrison? You have had plenty of time to read the bundles you were presented with before this trial started."

Things were not going in favour of the prosecution and Harrison quickly grabbed some papers from the table where he sat and hurried through them before looking over at George.

"Mr Collins, could you tell the jury where you currently live?"

"My present address is HMP Kirkham. It's an open prison for Category D prisoners and I'll be there for the next two to three years."

This statement got the whole of the court's attention. It made the prosecution lawyer cringe with embarrassment.

"Can you tell me how you know the defendant?"

"Yes, we went to school together and then went to work down the mine when we left school."

"And would you mind telling the court how you came to be in a wheelchair, please?"

"I'm paralysed from the waist down. It happened after an explosion when I worked down the mine."

"I see," Harrison said, moving on quickly. "So, when did you get involved in the drugs scene?"

"It was when Degsy, Derek Owens, got in contact with me and told me he had a connection to bring cocaine into the country."

"What, if any connections, did the defendant have in the importation of drugs from Belize?"

George thought for a few moments before giving his answer. "Noah was never interested in getting involved. It was something he never got involved in. The only ones who started importing were Degsy, Archie, and a bloke from Manchester, who I never met, but he seemed to be the main man who had the connection with the cartel in Columbia."

"What was his name?"

George shrugged. "I never met him, but I know his name was Adrian Chambers. He was the sergeant major in charge of everything when they were in Belize and then when they came back to the UK, as far as I know."

"Who told you Adrian Chambers was the main man, Mr Collins?"

"Archie Carmichael. He was the main man as far as I knew, but I was way down in the pecking order."

"Did you ever meet him or any other 'main men' in the organisation," Harrison asked, air-quoting the words 'main men'.

"No, I was just a gofer. I picked up the drugs that were being smuggled into the country by soldiers, as they had no customs and excise at the airport checks for the soldiers' personal belongings."

"What was the defendant's involvement in the operation?"

Esther was now staring intently at George, praying he gave the answer she hoped he would, which would almost guarantee an acquittal for her client.

"He had no involvement whatsoever, as far as I knew," George said, and Esther smiled and looked at the table in front of her.

Nigel Harrison didn't know what to say. He'd been led to believe the prosecution witnesses would most definitely incriminate Noah and this would be a closed case within hours. He hadn't expected it to go completely the opposite way. The case against Noah was becoming increasingly weak, and he slowly walked back to his seat, announcing that he had no more questions.

Esther stood up and looked around the court before resting her eyes on Noah and smiling at him. Then she walked towards where George sat in his wheelchair and smiled at him, too.

"Mr Collins, you say that my client, Mr Noah Burgess," she said, turning around to look at Noah before turning back to George, "had no involvement whatsoever in the importation and distribution of Class A drugs?"

"What I am saying is I did my job of collecting and distributing drugs throughout the Merseyside area."

"Could the defendant have been involved in some other way, say on the cash side of things, without you knowing?"

"I doubt it," George said. "All the cash I collected was given to Archie. What happened to it then was anyone's guess."

"Archie Carmichael?"

"Yes," George confirmed.

"Mr Collins, why are you here today as a witness for the prosecution?"

George smiled and then sighed before saying, "Because it was part of a plea-bargaining deal I was offered by the Crown Prosecution Service." The whole courtroom gasped.

"A deal?" Esther asked with fake shock in her voice. "What sort of deal?"

"I was offered a shorter sentence if I told the court about Noah's involvement in the drugs cartel."

"But you have just told the court that Mr Burgess had no involvement as far as you knew."

"I did, but all I have done today is told the truth, as far as I knew it to be."

"No further questions for this witness," Esther said, still smiling as she went to sit down.

Then Nigel Harrison stood up and approached the bench. "My Lord," he said, "I would like to re-address the witness in these unusual circumstances, if I may?"

"Granted," the judge said, and Harrison turned to look at George, lowering his head in a patronising manner as though George was inferior.

"Mr Collins, did you not tell the investigating officer that the defendant was involved at the highest level in the drug trade?"

George shook his head. "No, he told me he'd been told by other members of the organisation that Noah was the top man, which as far as I knew he wasn't."

"So, why have you turned up today on behalf of the prosecution to testify against the defendant?"

Turning and facing the jury, George said in a very firm voice, "I am in court today to tell the truth and nothing else."

The prosecution was contemplating on whether to ask George to expand but with one more witness still to testify, he decided to finish his questioning and went back to the table.

"Would you like to re-address the witness too, Mrs Epstein?" the judge asked, and Noah could have sworn he noticed a hint of sarcasm in his voice.

Esther stood up. "No thank you, My Lord."

"Then the witness can be excused," he said, and an usher quickly headed for the door and opened it to allow George to wheel himself out of the courtroom.

The session was then adjourned to the following morning, and everyone stood up to leave. Esther and Karen went to meet up with Noah, who was standing at the door of his cell getting ready to walk back to the hotel.

"It's going well," Esther said. "I think this will be over tomorrow. The prosecution hasn't done their homework and Chief Inspector Conboy has made a total fool of himself. You have two very good friends there, Noah."

He nodded. "I know. Loyal to the end, eh?" And then he strolled off in the direction of the Hilton Hotel, where he knew Brenda would be waiting for him in the bar.

The following morning, he turned up at the court with just twenty minutes to spare before the hearing was set to begin at 10am. Esther was a little frantic that he hadn't arrived an hour before, as he had been instructed to do, but he explained he couldn't stand sitting in that horrid little room on his own for five minutes more than he needed to, and if this trial went on longer than today, he'd be arriving fifteen minutes before it started tomorrow. Esther couldn't argue. She was confident the prosecution didn't have a chance in hell of winning this now.

"I'm quite sure Archie Carmichael hasn't turned up," Karen told Esther as they walked down the corridor towards the courtroom.

Chief Inspector Alan Conboy turned around as they got nearby. He'd been talking to Nigel Harrison, asking where Archie was.

"He hasn't turned up," they overheard Harrison say.

Esther looked at Karen and smiled. "In the bag," she mouthed.

Conboy looked around with a worried expression. Archie Carmichael was his key witness, the one to put a final nail in Noah's coffin. This was the worst news he could have been given.

"You've got to be joking," he shouted. "Where the hell is he?" he asked the detective.

"No one seems to know," Harrison replied.

"This doesn't look good, Chief Inspector."

Everyone made their way into the courtroom and took their seats, and within a few minutes the judge walked through the door situated behind the bench and took his seat, too.

Esther walked over to the bench and Nigel Harrison followed her, wanting to hear what she was about to say. "My Lord," she said, "the main witness for the prosecution has failed to turn up. No one can locate him, and it is believed he may have fled the country. My Lord, on this premise, as this witness is Mr Archie Carmichael, the man who planted the money in my client's garden, as we all saw from the recordings, my client has no case to answer to. I would therefore advise that this case against Noah Burgess be dismissed."

The judge looked at Nigel Harrison. "What do you say to this, Mr Harrison?"

"I don't think there is anything I can add, My Lord. Mr Carmichael was indeed our main witness and without his evidence, I must resort to the fact we have no chance of getting the defendant convicted."

"I agree," the judge said. Esther and Harrison both took their seats again, and Esther looked over at Noah and gave him a wink.

"Ladies and gentlemen of the jury," the judge began, "it has come to my attention that the main witness for the prosecution will not be giving evidence and therefore I have no choice but to call an end to this trial. You are all now discharged from your duty, and this case is dismissed."

He then stamped the gavel on the bench and stood up.

"All rise," the clerk said, to which everyone did, including Noah, who was allowed to leave the dock and go out through the court with everyone else.

"We did it," Esther said, shaking Noah's hand.

"We did, you were fabulous. Now I suppose I'll be getting your invoice for an extortionate amount," he said with a chuckle.

"I'm afraid I'm not a charity, Mr Burgess. But don't worry, at least the trial didn't last as long as we anticipated, which would most definitely have resulted in a much higher invoice."

He thanked both Esther and Karen, before walking back to the hotel. Brenda had got there just before him and ordered a bottle of champagne, sat waiting in an ice bucket on a table in the alcove.

"Are we celebrating something?" he asked, as he sat down.

"No, I thought we'd just splash out a bit," she said with grin. "We can celebrate properly when we get back to the room."

"That sounds like a good idea. Though I think I need to go back home now all this is over."

"Let's just stay tonight," Brenda said. "After all, my husband thinks I'm away on a business trip. He'll be asking all kinds of questions if I go home now."

Noah nodded and clinked his glass against hers. "You're right, let's indulge tonight. I reckon I deserve to!"

It wasn't long before they were joined by Bram and Lydia who wanted to join in the celebration.

CHAPTER TWENTY-TWO

It had been three weeks since the trial and Noah was just about settled back at home. The factory was running smoothly, and the extension was generating a massive increase in parts, which in turn meant a massive increase in profits. Noah had opened two bank accounts in Degsy and George's wives' names and put fifty thousand pounds into each. He felt it was the least he could do. If it hadn't been for George and Degsy, things could have turned out quite differently in court and he might not have had the freedom now to come and go as he pleased.

Bram and Lydia now held fifty per cent of both of Noah's business projects; the engineering factory and the ten apartments he owned. Financially, as had been the case for a long time now, he had piece of mind and a great lifestyle.

But he had recently started thinking about sharing it all with someone, wondering if having all the money he had was much fun at all considering he could only spend it on himself. He was contemplating buying a holiday home on one of the Greek islands or in Portugal, maybe even having one built to a high standard, but before he could make any plans, he got a phone call, out of the blue, from Shelley, telling him she was in Liverpool, which surprised him as he had disposed of all his old phones and bought two new ones: one for work and one for family, and Shelley had neither number.

"Noah," she said, "congratulations on your recent success. I'm in Liverpool and I'd love to catch up with you for a drink. Are you free?"

"How did you get this number?" Noah asked quite abruptly, which shocked her.

"That's nice," she scoffed. "I thought you'd at least be pleased to hear from me!"

"Nobody has this number, just family and close friends."

"So, I'm not a friend now?"

"Of course you are, but I got rid of all my phones. So, tell me, how did you get this number?"

"Well, how do you think I got it?" she asked.

"Someone's obviously given it you, I presume. Who?"

Shelley sighed loudly. "Okay, hand's up, I rang your factory and spoke to Lydia and pleaded with her to give me the number. Don't blame her, though. I told her it was an emergency."

"And she believed you?"

"Obviously. I'm sorry, maybe I shouldn't have done that."

Noah softened then, knowing that Lydia had probably been worried after everything that had gone on recently, and assumed something had happened, probably to Archie, and Shelley needed to speak to him to give him whatever news she had.

"No, I'm sorry," he said. "It was just a surprise hearing your voice, that's all."

"A good surprise, I hope?"

"Very much. And yes, I'd love to catch up. Are you staying at your mum's?"

"No, I'm at the Hilton. What time do you want to meet? I can be in the bar whenever you're ready."

"I can be there in an hour if you like?"

Shelley did like, this told her that he was keen to see her again. "Sounds perfect. I'll meet you at two in the bar."

"See you at two, then," he said, and she hung up. He then realised he was standing in the kitchen with a raging erection, having felt the stir a few moments ago when she mentioned she'd like to catch up with him. He hadn't been this excited for a long time!

Shelley had a similar feeling as she went to the wardrobe in her room and pulled out a pair of ankle grazers and a satin blouse, then rummaged in one of the drawers and changed into black lacey lingerie.

At 2pm, Noah walked through the entrance of the Hilton Hotel and made his way to the bar area, where he spotted Shelley sat on a stool sipping what looked like gin and tonic. He'd put his best suit on and made sure he looked extra smart.

"Hi," he said as he sat on the stool next to her. "What are you drinking?"

"Hi, yourself," she said. "Gin and slimline tonic, please."

Noah called the barman over and placed his order. Then Shelley leant towards him and kissed him on his lips, sending another tingle through both their bodies and causing Noah to develop another erection.

"Are you going for another interview?" she asked, hiding her smirk behind her glass.

"Cheeky," Noah said. "Thought I'd dress up a bit!"

"You look good. Shall we move to somewhere more private?" she said.

"Yeah, good idea," Noah agreed, and paid the barman before standing up and carrying their drinks to a table in the corner where it was much quieter.

Both sat down and looked at one another, seemingly waiting for the other to start the conversation. Both were smiling but it was Shelley who made the first move, stretching her arm out towards Noah's and putting her hand on him affectionately.

"I was so glad you got acquitted," she said.

"I think I had a bit of luck, to be fair. George and Degsy did good, they put their necks on the line in the way they gave their evidence. My lawyer was pretty sure the prosecution had been convinced I'd get convicted and end up with a lengthy jail sentence. But my barrister had other ideas. She was amazing."

What Shelley said next startled Noah.

"Your barrister was a terrier. I thought that chief inspector guy was going to have a coronary when she brought out her evidence. It was hysterical."

Noah sat looking at her, not saying anything.

"How did you know about all that?" Shelley shrugged and took a sip of her drink. "You were there in court, weren't you?"

She smiled now, knowing there was no use in lying to him. "I turned up, yes. You wouldn't have recognised me though, I made sure I wore a pretty good disguise and sat at the back. I didn't want to miss it."

"You should have told me you'd be there," he said. "You could have celebrated with us afterwards."

"Well, actually," she said, rather sheepishly, "I followed you, not knowing if you were going straight home, but when you walked along the road and came in here, I was going to let you know I'd been here all along. Only..." she paused. "Well, you went straight over to a woman at that table over there," she said, pointing to the alcove in the opposite corner, "and the woman you were with poured two glasses of champagne. Obviously, I assumed you'd found yourself a girlfriend, so I decided to leave you to it."

"That was just Brenda," Noah said in a nonchalant manner. "She works for me. She was just there for support."

"Hmm. So, how long have you been sleeping with her?"

"On and off for a while," Noah said. "But it's just a friends-with-benefits thing, nothing serious. She's happily married and got kids. Plus, she's a good worker and I don't want our working relationship to end, which it could do if her husband were to find out about us."

"And is it over now?" Shelley asked.

"Yeah, I guess it is."

"That's good to hear," she said. "Because I've got a proposition for you and if you've got a woman in tow, it isn't likely to happen."

"Okay, and what might that be?" Noah asked, taking a large gulp of his Guinness.

"I want to have a baby," she blurted out. "My biological clock's ticking way too fast and it's something I've been thinking about for a while."

"Wow!" Noah looked at her, his eyebrows raised.

"And I'd like you to be the father."

This shocked him even more. "What did you just say?"

"Okay, I'll put it another way. I want a baby and you're the man I want it with. There doesn't need to be any heavy commitments and we can share custody and all that, and you can have a say in bringing it up. But I've thought a lot about this, and I think you and me will make a beautiful baby together."

"Surely you must have somebody back in New York you could have a baby with, aren't you seeing someone?"

"I was, but he was much older than me. I lived with him for three years, but we weren't right for each other. He's a great guy, everyone loves him and respects him, and he's got money and brains. But he's also got grown up kids and grandchildren, too. I didn't want children until recently, so I settled for a ready-made family, but this has been building up in me for a couple of years now, and he doesn't want any more kids."

"Are you still together?" Noah asked, not wanting to get involved if she was still very much attached to someone else.

"No, we called it off. We wanted different things in the end, we decided to go our separate ways. There's no animosity between us, it was done amicably."

Noah's mind was running at a hundred miles an hour.

"I'd love to have a child, but I would want to be properly in its life, not just a sperm donor. If you were serious about me being involved fully in bringing the child up, then yes. But I must be honest with you, Shelley, I've always vowed I'd never want to bring a child into the world out of wedlock." He grinned then and took another large swig of the Guinness.

Shelley went quiet as she studied his face for a few moments. "Noah Burgess, are you asking me to marry you?"

Noah put his glass on the table and said, "Yes."

Shelley smiled at him and brushed his lips with hers. "Well, then I guess you've got yourself a deal," she said, wrapping her arms around his neck and kissing him with more passion than was probably acceptable in a hotel bar.

"Drink up then," Noah said, unwrapping her arms from him. "I think we should take the rest of the afternoon looking for an engagement ring, don't you?"

"Today is getting better by the minute," Shelley said, planting another kiss on Noah's lips and downing the rest of her gin and tonic before grabbing her handbag and standing up.

The next day, after spending an extortionate amount of money on a platinum diamond solitaire ring, Noah helped Shelley move her things from the hotel into his house and she wasted no time in calling her parents to give them the good news. It was a little awkward at first when they assumed she'd got engaged to Paul in New York, and she had a bit of explaining to do when she revealed her fiancé was actually a man she'd known for several years through work connections and was from Liverpool.

The second announcement was made to Bram and Lydia, after Noah invited them round for dinner. Bram nearly choked on his champagne when Noah introduced him to Shelley as his fiancé.

"Bloody hell, bro," Bram said, "you don't waste much time!"

"Well, we've known each other a while and there's always been an attraction between us. I guess it was just a matter of time. Only neither of us realised."

"Well, I'm happy for you. For both of you," he said, and raised his glass towards them.

Noah went into the kitchen to bring out another bottle of champagne and was surprised to find Lydia standing behind him.

"I'm happy for you too, Noah," she said. "You deserve this. Can I just ask one thing?"

"Sure," Noah said, waiting for Lydia's lecture.

"What about Brenda? I know you two have been seeing a lot of each other, and I know you're fond of her. Does she know about Shelley?"

"Not yet, but I'll tell her on Monday at work." He then took hold of Lydia's hand. "Look, Lydia, I know you care about Brenda and even more about me, but I've always been aware that Brenda's happy with her husband. She was never going to leave him and I always accepted that. We had a fling and it was good while it lasted, but it was only ever a fling, nothing serious."

"I'm not sure Brenda will see it that way. I think she was, and still is quite fond of you."

"Me and Brenda will always be close. But there won't be any intimacy between us now, not ever."

"I know. You're a good man, Noah Burgess, and I'm lucky to have you as my brother-in-law."

"I'm the lucky one, Lydia," Noah said. "I really am one lucky guy."

The next day while in his office, Noah and Lydia were going over the figures relating to their apartments when in walked Brenda. Lydia took this opportunity to leave the two of them alone, to have that much needed chat that Noah perhaps wasn't looking forward to. Brenda immediately guessed something was up by the way Lydia suddenly left the room and when she looked at Noah, it was more than obvious in his expression.

"What's up?" she asked.

Noah thought he might as well bite the bullet and tell Brenda the truth. "Lydia was just congratulating me," he began. "I got engaged last week."

Brenda, much to Noah's relief, didn't seem put out at all and in fact she congratulated him. "Is that the woman you were with last Saturday in town?" she asked.

Taken aback, he replied, "Yes, did you see us?"

Brenda nodded and smiled. "Yes, I was with my kids and husband when you walked out of the Hilton Hotel holding hands. Anyone could see you were a couple in love."

It was like a weight had been lifted from his shoulders as Noah felt the need to explain. "Me and Shelley go back nearly ten years. We've always had a thing for one another, but she had a long term partner and seemed happy. Then, out of the blue last month, she flew over to Liverpool from where she lived in New York, to tell me her relationship was over and she was moving back here to be nearer to her aging parents."

"So, you asked her to marry you, just like that?"

"No, she asked me."

"Well, I really am happy for you, Noah." What Brenda was really thinking was how lucky this Shelley was to land herself a catch such as him.

"Truthfully," he added, "she's in her mid-thirties and even though she's never thought about having kids, she realised recently that it's something she's ready for after all. The spark's always been there between us, Brenda, and I know what we had was special, but I love Shelley. I really do want her to be my wife and the mother of my children. I hope you understand."

"Of course I understand," Brenda said, and hugged Noah, gripping him tightly and holding on for just a little longer than was perhaps necessary. She'd enjoyed their fling and it had changed her for the better, plus it had helped rekindle her relationship with her husband, so she couldn't complain.

It was six weeks later that Shelley walked down the aisle of her local church to become Noah's wife. She hadn't told him but that morning she had taken a pregnancy test and it had shown up a positive result. She would tell him about the good news on their honeymoon in the West Indies. And when their first born, Lydia, was just eighteen months old, Shelley gave birth to their second child, a boy, who they named Henry after Shelley's father.

When Henry was a few months old, they decided to start sharing their wealth and made arrangements with Bram to donate all the interest made on their millions in several banks around the world, to various charities. It was their way of clearing their conscience on the way the money had been made in the first place.

Looking at his beautiful wife who had given him two gorgeous children, Noah realised on a daily basis that he had everything a man could possibly want in life and also knew he was one very lucky guy.

ACKNOWLEDGEMENTS

Thank you to my editor, Kathryn Hall, who is an absolute pleasure to work with. She is always supportive and candid in her feedback.

Thank you also to Beta reader, Lucy Sheffield, Elaine Denning for interior typesetting, and Josefa Altona for creating the cover design. Their commitment and passion is second to none.

Other books by John O'Neill

The Removal Man

From being a young boy evacuated from Liverpool to Wales during World War 2, Gerry Hamilton led a colourful life, one that most people would perceive as adventurous, eclectic, and perhaps even, dangerous. Respected and loved by many, he was also feared, but his heart was in the right place, and he looked after the people he felt deserved recompense. However, on a constant mission to put things right, his methods weren't always lawful.

Gerry grew up to be the man who would dish out the punishments, often to a grisly end, and he made his money through shady deals and being hired for his reputation in the city as a 'hitman'.

Then, one day, Gerry found love, and his zest for life was given a new focus. That was until the future he had planned disintegrated into a bloody mess. His confidence shaken and his life almost destroyed, he pulled himself from the brink of despair and concentrated on revenge. 'The Removal Man' made an explosive comeback that would shake Liverpool to its core. This is his story...

A Matter of Revenge

Liverpool lad, John Kelly, almost has it all, and at just sixteen, he wastes no time in trying to fulfil his ambition to make Dot Harper, his schoolgirl crush, become his girlfriend. Thinking he's finally done it, he soon discovers the love of his life isn't quite who he thought she was, and events begin to take a drastic turn for the worse.

A series of unfortunate occurrences follow, including a death in the Kelly family, which devastates John so much that he decides to start a new life in Jersey. Employed on a construction site as a foreman, John then embarks on a long-term affair with his wealthy boss, Renée, but starts to lead a double life when he marries Lesley and dreams of having a son to carry on the family name.

Things should be good for John Kelly now, but his determination for revenge is taking over what should be a happy family life, and along with his friends, he sets out to destroy the people who left him bruised and battered when he was a teenager. But does he manage to finally find the peace he yearns for? This is his story…

Bombay Scouse

Ambitious Liverpudlian, Joe Peters, marries into a wealthy Jewish family who at first worry that their daughter Kate, wants to spend her life with the son of a docker. It soon becomes evident that even though Joe comes from a working-class family, his ethics and morals are high and the love he has for his wife is, almost, unconditional.

However, family life takes an unexpected turn, bringing heartache to Joe, whilst giving Kate a high-flying career and expectations that far outweigh those of her marriage. When their youngest daughter Ellie, marries dangerous rogue Sanjay Patel, whose family business Joe, Kate, and her mother Esther invest in, it isn't long before tragedy and sorrow strike and Esther intervenes on a mission to take back control.

With determination on his side, Joe hooks up with Kam Kumar, who helps him unravel a string of events that could bring the Patel family down. But will their plans work out and will Joe succeed in keeping his own family together? Or will his problems escalate as he discovers the real reason why the Patels wanted their son to marry into his family?

Printed in Great Britain
by Amazon

45497173R00165